ALSO BY AMANDA FLOWER

FARM TO TABLE MYSTERIES
Farm to Trouble
Put Out to Pasture

IN FARM'S WAY

A FARM *to* TABLE MYSTERY

AMANDA FLOWER

Poisoned Pen
PRESS

Published by Poisoned Pen Press, an imprint of Sourcebooks
P.O. Box 4410, Naperville, Illinois 60567-4410
(630) 961-3900
sourcebooks.com

Printed and bound in the United States of America.
KP 10 9 8 7 6 5 4 3 2 1

For my favorite farmer, David

Chapter One

A Michigander knows snow—or at least she should. The northwest corner of the Mitten gets ten to twelve feet of snow a year. In a ranch home, that's snow up to the roof. Snow was something Michiganders understood most of the time. But that wasn't the case when a Michigander moved to LA and came back.

I knew this because I was sitting in my father's old pickup truck in a ditch. The front end of the truck was half buried in the snowdrift on a dark January night on a lonely country road.

I gripped the steering wheel and let out a breath. My tires had lost traction on some black ice. My saving grace had been the lack of other vehicles on the country road and the fields on either side, so there weren't any trees or large brush to hit.

The problem was the ditch and four feet of ice-cold Michigan snow.

Huckleberry, my beloved pug, was on the floorboards of the car, having rolled off the passenger seat when I lost control of the truck. Luckily, his dog bed on the floor had broken his fall. If Huckleberry had been hurt, I would have never forgiven myself.

He shook his head and the metal tags on his collar clacked together. I reached down and scratched him on the head. "You okay, buddy?"

He snuffled at me. Snuffle was the pug answer to everything.

I rested my forehead on the steering wheel. "I'm so sorry, Huckleberry. I thought driving in the snow was like riding a bike. Clearly, it's not." I straightened up. This was no time for a pity party. I might have gotten into a jam, but I was okay. Huckleberry was okay. It could have been so much worse. I knew that better than most. A car accident snatched my fiancé, Logan Graham, from my life nearly sixteen years before when I was twenty-three years old.

I cleared my throat, refusing to allow myself to dwell on what might have happened and what had happened in the past. "I just have to find my phone and we'll call for help. The truck has plenty of gas. We'll be toasty warm until someone can come and get us. That's what AAA is for, right?" I knew my singsong voice was more to calm myself than the pug.

Huckleberry hopped back on the passenger seat and licked my hand.

I unbuckled my seat belt and started looking for my phone. Of course, it wasn't on the console where it had been when I hit the snowbank. Most likely, it was under one of the seats. I reached under my seat and then Huckleberry's, running my hand back and forth over the rubber mats. Nothing.

"I hope all those yoga and Pilates classes I took in LA made me as limber as they promised," I told Huckleberry as

I contorted my body to reach under the seat again. I swiped my hand back and forth like a metal detector on the beach. I reached under as far as I could, and on the second pass, I hit what I thought was my phone. Except instead of grabbing it, I knocked it deeper under the seat. I groaned.

Huckleberry tipped his head back and let out a high-pitched howl. Usually a pug only howled when it was stressed.

"Oh Huck. It's going to be okay." I righted myself and lifted the dog from his seat into my lap to hold him close. "As soon as I find my phone, we'll get out of here. I know it's under there. Don't worry, buddy."

He whimpered.

Headlights bobbed in my rearview mirror and came to a stop right behind us. It was either a Good Samaritan or a killer. As far as I was concerned, there wasn't anything in between. As a television producer of true crime for over a decade, I had a chronic inability to believe it was ever the former. I set Huckleberry back on his seat, confirmed the doors were locked, and grabbed the ice scraper from the small back seat. It wasn't much of a weapon.

Someone knocked on the driver's-side window.

I jumped, and Huckleberry yipped in excitement. He'd been frightened just a moment ago, and now he seemed perfectly at ease. He wagged his curled tail back and forth. This told me it was friend not foe at the window.

I dared to look. A man stood there holding a flashlight. He wore a navy-blue paramedic ski jacket and a matching navy-blue stocking cap on his head, and he was smiling.

Of all the people in Cherry Glen, of course it would be firefighter Quinn Killian who just happened to drive by when I was in a predicament.

I groaned, but not because Quinn wasn't capable of helping me. He was probably the most capable EMT and fireman in the Glen, as the locals called our town. He'd spent most of his firefighting career working in Detroit, Michigan's largest city. He was also a close neighbor to the farm I shared with my dad. And when I say close, I mean a couple of miles away. We were in farm country after all.

It was just plain embarrassing to think of the number of times I had humiliated myself in front of Quinn since I'd moved back home from LA. I'd only been back six months, and it seemed like I was going for some kind of record to make myself look like a fool in front of this handsome man.

His handsomeness was just a statement of fact, such as the sky was blue or my face was bright red. He was clean shaven and always well-groomed, even when he was out of uniform. Years of athletics and working a physically demanding job kept him in amazing shape. I couldn't see his hair now, but I knew it was brown and slowly fading into gray. I would even venture to say he was more handsome as a distinguished grown man than he ever had been as a high school athlete. But like I said, my recognition of this was purely observational.

Quinn knocked on the window again. "Shiloh, open up. Are you okay?"

I rolled down the window, and when I say rolled down the window that was exactly what I meant. I cranked on the lever by the door. My dad's truck was so old it didn't have power windows. However, it did have a really sweet tape deck.

I smiled. "Quinn, fancy meeting you here tonight. Out for a night drive in the snow?"

"I take it you and Huckleberry are all right. You wouldn't be cracking jokes if Huckleberry was hurt."

"Huckleberry is fine, if not a little bewildered by what happened. As for me, the only thing injured is my pride." I let out a breath. "But I am grateful you happened by."

"So am I. When I saw the truck on the side of the road, I knew you or Sully had to been in it. You need to be more careful on these icy roads. What if there'd been oncoming traffic? You could have been killed like…"

Like Logan, he was about to say. Not only had Logan been my fiancé but he had been Quinn's best friend. I didn't need Quinn to remind me of what happened. I knew all too well.

"I hit a patch of black ice, and the truck spun out. And you know I would never let Dad behind the wheel on a night like this."

Since Thanksgiving, Cherry Glen had been in a constant state of on-and-off-again snow. So far, I'd been able to drive my father everywhere he needed to be or found someone to give him a ride. My spare driver was usually my cousin Stacey or Quinn.

"I'm really glad you aren't hurt. I don't know how I'd explain it to Hazel if something happened to you. She would hold me accountable."

Hazel was Quinn's twelve-year-old daughter and my

partner in crime when it came to solving a two-decade-long mystery at Bellamy Farm, which I co-owned with my father.

"I'm fine," I said brightly. "And I think the truck is fine too. It's just stuck. Can you pull me out? I need to get to town. I'm already running late."

"Late for what? It's eight o'clock at night. You've never struck me as a night owl."

I barked a laugh. "Eight o'clock is night owl status?"

"It is in Cherry Glen in the middle of the winter. The town rolls up the sidewalk at this time of night when it's this cold."

He had a point. The freezing wind coming south from Canada over frozen Lake Michigan didn't help.

"I was on my way to the brewery. Kristy invited me to a party. She said the owner is going to make some kind of big announcement that involves her husband, Kent, and she wants me there to hear it."

"Do you even like beer?" Quinn asked.

"It's okay…"

He laughed. "You lived in LA too long and became a wine and champagne girl."

I rolled my eyes. "Coffee. I'm a coffee girl." I cleared my throat. "You should come tonight. The food is supposed to be great. At least that's what Kristy said. Likely to entice me since she knew the mention of beer wouldn't do it for me."

"I can't. I'm picking up Hazel from my parents. I don't think beer tasting is an appropriate school night activity for my seventh grader."

I supposed not. "Well, in that case, you shouldn't be standing out in this weather. And I need help out of here."

He pulled down on his winter hat. "Let me get my chain."

"Hopefully I'm not so stuck that we'll have to call a tow truck."

"A tow truck? You really have been away too long. Any pickup worth its salt can get you out. Just shift your truck into neutral."

When Quinn left to get the chain, I turned to Huckleberry. "This is one of those stories that's going to make the rounds at Jessa's Place, isn't it? And I'll have to hear about it for years to come."

He grunted. In pug that meant yes.

Quicker than I expected, Quinn knocked on the window again.

I opened the door.

"You got it in neutral?"

I nodded.

"Good. Then you and Huckleberry should probably get out just to be safe. Wait in my truck."

I hopped out of the truck and stuck my hand under the driver's seat once again. This time, my fingers brushed against something. *Got it!* I shoved my phone into my coat pocket, then scooped up Huckleberry and snuggled him against my chest to keep him warm. It took all my balance not to fall in the snow as each step went up to my knees. Quinn gave me his arm and helped me out of the drift. I trudged toward the headlights of his truck, opened the door, and lifted Huckleberry up into it. Once I was on the leather seat, I let out a sigh of relief.

The truck was tidy. The only trash was a disposable coffee

cup that I recognized from Jessa's Diner in the cupholder.
Everything else was neat as a pin, except for a collection of
stickers along the dashboard that ranged from flowers to cars
to smiley faces. There were at least two dozen of them. They
looked aged and worn, as if they'd been cleaned several times
over the years.

They had to be from Hazel when she was younger, and it
was endearing that big, tough Quinn Killian would proudly
drive around rural Michigan with princess stickers on his dash.
That said a lot about who he was as a father—and as a man too.

The driver's-side door opened, and Quinn jumped in like
this was the Wild West and he was jumping onto his steed.
"Here we go."

After checking for nonexistent traffic, he shifted into
gear. The wheels spun on the icy pavement.

I held Huckleberry close to me. The wheels spun more.

"If you can't get it, we can call AAA. I think my membership is still current."

"Patience. I haven't even tried yet."

It looked to me like he had been trying, but I clamped my
mouth shut.

He changed gears, revved the engine, and pressed down
harder on the gas. My father's truck inched backward.

"Now, I got him," Quinn said, as if he was the old man
from *The Old Man and the Sea*, about to bring in the marlin.

Finally, the two rear tires of my dad's truck were on the
pavement and after that, the rest of the truck came out relatively easily. It stood in the country road blocking both lanes
of traffic.

"Oh my goodness, thank you!" I cried. "I don't know how I can ever repay you for this."

"You don't have to make it up to me. You watch my daughter several days a week after school and won't let me pay you. The least I can do is pull your truck out of a snowdrift."

"There's that," I said with a smile. "But honestly Hazel is a great help on the farm. I would feel guilty for taking your money and then putting her to work."

"She doesn't see it as work. She thinks it's fun. She's talking about being a farmer now, much to my mother's chagrin."

"What does your mother have against farmers? She's surrounded by farms," I said.

Quinn shrugged. "She's a townie," he said, as if that were explanation enough, and maybe it was.

"Thank you again. You've been a great friend to Dad and me."

A strange look crossed his face. "Being a friend to *both* of you is important to me. I know that it's been awkward since—"

"Oh wow," I said, making a show of looking at my watch. "I had better get going. I at least owe you one of my homemade pies for this."

His face fell because I knew what he was going to say, and I wasn't up to hearing it again. Three months ago, I thought that it maybe it was just possible that Quinn and I could be something more than friends, but he squashed that. He wasn't ready after the death of his wife, and he was still conflicted after all these years about Logan. I didn't want to rehash it. I just wanted to move on and concentrate on my farm and caring for my dad.

"I'll see you tomorrow?" he asked after a beat.

I frowned and then if dawned on me. "Right. I'll be bringing Dad to the ice fishing derby. Thank you again for letting him fish with you and Hazel. Ice fishing really isn't my thing, and he'd be so disappointed if he couldn't go. He's gone every year no matter how bad he's feeling."

"It's no problem, and it will be a fun day. I think he can teach me a thing or two about catching a muskie."

"He probably can." I shifted in my seat. "Well, again thank you. I'd better get going. I was running late as it is for the party. Kristy is going to start blowing up my phone at any moment." Balancing Huckleberry on my lap, I started to open the door.

Quinn grabbed my arm. "Shiloh, be careful. I would hate for anything to happen to you." He paused. "For Hazel's sake. She really cares about you."

I swallowed. "And I care about her too. She's a great kid."

"Good. Good." He punched me in the arm lightly as if I was an old football teammate. "You have my number. Remember, if you ever get into trouble, you can always call me for help. I'm a fireman, after all. It's my job to rescue people."

"I know." I cleared my throat. "Thanks again." I gathered up Huckleberry and slipped out of the truck.

As I drove away, I felt Quinn watching me.

Chapter Two

"Ohmigosh, Shi, you're here! I was just about to call you," Kristy Garcia Brown said as she tiptoed toward me on four-inch heels. She wore a black cocktail dress that was a perfect fit and showed she was back into prepregnancy shape just nine months after the birth of her twin daughters. She wore her black hair slicked back and dark eye makeup. I blinked. I hadn't seen her this dressed up since we were in college.

Kristy was the director of the Cherry Glen Farmers' Market, so most of her days were spent in jeans, sweatshirts, and boots.

I looked down at my black leggings, boots, and black sweater. I felt immensely underdressed, but at least I got the color of the night right. I set Huckleberry on the floor and snapped on his leash. "Are you sure it's okay for him to be in here?"

"Oh yeah. The owner's wife has a bunch of dogs that are here all the time. I'm surprised they aren't here tonight. Now why are you late? I was getting worried. I thought you bailed again."

I grimaced, since she had reason for making such an assumption. I wasn't the most social person in the world. After years in LA where social events were made to rub shoulders and network for that next big project, I was burned out on parties and even more on small talk. Kristy had invited me to so many events since I'd returned to Cherry Glen, but I had only gone to a handful. I wasn't even sure why I agreed to come here tonight other than my best friend had begged me.

"I've never bailed without giving you warning," I said.

"Not much warning. You told me just three hours before our double date last week that you couldn't come."

The double date had been a setup by Kristy with one of Kent's friends. It was a blind date for me, and it was true, I hadn't wanted to go. I agreed to it because Kristy was my friend. However, that wasn't the reason I canceled.

"We were in the middle of a blizzard that night. No one was going anywhere."

She sniffed, as if the weather hadn't been a factor at all.

I glanced around the crowded room. The building had once been a granary. Behind me there was a glass wall that looked into the brewery itself, with its large copper fermentation tanks, tubing, and gauges. The restaurant and bar on the right side of the building served the brewery's selection of beers but was no longer the only place selling the beverage. Fields had recently made the leap to distribute through local retailers. I knew very little about the owner, Wallace Fields, but I'd heard from chatter at Jessa's Place he was an ambitious man. Local retail was just the beginning. He wanted to go national.

"I was late because the truck slid off the road and into a ditch," I said.

Her mouth fell open. "What? Are you okay?"

"I'm fine. I'm fine." I waved my hands back and forth before she could get the wrong idea. "Huckleberry and I weren't hurt, and my dad's truck is fine too."

"Nothing can hurt your dad's truck. It's as sturdy as the tank."

The tank was the old World War II Sherman tank sitting at the end of Michigan Street, the main road in Cherry Glen. It was also the same road that pretty much all the businesses were on, including Fields Brewing Company. The tank had been a donation to Cherry Glen by a local collector—don't ask me how someone goes about collecting tanks—and had sat at the edge of town since before I was born.

"How did you get out?"

"Quinn happened by before I could even call for help and pulled the truck out of the ditch."

Her demeanor immediately changed from concerned to amused as her dark eyes sparkled. "Quinn saved you, huh? Maybe I don't need to set you up with someone else when you already have a man in shining pickup in your corner."

I frowned back. Kristy had made it no secret that she thought Quinn and I would make a good couple. We'd all gone to high school together. I think for her, Quinn and I being together would be a chance to relive those past days. She just didn't understand or accept it was never going to happen. The memory of Logan was just too big a hurdle for Quinn or me to jump over.

"As a fireman, he has to save people. It's his job."

"Okay," she said in a voice that told me she wasn't going to drop this anytime soon.

Time to change the subject. "So what is this party about anyway?" I asked as I looked around the room. "You told me very little about it. I'm not sure why I'm even here."

"I know, I know. I've just been so frantic between this event and the derby tomorrow. You'll be there at seven, right?"

"I will," I promised.

The derby was the Lake Skegemog Ice Fishing Derby, an annual event in the region. This year, Cherry Glen had a booth to share information with the hundreds of fishermen at the derby. The fishing began as early as six in the morning, but the booths and vendors started at eight, which was about the time the spectators started to arrive. The Glen's booth had been Kristy's idea. She thought it would be a great opportunity to showcase all that the town had to offer. We had the brewing company, a local theater, boutiques and shops, and Kristy's pride and joy, the farmers' market that ran from April to October.

"Good. I'm so excited about how many of our business and community members are on board. It's going to be an amazing opportunity for Cherry Glen."

I nodded. "So what's big announcement tonight?"

"It's an announcement of the brewery's new specialty beer. There's a tasting and then we all vote to see which one wins."

At that moment, a waiter walked by with a tray of

flight-size beer glasses. Kristy stopped him and took one of the glasses from the tray. After she thanked the waiter, she started to hand it to me. "Try it. It's delish."

"I'm not much of a beer drinker," I said. "I don't know if I'll be a great judge of how it tastes."

"I know you're not. That's why you need to try this. You're the perfect one to taste it. If *you* like it, a lot of people will."

I wrapped Huckleberry's leash more tightly around my wrist and took the glass in my other hand. I studied it before I drank. The lighting inside the restaurant side of the pub was lowered, but even in the dimly lit room I could see the beer had a slight reddish tint.

"It's red," I said.

She rolled her eyes. "Just drink it. You don't have to analyze everything before you do it."

Didn't I though? It was always the times I *didn't* analyze something that I made the wrong decisions.

Shaking my head, I took a sip. It was sweet, a little bitter, but not in a bad way, and had just enough hint of an alcoholic kick to it. "It tastes like a cherry," I said.

Kristy clapped her hands. "Yes. I'm so glad that you got it on the first sip. It's tart cherry beer. If it goes well, they will put it in production for the summer's cherry festival. Fields Brewing Company has been selected as the official brewer of the festival, so Wallace wanted to have a new cherry beer to debut for the event. You know what a big deal that is."

I did. The cherry festival in Traverse City was the biggest event of the year in Western Michigan.

"That's pretty impressive that a brewery from Cherry

Glen was selected. There are microbrewers all over the area and several in Traverse City."

"I know!" she said excitedly.

I squinted at her. Kristy was usually happy about good press for Cherry Glen because ultimately it helped the farmers' market, but she seemed *really* happy over this tart cherry beer. "So this is a shoo-in to win?"

"It should win. I mean it *will* win; everyone is saying that it will. It just hasn't been announced yet until the voting is over." She checked her watch. "In about twenty minutes. You need to vote for this one." Her tone left no room for discussion.

"What's the other beer? Shouldn't I taste that before I vote?" I asked.

"It's a cherry stout. It's boring, and something people have seen at the festival before. This one is completely new. You have to vote for it."

"Is there a reason you're so insistent I vote for it without tasting the other one?"

"Because Kent made this one!" She glanced around as if to see if anyone was watching us. No one even gave us a second glance in the crowded room. "If he wins this could change everything for us."

Kent was Kristy's husband, a quiet high school teacher who appeared to be perpetually in a state of concern. His apprehension had become even more apparent since he'd become a father.

"I didn't know Kent worked on the brewery side of things. I thought he only tended the bar here on the weekends and in the summer."

"He's dabbled for a long time. You should see my basement. It's like a science test kitchen down there, and Kent has this huge cooler with his equipment inside. He's been working on it for months. He even has a second fridge in our basement dedicated to his home brewing."

It made sense to me that Kent was drawn to beer making. He was a science teacher. Fermenting things was science.

"He did it for fun," she went on. "And never expected that a great opportunity would come from it, but it has."

"How's that?"

"Wallace lost his master brewer, and he's been on the hunt for a new one with no luck. So, he had the idea of having a contest among his employees to enter their own beers. The winner receives five thousand dollars and the job of brewmaster. It'd be a massive boost in Kent's salary. Do you have any idea what we could do with the money? It would be a godsend."

My eyes went wide. "Would Kent leave teaching to work at the brewery full-time?"

Kristy bit her lower lip. "It's a lot of money. He'd do it for the money, and we can certainly use it."

Since the twins were born, I knew money was tight for Kent and Kristy. Kristy loved her job as the head of the farmers' market, but it paid very little. As a teacher, Kent wasn't making a ton of money either.

Kristy wrung her hands. "But it's such a gamble. There's not much money in teaching, but it's stable. He also gets the summers off to spend more time with the girls. I know Wallace, he'll demand all of Kent's time. He's a workhorse himself and expects everyone around him be the same way. So Kent wouldn't have as much time with the girls or with me. It's hard to know what to do."

I adjusted Huckleberry's leash in my hand. I knew all about taking a job just for the money. As a television and film producer, I'd taken several jobs that hadn't been worth the bigger paycheck because of disgruntled staff or outrageous actors, but at least I'd always known it was short term. Film and television productions wrapped. If Kent walked away from twenty years of teaching now, he might regret it. However, I didn't say any of this to Kristy. It wasn't my place to give her or her husband life advice. And anyway, I'd made plenty of really dumb choices in my own life, so who was I to be passing out nuggets of wisdom?

I looked around the crowded room. "Where's Kent now?"

"He's working at the bar."

"He's bartending tonight when he's one of the two finalists? He couldn't get the night off just to celebrate?"

She shifted back and forth in her heels. "He was happy for the extra hours. The voting box is right over there." Kristy pointed at the bar. "Hurry! Go vote before it's too late. He's 'A.' Vote for 'A.'"

At the end of the long, polished bar sat a golden box. The side of it read, "Votes." I didn't know if the brewery could have made it clearer if they tried.

I had to weave my way over there as the bar itself was three deep with people waiting for drink. When I broke through the crush of people, I spotted Kent behind the bar with two other bartenders. They were frantically seeing to all their customers as they smiled and chatted. I didn't envy them. When I first moved out to LA, I lasted as a bartender for two weeks before I quit. It wasn't an easy job and required some serious multitasking skills.

Maybe if Kent became brewmaster he wouldn't have to work behind the bar again.

A man and woman stood right in front of the golden voting box, blocking my path. I glanced at my watch. I had four minutes to cast my vote before the cutoff. If I didn't vote for Kent, Kristy would kill me.

"This is another way that he's using talent to his own advantage. He doesn't know how to make beer himself. He cheats," the woman said. I would put her age as close to sixty. She had a sleek silver bob haircut that brushed her shoulder and was dressed like she was making a bid for senator in a navy-blue pantsuit.

"He knows how to get what he wants. If only we all were so strategic, we would be farther ahead too. I, for one, would prefer to be authentic over successful. I know not everyone feels that way. If I wanted to have all that Wallace has, I could, but I choose to do it the right way. That's the difference," the man said. He was a bit older than the woman. My guess was closer to seventy than sixty, and he had curly gray hair and a short beard. While the woman was dressed for a political rally, he was dressed to go fishing in cargo pants and a thick sweater.

Next to him, I didn't feel underdressed at all.

"I hate to think what my husband would have thought of all this," the silver-bobbed woman said.

I didn't want to interrupt them, but I had to cast my vote. I cleared my throat. "Excuse me. I'd like to cast my vote."

The woman eyed me. Her eyes were a steely gray not much different from her hair color. It was a bit disconcerting to be honest. They didn't look natural, and I wondered if she wore colored contacts. "Go ahead." She stepped aside and let Huckleberry and I through. "There's not much point to it since the winner has already been chosen."

I gave her a wan smile. Whatever the two of them were complaining about, I didn't want to know about it or get involved. I slipped past them to the box, Huckleberry right at my heels.

There was a stack of voting sheets next to the box, and I was just marking "A" when someone said, "Shiloh, I didn't know you would be here tonight. We could have ridden together."

I popped my vote into the box and turned around to see Tanner Birchwood standing directly behind me. He was so close that I had to sidestep so the two of us weren't touching. I scooped up Huckleberry and held the pug close to my chest.

"Oh hey, Tanner, nice to see you." I hoped my words came out more genuine than I felt.

Tanner was my closest neighbor. In fact, he lived on Bellamy farmland—or what used to be Bellamy farmland before my cousin, Stacey, sold her half for a pretty penny to buy and restore the Michigan Street Theater just down the street from the brewing company.

Tanner had a wide smile, high cheekbones, and sandy blond hair that was always perfectly styled in a casual, tousled sort of way. After a successful financial career in Chicago, he'd bought into Cherry Glen because he'd wanted to know what it was like to live off the land and start Organic Acres, as he'd renamed the property.

He was a very nice guy, but there was just something about him that didn't sit well with me. One minute he could be the friendliest neighbor in the county, and the next minute I felt like he was sizing me up as competition. Although I guess I was, since I'd started the process of having Bellamy Farm certified as an organic farm as well.

He shook his head. "I should have known you'd have thought to come here too."

"Thought to come here?" I had no idea what he meant. Being at the brewery was the last thing I wanted to be doing tonight. If I had my way, I'd be tucked up in my little cabin with a good book, Huckleberry on one side, and Hazel's cat, Esmeralda, who lived with me on the farm, on the other. This party was not my scene at all.

He shook his finger at me. "I know you're here to meet with MOBA."

"MOBA?"

"You know, Michigan Organic Beer Association. I saw you speaking with two of the members."

"When?" I asked. "The only person I have spoken to since I arrived is Kristy."

"You were standing with Annette Woodhall and Sidney Tucker for quite some time."

"You mean those two people who were blocking my way to the voting box?"

He chuckled. "You're being very closemouthed about this. But I'm sure you know all the MOBA members are here tonight. Wallace Fields in a prominent member of the group, so they are all here to support him tonight. I don't doubt for a second that, like me, you're hoping to work out some agreement with some of the members so you can provide them with the organic grains and hops they need for their beers."

I tried not to look surprised. The last thing I wanted was Tanner to think he had one up on me, even though he did. I knew nothing about MOBA or Wallace's involvement in it. However, it did sound like an interesting business opportunity for the farm.

"I knew you were a savvy farmer," Tanner said and sipped the beer in his hand. "A friendly rivalry is a good thing, but I think we can be more than that. Have you thought—"

"Excuse me!" A trim, fiftyish woman in a formfitting dress picked up the ballot box and carried it away, stopping Tanner before he could ask his question. It seemed the voting was over.

I took her interruption as an opportunity to slip away. I knew what Tanner was going to ask anyway. He wanted to know if I'd thought about how our two farms could collaborate and work together. It wasn't the first time he'd asked, nor did I expect it to be the last. It wasn't a bad idea…if I could trust him. Unfortunately, I couldn't say that I did.

Chapter Three

Kristy and I sat at a high-top table in the back of the restaurant, watching as a man in a tuxedo stepped onto the small stage at the opposite corner of the room. I had never seen anyone wear a tuxedo in Cherry Glen before. At least, never outside of a wedding or prom. He moved with the confidence of an athlete and had thick blond hair that kept falling in his eyes. His hair and build made him seem younger than I suspected he was due to the slight wrinkles on his face. He appeared to be the kind of man who was in a lifelong quest to stop the aging process. I'd seen his type a lot in Los Angeles, where aging was seen as a fate worse than death.

Kristy must have noted the direction of my gaze, because she said, "That's Wallace Fields, the owner of the brewery." She lowered her voice. "When he first bought the granary and said he was going to transform it into a local brewery and restaurant, the townsfolk were suspicious. You know change is hard for people in the Glen."

I nodded. From my own personal experience, the citizens of Cherry Glen could definitely be suspicious.

"But Fields Brewing Company's success really was the catalyst that started the renaissance in our town. I really believe we otherwise wouldn't have the theater or any of the little shops and boutiques that are so popular with tourists. He really changed life for everyone in Cherry Glen, but I wouldn't say everyone was grateful for it."

I wanted to ask more about Wallace, but before I could, he removed the cordless microphone from its stand. "If I could have your attention, please. Your attention."

Slowly, all the chatter in the room subsided. I let out a sigh of relief. The noise of so many people talking at one time had been deafening with the high ceilings. The sound just seemed to reverberate all around us. Only when it was mostly quiet did I realize how loud it actually had been.

"Welcome to Fields Brewing Company! I'm Wallace Fields, and I'm so happy that you are all here tonight for our big announcement. For those of you who might not know, for the last eight months I have challenged my staff to come up with their cherry-flavored beer recipe to be used as our signature drink at the Cherry Festival this summer. Field Brewing Company has been selected from hundreds of candidates to be the official brewer of the annual Cherry Festival in Traverse City."

Clapping broke out in the room.

"Thank you." He waited for the applause to die down. "On the line for those entering the competition is a cash prize of five thousand dollars." He waited for the claps and hoots to die down again. "And the opportunity to work full-time as a brewmaster right here in Fields Brewing Company.

As you know, we tragically lost our last brewmaster, Bastian Woodhall, to a heart attack last February. Since then, we have been making do. We would not be where we are today without his leadership at the start of this business. I personally loved him like a brother."

Woodhall? The name rang a bell in my head. Didn't Tanner say that the woman I had seen by the voting box was named Annette Woodhall? Cherry Glen was a small town. They had to be a relation of some sort.

"Twelve members of our staff entered the competition," Wallace went on. "And now we are down to the two finalists. The finalists are Jason Brennan and Kent Brown. Jason, Kent, will you two come to the stage now?"

The crowd cheered. Kent was the first to reach the stage. He pulled at his short beard, and his face was bright red. A younger man joined him on the stage. He was a head shorter than Kent and had thick black hair. He wore a bright red dress shirt that was in perfect contrast with his hair. He waved to the audience while Kent clasped his hands in front of himself and looked like he'd rather be anywhere else on the planet but there. Jason oozed sex appeal and confidence. He reminded me of some of the young men who'd come into my casting calls and then blamed the casting directors when they didn't get a part.

I shook my head, trying to dispel my judgmental thoughts. It seemed I'd spent too much time in Hollywood to give anyone a fair shake. I was always assessing them as to what role I should put them in by their attitude, persona, and—as superficial as it was—by their looks. It had been part of my job for so many years. I needed to retrain my brain to stop that. I wanted to stop, so as best I could, I set aside my quick judgment of Jason Brennan...for the most part.

"These two employees are talented brewers in their own right. Jason works in the office and is my right-hand man in running the day-to-day operations of the company. I never knew he had an interest in brewing until this competition. And Kent is one of our best bartenders, so reliable. You never have to wonder if Kent will show up for his shift, and he's always willing to take on more. You might have seen him at the bar tonight!

"I have to tell you, over the last few months, watching this competition has been thrilling. I never thought that employees would be so enthusiastic about it. It means a great deal to me, as well as my wife, Chanel, that the staff here at Fields Brewing Company is so invested in the business. On the behalf of my wife and myself, I want to thank each and every one of you who have entered the competition.

"And now it's my great honor to announce the winner, who will be awarded five thousand dollars in cash and full-time position as master brewer for the company and have his beer featured at the annual cherry festival in Traverse City." He looked at the piece paper in his hand. "This was close, folks. This person took the crown by two votes. That's right, you heard me, two. With no further ado, the winner is..."

Kristy grabbed my arm and dug her nails into my sleeve. At least the sweater was thick, which protected me for the most part.

"Jason Brennan!"

"What?" Kristy cried.

I winced, but it seemed like Kristy wasn't the only one shocked with the results. There wasn't a single cheer of a congratulations. Instead, murmured confusion filled the room.

"I didn't vote for him," a woman said behind me. "Did you?"

"Did you taste Jason's beer? It was B. I didn't think it was at all good. It was far too sweet. I thought my teeth might rot right out of my head."

"I wanted Kent to win," another voice said. "He's a decent guy and his beer was better by a long shot."

"No, I tasted Jason's and thought it was better," another person said. "Try it."

I looked over my shoulder, and a couple stood right behind me. The man handed his beer to the woman. She tasted it. "That's not what I tasted earlier this week. I guess he changed the recipe." She shrugged.

"Is he allowed to do that?"

She shrugged again. "I don't make the rules."

"You're assuming there are rules when it comes to something Wallace Fields has done."

I frowned and looked forward again.

While all this chatter was happening, Kristy's grip on my arm grew harder and harder until I was certain she would snap the bone.

Despite the rumblings, Jason went up to the podium, all smiles. "Thank you, Wallace. I just have to say I'm honored for this opportunity. This really is a dream come true for me.

I started working in the office because I wanted to be a brew-master in the future and have my own brewery." He smiled at the brewery owner. "I might even take your job one day, my friend."

Wallace plastered the fakest smile on his face I had ever seen.

"It's rigged," Kristy stage whispered to me. "He works in the office. He would know how to throw the votes his own way."

"Kristy," I said, looking around us to see if anyone over-heard. By the ears turned in our direction, I was sure many of them had.

"This recipe," Jason went on, "is one I've been working on for a long time. I'm so glad that it has finally received the recognition it deserves."

"He's a liar! He stole that recipe from me," a hoarse male voice called from the back of the room.

Jason narrowed his eyes. "Would someone show the man causing the commotion out?"

Two waiters moved to the back of the room. Kristy and I turned around to see the waiters stand in front of someone. All I could see of this person was a bit of gray hair and a pale fist waving about. With very little trouble the guards ushered the man from the restaurant.

"I wonder what that was about," I said and wished I had seen the man's face.

Kristy and I returned our attention to the stage.

"Now with that done," Jason said. "Let's party!"

Kent quietly stepped off the stage.

Chapter Four

"I should have been out on the ice by now," my father said as we bumped along the interstate on our way to Ballden, the small village on the banks of Lake Skegemog, where the ice fishing tournament was about to begin.

My father had fished at the derby every year for the last fifty years, but this was the first time he wouldn't be on the ice as soon as permitted. Fishermen were allowed out as early as three in the morning to set up their fishing shanties and tents. However, lines weren't allowed in the water until six o'clock sharp, which would be about the time Dad and I were set to arrive.

Huckleberry sat in the back of the truck in his puffy orange winter coat and matching boots. He did not like the boots and whimpered when I put them on. All he needed was a pointed orange hat and he could pass for a traffic cone.

As we drove along the road above the lake, we had a bird's-eye view of the proceedings below. A hundred yards from Ballden's docks, there was a square mile of plowed ice. That small part of the lake was dotted with shanties and lights. It seemed like there were several hundred on the lake, and each one represented a fisherman or woman who had claimed a spot to fish the derby that day.

"There's not going to be any good spots left," Dad complained.

"That's not true. Quinn is fishing today and promised to save you a spot near him," I said as we followed the winding road down into Ballden.

"He had better pick a good one. One year he got all tangled up in boulders on the bottom on the lake. It was embarrassing."

"I'm sure he remembers that too and is being careful."

My father grunted and leaned back in his seat. While he grumbled under his breath over his chances of catching any keeper pikes and trout because of this late arrival, I couldn't get my mind off the party at the brewery the night before. Kristy had been crushed over Kent's loss, but surprisingly, Kent had actually seemed relieved. This made me think he hadn't really wanted to leave his teaching position to be a brewmaster. I knew Kristy might be disappointed for a day or two, but maybe everything had worked out just like it should.

The weather was supposed to be frigid but clear, with little wind. It was perfect ice fishing conditions, or so I had been told. I had never participated in the sport myself, even when I was a kid. It was something my father did with his friends, and he wouldn't take his bookworm child along. I'd always stayed back on the farm with Grandma Bellamy to do chores and read.

Finding a parking spot was a bit trickier than I had expected it to be, but I finally found one close to the dock.

Outside of the truck, as the cold bit into my skin, I wished chores and reading had been my agenda for this Saturday morning too.

Thankfully, I didn't have to stay all day. I was assigned to work the Cherry Glen booth from eight to ten, and Quinn had promised to bring my father home when the first day of the derby ended at three that afternoon.

Huckleberry jumped out of the pickup and landed on his new boots. He shook each leg in turn as if he was trying to flick them off. When the boots didn't budge, he looked up at me with the question in his eyes: "How could you do this to me?"

"It's just for a few hours, Huckleberry," I told him. "You can take the boots off on the way home. You don't want to get frostbite on your paws, do you?"

He snuffled and I took that to mean, "This isn't over."

"Shi!" a high-pitched voice called to me as I went to the passenger side of the truck to help my father out.

I turned and spotted Hazel Killian waving frantically. Her long, dark hair was tied in a ponytail and bobbed from the hole in her stocking cap, specifically made for the purpose. She was dressed in teal from the hat to her coat and snow pants to her boots.

I waved back and opened the door for my dad. By the time he was standing on the pavement gripping his walker, Hazel was at our side.

She bounced, her eyes sparkling. "Isn't this so much fun? I've never been to a fishing derby before. I bet I'll catch at least three pike!"

Dad held on to his walker. "I don't doubt for a second you will, and I'll make sure of it. I'll teach you everything I know about ice fishing. Did you know I won the Western Michigan Junior Ice Fishing Derby in 1957?"

"No!" Hazel cried, clearly impressed.

"It's the truth," Dad nodded. "You're speaking to a champion. You couldn't ask for a better teacher."

I bit the inside of my lip as I watched Hazel and Dad joking together. It was the kind of relationship that I had wanted with my father growing up, but Dad had been in a different place then. My mother died suddenly, and he was left alone with a young girl he didn't know how to raise. He threw himself into the farm and learning all he could about Michigan history and left the child-rearing to his mother, my Grandma Bellamy. I loved my grandmother dearly. She had been more like a mother to me than a grandmother, but I'd wanted a dad too.

"Do I hear Sully bragging about his angling prowess again?" Quinn asked as he walked up to us.

"It's not bragging if it's the truth," Dad retorted. "Now, I want to get onto the ice and see my spot."

"I got us a good one," Quinn said.

"You had better. If my line gets caught up on some boulders, you'll have to answer to me."

"I'm never going to live that down, am I?" Quinn asked with a grin.

Hazel grabbed my hand and swung my arm back and forth. "Shi, are you coming out to see our shanty? It's really cool!"

"Cool" being the operative word there.

I lifted our joined hands and peered at my watch. "I promised Kristy I'd be at the booth by seven, so I have a little time to ride out with you all to see your setup."

Hazel beamed up at me. "You'll love it, Shi!"

After unloading Dad's gear and putting it on a sled to be pulled behind Quinn's ATV, Quinn helped Dad into the passenger seat of the recreational vehicle, while Hazel, Huckleberry, and I piled in the sled. We tucked Dad's walker in front of our knees. It was a little tight, but we made it work.

Slowly Quinn drove the ATV and sled out onto the ice. My breath caught as I thought of all the weight we carried and the cold water below. As the sun came up and shone on the ice, I took comfort in the deep blue surface. We were going to be just fine. The clearer and bluer the ice, the thicker and safer it was to be out on.

Quinn and Dad waved and called out to other fishermen as we drove by. The fishing shanties ran the gamut. There were ones that looked like outhouses and others like playhouses, but the majority of them were tents. Thankfully, there was no wind forecast because the tents wouldn't have stood a chance against the gusts that traveled across the interior lakes in this area.

Quinn and Hazel's shanty was something in between. It was a sturdy wooden frame, and while one wall was Plexiglas, the rest was tent canvas. Fishing poles and a hand auger for drilling the fishing holes in the ice sat outside of the shanty.

"Be careful on the ice," Quinn warned as he helped Dad out of the ATV.

I held the walker until my father had a steady grip on it.

"This is a nice setup. Where's my hole?" he asked.

"You can either have the one inside of the shanty, or I have another about ten feet away outside."

"I'll take the outside hole to start. I believe fish can sense the shadow of the shanty and it keeps them away."

"I thought you might say that." Quinn smiled at me over my dad's head and helped him to the outside hole.

There was a lawn chair already set up in front of the hole, and Quinn settled my father into it.

I unhooked the sled from the ATV and pulled it over to my father. "Do you have everything you need, Dad?"

My father squinted into the sunlight. "I do."

"I put an extra winter coat and your favorite cookies in your pack."

"Good, good." He waved my away. "Stop mothering me, Shiloh."

I winced and stepped back.

"The fish will be biting today. I can feel it in my bones," Dad said, completely unaware of how his comment affected me.

"I know you're right," Hazel agreed and then turned to her father. "Can I start the day out here with Sully? He promised to teach me everything he knows. He's the 1957 champion."

"I can't argue with that," Quinn said. "I will leave it to Sully to teach you, Hazel. He's a lot better at this than I am."

Dad looked up at Quinn. "That is the truth." He turned to Hazel. "Now, the first lesson we have to talk about is ice safety. What happens if you fall into the ice?"

She pointed at the twelve-inch hole in the ice. "There is no way that I could fall into that."

"You'd be surprised," my father said. "Conditions on the ice can change quickly, and you need to know what to do."

She nodded solemnly and listened.

"First of all. The bluer the ice, the thicker it is. White ice is fragile."

My heart constricted as I listened to Dad speak to Hazel about the ice. It was something that he said to me when I was about her age. It was one of the few things that he bothered to teach me.

"White ice is fragile," she repeated. "Got it."

"Second. If you were to fall in, there are three things you can do to save your own life, especially if there is no one around to help you. Number one: don't panic. Try to remain calm. Number two: swim out of the hole."

"What do you mean when you say that?" Hazel tugged on her ponytail.

"You want to get your upper body up over the edge of the ice and kick like you are swimming."

She nodded.

"And number three: if for any reason your head goes under the water, do not lose sight of the hole in the ice. If you go under the ice slab, you're done."

Hazel's eyes were wide.

"Okay," Quinn said. "I think that lesson is done. It's important advice, but don't worry, Hazel, you will never have to use it. 'The ice here is thicker than the whole length of my arm"—he held out his arm to show her, then flexed it with a wink—"and it won't go above freezing today. When the ice is melting, that's when you should just stay away from it altogether."

"Good advice," my father agreed.

"Looks like you all are all set," I said, changing the subject. "I'm sure you're going to have a great day on the ice. I, however, had better head back to the shore and meet up with Kristy. If you need anything, just shoot me a text."

Dad was already in the process of showing Hazel how to bait the line, so I wasn't sure he'd even heard me.

Quinn followed Huckleberry and me over to the ATV. "Hey, are you okay?"

I gave him a half smile. "I love seeing Dad with Hazel, but…"

"You wished he was like that with you." He touched my hand.

I pulled my hand away to brush imaginary snow from my sleeve. "Just never take for granted what you and Hazel have. It's special. Very special. Not every girl gets that kind of close relationship with her father, no matter how much she may want it or try to have it."

"I don't take it for granted," he said. "I don't take *anything* for granted."

I squinted at the sun because I knew he wasn't talking about his daughter any longer. "Will you look out for Dad today? I have to say I'm worried about him sitting out in the cold for so many hours. He's stubborn, and he wants to win. He doesn't always listen to reason. At least he doesn't listen to *my* reason. He might do better if it's coming from you."

"I'll make sure he's well cared for. You don't have to worry about a thing."

I smiled. "I am grateful you're an EMT."

He chuckled. "It helps."

"Before I leave, I'll stop by and see if you all need anything."

"Your dad and Hazel would like that." He paused. "And I would too. I love spending time with you."

I swallowed and couldn't think of anything to say in return.

"Do you want me to drive you back?" Quinn asked after a beat.

I shook my head. "I think a walk on this crisp morning will do both Huckleberry and I some good. Right, Huck?"

The pug looked at me and tried to shake off his right front boot.

"He doesn't like those boots," Quinn observed.

"Not even a little bit," I agreed and started to walk away, but my foot slipped on the ice; Quinn's hand shot out to steady me, holding my arm in a comforting grip. "You need to be careful. I can drive you, really. It's no trouble."

I felt my face turn red. My brain swirled over him saying "I love spending time with you." Why would he say that when he made it clear we were just friends and would always be just friends?

"No, no, you stay here with Dad and Hazel," I said. "I'll be fine. I just need to get my ice legs under me."

He grinned. "Ice legs? I've never heard that term before."

"That's because I just made it up." I said goodbye one

more time and started—much more slowly this time—to cross the ice. The outside chill permeated my coat, but the place where Quinn had touched my arm felt like it was on fire.

Maybe twenty yards from the shore, Huckleberry whimpered and started pulling against the leash. He wanted to go to the left.

I tugged on his leash. "Huck, Kristy and the booth are this way."

He pulled harder.

Thinking that he needed a potty break, I said, "All right. You lead the way."

The little pug took an abrupt ninety-degree turn and walked to the edge of where the ice had been plowed free of snow. I went along, knowing my dog could be finicky about where he went to the bathroom.

However, when he reached the edge of the snow, instead of going potty like I expected, he pawed at the ice and snow. Then he bent his neck and howled into the sky. It was the most haunting sound I'd ever heard from my little dog.

"Huck, what's wrong?"

He pawed at the ice again and looked at me.

Shaking my head, I walked over to see what he had seen.

I screamed. There was a dead man under the ice.

Chapter Five

I shivered under the blanket wrapped around my shoulders. Everything that had happened after Huckleberry and I made our gruesome discovery was a bit of a blur. My scream had made people come running. I remembered shouts and being pulled away from the man under the ice. Fishermen immediately started sticking their augers into the ice to cut the man out.

I held Huckleberry to my chest as if my life depended on it. I found myself sitting on the bay of an ambulance, which was already on the lakeshore because of the potential of fishing injuries during the day. I told the EMT that Kristy was waiting for me and asked someone to tell her what happening. I texted Quinn.

Just as I finished the text to Quinn, a man in a sheriff's uniform walked up to me. "Ms. Bellamy? I'm Sheriff Milan Penbrook from the Antrim Sheriff's Department. I'd like to talk to you about what you found this morning."

He was a handsome Black man with a trim goatee and close-cropped wave haircut. He wore black plastic-rimmed glasses. The sheriff's badge shone in the morning sunlight on his chest.

I cleared my throat. "Yes, of course. I don't know much at all."

"Just start at the beginning."

I swallowed and told him about going with Quinn, Hazel, and my father on the ice and walking back to the shore with Huckleberry. "To be honest, I just thought he had to use the bathroom." I felt my face warm. "It wasn't until he howled that I knew something was wrong."

He looked down at my pug in his orange coat and boots. "Pugs howl?"

"Oh yes, especially when they're upset."

His eyebrow went up as if this was brand-new information. He then squatted in front of Huckleberry and held out the back of his hand to the little dog. Huckleberry sniffed his hand and then licked it.

The sheriff smiled and scratched Huckleberry under the chin. "You're a very brave little pug."

Huckleberry's back end wiggled back and forth under the sheriff's praise, and my heart gave a little leap inside of my chest.

Sheriff Penbrook stood again.

"I keep thinking about one detail over and over."

"What's that?" the sheriff asked.

"His boot. I could see that he was wearing only one boot. The one he had on was black and looked expensive. It had some kind of designer insignia on it that I couldn't see clearly. I don't know why that's bothering me so much, but I keep thinking of how cold that bare foot must be." I shook my head. "I know that doesn't make sense. In freezing water,

all of him would be cold whether or not he had clothes on."
I looked up at Sheriff Penbrook. "Do you have any idea who
the man under the ice was?"

"We do." He paused. "Did you recognize him?"

I pressed my lips together. "I—I thought for a second
he looked like Wallace Fields. He's a prominent citizen in
Cherry Glen, the town where I live. It's about twenty minutes from here in Grand Traverse County."

He nodded. "I know where it is."

"I can't say for sure it was him because he was so…blue." I
closed my eyes for a moment as the image came back to me.
"And his face was bloated. It was hard to see his features at
all." I looked up at the sheriff. "Am I right?"

The sheriff folded his arms. "You are."

I sucked in a breath. It was the answer I'd been expecting
to hear, but it still came as a shock, especially since I'd been
at his brewery less than twelve hours ago.

"When was last time that you saw Mr. Fields alive?"

"Just last night." I went on to tell him about the party at
the brewery. However, I held back any mention of the contest or Kent Brown. Something told me I had better keep
that to myself.

"That's interesting," Sheriff Penbrook mused. "But it's
helpful. It gives a small window to account for his move-
ments. The smaller the window, the more likely we are to
find out how he ended up under the ice."

I grimaced. "Will the ice fishing derby continue?" I asked.

He sighed. "Yes, the county commissioner wants it to
go ahead. It's a big revenue draw for Ballden and the county

as a whole. The body was found far enough away from any fishermen or shanties that we can cordon off the area without impacting the competition. Unfortunately, an under-ice crime scene like this is almost impossible to investigate. I have some guys coming in to do a dive, just to search the area. But with all the special equipment they need because of the freezing temperatures, they won't be able to get under the ice for a few hours yet. A lot of evidence can be lost in that time. Not to mention, the anglers did a number on the surrounding ice trying to cut him out." He shook his head.

"How did Wallace get under the ice?" I asked. "It's at least a foot thick, more in other spots. And an auger hole is far too small to fit a person inside."

"We don't know just yet, but I have deputies searching the lake to see where he might have gone in."

"So you think he fell in, that this was some sort of accident?"

"I didn't say that."

"Then it's murder." I held more tightly to Huckleberry's leash where it was wrapped around my gloved hand.

He pressed his lips together before he spoke. "I didn't say that either."

"Shi! Are you all right?" Kristy cried as she ran toward the ambulance. "I just heard everything! How does this keep happening to you? Like, stop finding dead people!"

Sheriff Penbrook stepped back. "Stop finding dead people?"

Kristy hugged me and looked at the sheriff, as if seeing him for the first time. "She didn't do anything wrong."

I appreciated my friend coming to my defense so quickly, but I put a hand on her arm. I didn't need her putting the idea into Sheriff Penbrook's head that I might have something to do with Wallace Fields's death.

"Sheriff Penbrook, this is my friend Kristy Brown. She's from Cherry Glen too."

"I am. Shiloh and I were set to work the Cherry Glen booth this morning at the derby. When she didn't show up, I knew something had happened. That's when I heard about the dead man." She looked to me. "Are you okay?"

I removed the blanket from my shoulders and stood up. "I'm fine. The most helpful thing I can do right now is put it out of my head for a little while."

"Are you planning on leaving?" the sheriff asked.

He examined my expression so closely, I felt like a bug under a microscope. It wasn't a great feeling.

"No," I said. "I came here to help out in the Cherry Glen booth, and that's what I plan to do."

He nodded. "Good. I'll send one of my deputies over to get your information in a little bit. Do not leave the derby without telling me."

I swallowed. That sounded like a warning.

The sheriff nodded to Kristy and me in turn. "I'll talk to you later on today, Ms. Bellamy."

"You can call me Shiloh," I said.

Sheriff Penbrook nodded and strode away.

Kristy grabbed my hand. "You have to tell me everything!"

"Can I tell you when we get to the booth? My head is sort of spinning."

"Let's go."

The Cherry Glen booth was decked out in, well, cherries. The awning over the booth was cherries, the tablecloths on all three tables were covered in cherries, and all the signs and labels were decorated with cherry graphics.

"I'm sensing a theme," I said to Kristy as I stepped behind the table.

"Hey, I make no apologies for my cherry decor. In a place like this, you have to stick out. There are dozens of towns and villages with tables and booths at this derby. We need to be noticed. It's for the good of the Glen."

I raised both hands in surrender. "I wasn't criticizing it. I love cherries. I *grow* cherries."

She narrowed her eyes, as if sizing me up to see if I was lying.

A group of women walked by the booth, and one of them said, "Did you hear it was Wallace Fields under the ice? How awful!"

Kristy spun around and faced me as the women melted into the crowd. "When were you going to tell me *that*?" she hissed.

"I wasn't keeping it a secret," I said. "I thought it might be him when I saw the face under the ice, but it wasn't until the sheriff confirmed it that I knew for sure. I was going to tell you."

"I know you were." She let out a breath. "I'm sorry I snapped at you." She opened a canvas bag and removed a plastic container of dog treats. She opened the container and gave two to Huckleberry. "You're a good cadaver dog. What is this, body number two for you?"

I grimaced. "He's not a cadaver dog."

"Maybe not officially." Kristy chewed on her lower lip.

I leaned against one of the tables and folded my arms. "What's wrong?"

She wouldn't look at me. "Is the sheriff sure that it's Wallace? One hundred percent sure?"

I cocked my head and imagined I looked much like my pug when he had the same expression. "He didn't give me a percentage of how sure he was, but he also didn't give me a sense that he doubted the victim's identity."

She blew out another breath. "What time did he die?"

"The sheriff didn't know, but I told him I saw Wallace at the party as late as ten o'clock last night. He thanked me for the information, because he said it would narrow down the time of death."

She took another deep breath.

"Kristy, what on earth is going on here? You look like you might be sick." My eyes went wide. "You're not pregnant again, are you?"

She rolled her eyes at me. "No. I'm not getting pregnant ever again. Two is more than Kent and I can really handle in the first place."

I touched her arm. "Can you tell me what's going through your head?"

She looked me in the eye. "I'm scared."

My heart sank. "Why? What happened?"

"I'm just so shocked that Wallace is the person you found under the ice. I can't wrap my head around it."

"Why? Why do you need to? It's a terrible tragedy."

"It is." She licked her lips. "But it's more than that."

"Why?" I asked again, feeling like a broken record.

Kristy looked around and then turned her back to the people walking by along the shoreline. "Because my husband might be the last person to have seen him alive."

Chapter Six

W hat?" I yelped.

She clapped her hand over my mouth. "Shhh! Don't talk so loudly. You'll get people's attention."

Like her covering my mouth wouldn't get a lot of strange looks. But I decided not to argue with her since she was clearly so upset.

I removed her hand. "Tell me everything."

"Wallace and Kent were here last night after the party."

"What?" I asked. "Here? Why would they come all the way out to Ballden?"

"The brewery was set to have a booth here. They had their own booth but were participating with MOBA as well. Do you know what that is?"

I remembered my conversation with Tanner at the brewery. "I do. I just learned about it last night."

She nodded and leaned in closer to continue with her story. "After all the guests left the party last night, Kent was cleaning up the bar like he always does at the end of a shift. He's meticulous about it. He'll never even leave one glass out of place. He was the only one there doing that. All the other employees—including the new brewmaster, Jason Brennan—had left over an hour beforehand. I stayed to keep Kent company, but we didn't have much time because we only booked the sitter to eleven thirty. Wallace came up to the bar and asked Kent if he would be willing to go with him to Ballden."

"And Kent agreed after such a long shift working at the party?"

Kristy nodded. "Wallace said he would pay him for his time. He said he was going to Ballden to pick a spot for the brewery's booth. Somehow, he'd heard that people were already at the lakeshore picking their spots. Wallace hated to be the last person to know about anything. He wanted to go right then and claim Fields's spot." She shook her head. "I wasn't too keen on the idea of Kent going. It was a very cold night and Wallace had just passed him over for the promotion. I don't trust that voting system at all. Kent didn't owe him anything." She took a breath. "But since the twins were born it has been so hard for Kent to turn any job down. He stays up at night murmuring about paying for college and weddings. It's really gotten out of hand." Tears came to her eyes. "That's why I was happy that he might get the promotion. I thought it would help him worry less if he was making more money on a regular basis."

I frowned. It had been my impression after the announcement that Kent was relieved he hadn't won the position. Could it have been a little of both? And I had a feeling Kristy's story was about to get much worse.

"Kent agreed but he opted to drive separately because we

live in the opposite direction from Wallace. I went home to the twins and let the sitter leave. Kent got home a little after one in the morning. I know because I checked my phone when I heard him come into our bedroom. I asked him if they found a spot for the brewery. He said they did, and I went back to sleep. The twins woke me up a couple hours later."

"What did Kent say the next morning about it?" I asked.

"He told me they'd gone to the site and marked where the brewery booth would be. He'd also said he was glad they went because, just like the anglers staking claim for the best fishing spots on the lake, businesses were grabbing up all the prime areas along the shoreline. Even so, he said he got a perfect spot."

"He got the spot? By himself, not with Wallace?"

"Wallace never showed up."

I stared at her. "Kristy, you have to tell the sheriff all of this. It narrows down the time of death even more and explains why Wallace's body was found here at the lake, so far away from the brewery."

"I can't do that," she whispered. "Do you know how bad this will make Kent look? He was just passed over for a promotion by Wallace. Now Wallace is dead, and Kent was the last person to see him alive..."

She had a point, but I knew it'd be much worse if the sheriff found out about it on his own. I'd been involved in several murder investigations in Cherry Glen, but in those cases, Chief Randy—Quinn's father—had always headed up the investigation.

"Where's Kent now?" I asked.

"Home with the girls," she said. "It's way too cold for the girls to be here all day."

"Was he going to work the brewery booth today?"

"No, and as far as I know, Wallace didn't ask him to. Kent has a shift tonight at the bar, but I'll be home long before that to take the girls." She paced back and forth in the booth. "I need to talk to him, but I can't do it here over the phone. Someone might hear me. I need to go home."

I really thought she needed to speak to the sheriff first, but maybe I wasn't correct about that. Maybe it would have been better find out exactly everything that happened between Kent and Wallace last night first and then talk to the police. In any case, Kristy or Kent, hopefully Kent because it would be much better coming from him directly, needed to come forward with this information.

However, saying any of that to Kristy at the moment wasn't going to make her feel any better. Instead, I said, "Go. I'll take care of the booth. I've got it covered."

"You might be stuck here all day, though. I signed up for the whole day. You were only supposed to be here until ten. I couldn't find anyone to help after that. It's a big ask to have someone stand out in the cold and hand out brochures."

"Don't argue with me. I'll be fine. Just go home to your husband and get this straightened out. Everything is going to be okay," I said, even though I wasn't one hundred percent sure of that.

She nodded and gathered up her things. She left the container of dog treats on the table. "I brought this for people who come by with dogs. Huckleberry can have as many as he wants. And you have to—"

"Kristy, I have produced award-winning shows in Hollywood. I can watch an information booth about the town I grew up in for a few hours. Just leave and talk to your husband before..."

"Before the police do," she finished for me.

After Kristy left, I familiarized myself with the booth and read over the detailed notes Kristy had left. It even included a script so the person working the booth wouldn't forget to mention all the wonderful things Cherry Glen had to offer tourists and locals alike.

I didn't pay much attention to the written prompts, to be honest. I may have been away from Cherry Glen for years, but I knew the town like the back of my hand. I knew what to say and what not to say about the Glen.

I texted my dad to see how he was doing out on the ice. Unsurprisingly, he didn't text back. I hadn't heard from Quinn either. I debated leaving the booth to make sure Dad was okay, but I reminded myself that he was in very good hands with Quinn.

For the next little while, people stopped by the table and entered the raffle for a gift basket, and I passed out treats to their dogs when the owners gave permission. The gift basket was a compilation of all the Glen had to offer. It included two free tickets to one of the plays at the Michigan Street Theater during the upcoming spring season, coupons and small gifts from the shops in town, and a gift certificate to the Fields Brewing Company valued at one hundred dollars.

With Wallace dead, I wondered if that gift certificate was still valid.

People stopped to enter the raffle and pick up freebies provided by town merchants. A middle-aged woman asked me about places to shop in the Glen, and I was happy to answer her questions to get my mind off Wallace.

"If you stop by Cherry Glen, I highly recommend you have breakfast or lunch at Jessa's Place," I told an older couple all bundled up in hats, gloves, scarves, and coats that made them look three sizes bigger than they actually were. "It's where the locals like to eat. The pancakes are the best in the Mitten State, and they are served all day. Get the cherry pancakes. You won't be sorry."

"Thank you," the woman said. "We will do that. I love pancakes, and it only seems right to eat something cherry in Cherry Glen."

"Be sure to ask for Jessa's cherry syrup too."

She promised she would.

"Shiloh!" Quinn called as he hurried through the crowd to my booth. His eyes were wide. "Are you okay?"

"Quinn! How's Dad? Is he doing okay? Is he warm enough?"

Quinn stopped in front of my table. "Your dad is having the best time. He's already caught three fish. I don't know how he does it. I've caught nothing, not even a boulder. At this point, I would be happy for my hook to sink into something. Anything."

I let out a sigh of relief. I knew I had been worried about my father for no reason. Maybe it was the gruesome discovery I made that made me so anxious to know he was okay.

Quinn looked me over and not in a romantic way, but in a way a doctor—or in his case, an EMT—checks you out for any noticeable sign of injury. "Are you hurt? I couldn't believe it when I read your text. I'm so sorry it took me so long to get over here and check on you. Your dad was pulling in an eight-inch pike right when the text came, and I didn't hear my phone. Both he and Hazel were shouting their heads off."

I smiled at the image of my dad and sweet Hazel having such a great time together.

"No, no, I'm fine." I peered behind him. "Thanks for checking on me. Are Dad and Hazel still on the ice?" I asked.

"They're still fishing. I thought they'd be okay for a few minutes. I told one of my buddies, who is in the next spot over, to keep an eye on them. Not that I think they'll need any help. I'm certain your dad has no intention of moving from his spot until he's caught every fish in the lake."

"He's a stubborn one. Runs in the family," I replied.

Quinn didn't laugh at my joke like he normally would. "Why didn't you come back to the shanty after you found the body? Why didn't you call me?"

I licked my lips. "I had to get to the booth. I promised Kristy I'd work it today."

"Where is Kristy?"

"She had to run home. Unless she comes back, it seems that I'm stuck here for the rest of the day."

A strange look crossed his face. "Why would she leave you like that when she knew what you've just been through?"

"Mom stuff," I said. "I totally get it."

Quinn's face cleared, and he nodded.

I let out a breath. I hoped I wouldn't have to tell anyone what Kristy had said about her husband and last night, now or ever. I just hoped Kent would speak to Sheriff Penbrook soon.

"Besides, by staying here, I will be around in case you need any help with Dad."

He chuckled. "It might come to that. He takes ice fishing very, very seriously."

"Oh, I know." I smiled. "I was never good at it, much to his disappointment. I'm glad that Hazel can fill that void for him."

His eyebrows knit together in concern.

A few passersby stopped at the booth. I greeted them and encouraged them to enter the raffle while Quinn looked on. When they left, he said, "Wallace Fields was the victim."

"I know that's the rumor around the derby," I said unsure I should confirm what I knew until I heard from Kristy.

"I didn't hear it from a rumor. My dad called me, and he's up in arms because he says he's being boxed out of the investigation, even though it includes one of his community members. He knows I'm here today, so he wants me to keep an eye on things. To be honest, I wouldn't be surprised if he didn't roll up in a few minutes and start asking questions. He's not going to let Sheriff Penbrook run this investigation without him."

I grimaced, but I wasn't surprised to hear that. I knew Chief Randy didn't like to share investigations with other law enforcement. He hated sharing them with me even more. However, I couldn't see the sheriff playing along with the short-tempered chief. If Quinn was right about his father's intentions, the police chief and the county sheriff were about to bump heads in a big way. I didn't want to be around when that happened.

Quinn cleared his throat. "I just wanted to make sure you were okay."

I smiled at him. "I'll be fine, Quinn. I promise."

He nodded and said, "I had better get back on the ice. If Hazel catches a fish and I'm not there to see it, both of us will be disappointed."

I nodded. "If Kristy isn't able to come back, I'll probably be here all day, so I can take Dad home myself." I cleared my throat. "I'll let you know either way. Thank you for keeping an eye on Dad. It means a lot to me. It really does."

He nodded and then melted into the crowd.

After Quinn left, I needed a break from making small talk with strangers about everything Cherry Glen had to offer. My cheeks ached from fake smiling for so long. I placed a "Be Back Soon" sign on the table, snapped on Huckleberry's leash, and left the booth.

I looked down at the pug. "Let's go see if we can find out more about Wallace Fields, okay?"

He shook one of his boots at me.

Chapter Seven

W alking down the line of community tables and vendors selling hot coffee, soft pretzels, and fishing gear, I inhaled the crisp winter air. Snow and ice crunched under the soles of my boots, and snowflakes landed on my eyelashes. I tried to concentrate on those sensations, but it was difficult. My mind kept returning to what Huckleberry and I had seen under the ice.

Thankfully, the pug didn't seem haunted by the memory as he tried to catch snowflakes on his tongue. At the end of the line of vendors sat the brewery booths. To my surprise, I saw Field Brewing Company was open. There was a young woman in the booth handing out samples. She was tall and thin, and her black hair was held back from her face in a braid that looked both carefree and complicated at the same time. She wore bright red earmuffs rather than a hat.

I glanced at my watch. It wasn't even ten in the morning, and the beer was already flowing. I reminded myself that most of the anglers had been out on the lake since three o'clock. This would feel like the middle of the day for them.

Next to the woman in earmuffs stood Jason Brennan, the

young hipster who had beat out Kent for the brewmaster position. Neither of them looked as upset as I expected they might upon hearing the news that their employer had been found dead not long ago.

It was a little too early in the morning for beer for me, but it seemed that was all they were giving samples of or selling. The line to the Fields's booth was five people deep.

"Would you like a sample?" the young woman asked when I finally made it up to the counter.

I nodded. "I'd heard you had a new cherry beer. Would I be able to try that?"

"No, we—"

"Don't tell her no, Lila Rae," Jason interrupted her. "We do have a few bottles left."

Lila Rae pressed her bright red lips together. "I thought we were saving those for MOBA members."

"One sample for one pretty lady won't hurt anything." Jason smiled at me and then brushed his hair out of his eyes in a practiced way.

I held up my hand. "I can try a different one if you need to save those."

He poured the beer out of a growler into a small disposable cup. "Here. Have a taste."

I accepted the beer from his hand. It smelled like cherries. I took a sip. It was sweet and tart, and honestly delicious.

Everyone was so certain that Kent was going to win, but this beer, at least to my unrefined palate, was the better of the two. It reminded me of the conversation I heard last night after the winner was announced. Someone had said that Jason's beer was better than Kent's and Jason must have changed the recipe.

"This is the beer that won the competition at the brewery?" I asked.

Jason played with the skull and bone rings on his hands, which were red from cold. "It is, and it's mine. I will be the brewmaster at Fields Brewing Company going forward."

Instead of telling him to put on gloves to cover his freezing hands like I wanted to, I took another sip of the beer. It really was good. "Is this the original recipe that you submitted?"

His face reddened ever so slightly. "Of course it is." He folded his arms. "I made some tweaks to it, but it's the same."

Lila Rae gave him a sideways glance.

I held up my cup. "Well, it's very good. I may be back to get more, but I'm working the booth from Cherry Glen just down the line there. I have to have my wits about me."

"You're from Cherry Glen?" Lila Rae asked.

I nodded.

"You must have been to Fields before, then."

"I have," I said. "I was just there last night for the announcement." I nodded to Jason. "Congratulations."

He narrowed his eyes as if questioning whether my congratulations were genuine.

"I'm surprised that your stand is open. I—I heard what happened to the owner," I trailed off.

Jason's face changed into a stony scowl.

Lila Rae spoke up. "My mother thought it was the best

way to remember Wallace today. She doesn't want the business to falter over what has happened. We're upset, yes, but we can't just stop because something bad has happened. We have to keep moving forward."

"Chanel is wise," Jason said. "We have to keep moving forward. As sad as we are, under her leadership, the brewery will be just fine."

I swallowed. "Chanel Fields is your mother," I said to Lila Rae. "Was Wallace your father?"

"He was my stepdad. There's a difference," she said with no emotion, leaving the comment to hang in the frigid air. It made me think there was something more to it.

"I'm glad to hear the brewery is staying open." I almost added that Kent was a friend of mine but decided to keep it to myself for the moment. "I heard the competition was very close."

"It wasn't, really." Jason said. "That was what Wallace wanted people to think to build up excitement for the party. However, there really wasn't any doubt in anyone's mind that I would win."

Lila Rae watched Jason from under her fake eyelashes with a scowl on her face. I couldn't tell if these two were friends or frenemies. There was definitely something going on between them.

"You mentioned MOBA. I've heard of the group before. Is Fields a member?"

"We are," Jason answered. "In fact, Wallace was set to be sworn in as the organization's president. I don't know what they'll do now."

"They'll go to the elected vice president," Lila Rae said, as if she couldn't believe he was so naive on the matter.

"Well then, Annette Woodhall must be one very happy woman. I'll have to congratulate her," Jason said.

Annette Woodhall? That was the name Tanner had called the woman with the silver bob at the brewery party last night. She had been the one complaining to the man, Sidney Tucker. Was that significant?

"Annette's the vice president now?" I asked. "I was hoping to talk to the organization. I'm an organic farmer, and I thought there might be a good opportunity for local farms and brewers to work together."

Jason nodded. "That sounds like just the kind of discussion that Annette would want to have. If you are looking for her, she should be at the MOBA booth at the end of the line. No one is more passionate about MOBA than she is. Honestly, I was surprised when she wasn't named president in the first place. She certainly put her time in. She and her husband both did."

"Who's her husband?" I asked.

Lila Rae and Jason shared a look.

"He used to work at Fields," Lila Rae said.

"He doesn't any longer?"

"No," Jason said. His tone had finality to it that didn't invite more questions.

While I had stood there, the line grew long again. I held up my plastic cup and thanked them for the sample before I moved on. I debated whether or not I had time to talk to Annette at the MOBA table. I had been away from the

Cherry Glen booth for a long while now. I bit the inside of my lower lip and decided I would just introduce myself to Annette and then be on my way.

The MOBA booth was at the very end of the line, as Jason had said, and I noticed it wasn't getting nearly as much traffic as the breweries themselves. I wasn't surprised. MOBA wasn't giving out samples of free beer. It wasn't going to have much luck competing against that.

Annette and Sidney stood behind the booth waving to people as they walked by. Annette stood as I approached the table. "Good morning! Have you heard of MOBA before?" She asked it in such a way that I guessed she had asked that question many times already that morning.

"I have," I said with a smile. "You're the beer association, right?"

She nodded. "The *organic* beer association. MOBA stands for Michigan Organic Beer Association. We started in Traverse City, and I can tell you that we are sweeping across the state. People want to enjoy their brews without having to worry where the grain, hops, and other ingredients came from. We certify brewers as organic, and customers can buy our members' brews with the confidence that only the very best organic ingredients were used." She took a breath.

It was quite a speech and clearly one she knew well.

"That's what I've heard. I'm an organic farmer from Cherry Glen, and I was interested in information about your group. Perhaps there are ways we can partner?"

She smiled. "You know I've already been talking to

another organic farmer about a partnership with MOBA. He said he was from Cherry Glen too." She tapped her cheek. "I can't remember his name off the top of my head, but he was very handsome. If I was thirty years younger, I would've asked for his number!"

There was only one handsome organic farmer in Cherry Glen.

"Tanner Birchwood?" I asked.

She nodded. "Yes, I do believe that was his name. So handsome and polite. They don't make young men like him anymore. I can assure you my three sons didn't turn out like that." She shook her head.

"If you're from Cherry Glen, you must know Wallace Fields." Sidney spoke up for the first time. "In fact, didn't I see you at his party last night? You were with Kristy Brown."

I glanced at him. "I was there," I said. "To support Kristy's husband Kent."

The man shook his head. "It was a real shame Kent didn't win. He's a nice guy. However, when you taste the other brew by that Jason fellow, Kent didn't stand a chance. It was that good."

"I just had a sample." I help up my empty plastic cup. "I will admit that it was good, though to be honest I don't drink much beer."

Annette shifted back and forth where she stood. "Yes, well, I know we are all so terribly sad about the accident."

"I severely doubt that everyone is upset over Wallace's accident," Sidney said. He wore circular glasses and had a gold earring in both of his ears that I hadn't noticed in the dim light at the brewery. "In fact, I would venture to say that there are many people who are quite pleased with it."

"Sidney!" Annette gasped. "That is a horrible thing to say."

"It's not horrible if it's the truth. People didn't like Wallace, and for good reason. He was a cheat."

Annette's face turned bright red. "I don't believe that's how you should speak about the matter."

"When I start caring how I speak about matters, you'll need to check my pulse because I'll be dead."

Annette wrinkled her forehead as if she didn't understand exactly what he meant. I was with her on that.

"It's been a shock," I said. "I remember seeing you at the party last night too, but we haven't met."

"This is Annette Woodhall, and I'm Sidney Tucker. I live near the lake. I'm not usually given credit for it, but I'm the reason MOBA started in the first place. There wouldn't be an organic beer movement in Michigan without me."

Annette frowned. "Brewers in the state have been making organic brews for years, if not decades."

"Sure, but I was the one who mobilized and organized them into this group. When it comes to pricing and laws, a group will always be more powerful than the individual. I gave them that."

Annette twisted her mouth like she wasn't in complete agreement, but she wasn't going to argue in front of a stranger like myself.

Annette handed me a brochure. "We would be happy to get information about your farm, including what you grow."

She set a clipboard with a blank piece of paper in front of me. "We would need your name, number, website, and crops. If we're interested, a contingent from our group would come out to your farm to examine your farming practices. Are you a certified organic farmer?"

"I'm in the middle of the certification. We've only been making the transition to organic over the last six months. As you know, it's a process."

"Well, if you're not ready... It seemed to be that the young man Tanner was ready. Maybe we should start with him."

"Our cherry orchard is ready," I said quickly. "And our fields will be by planting season."

She narrowed her eyes as if she wasn't sure she could believe me.

I quickly wrote my information on the piece of paper.

Annette picked up the clipboard, skimming it quickly. "Thank you, Shiloh" she said with a finality that told me this conversation was over.

I turned to go.

"Hey, Shiloh," Sidney called after me. "You should come to our next MOBA meeting and find out what we're really about. You can meet brewers there."

"Our meetings aren't open to the public," Annette interjected in a chilly voice.

Sidney folded his arms. "She's not the public. She's a farmer who is looking to do business with our brewers. It could be advantageous to lots of people."

Annette looked like she was going to argue some more when Sidney went on to say, "Besides, you invited that

Tanner fellow. I don't see why this girl should be treated any differently."

"I'm the president of the group. It's my decision who is and who isn't allowed to attend our meetings."

"You're not the president yet. You have to be sworn in. That won't happen until the meeting," Sidney argued. "You could be contested."

"No one will contest me. Being the president of this group is a thankless job."

This made me wonder why Wallace or Annette would want the position.

"I'm the acting president," Annette insisted.

"That may be, but you're not ruling in a dictatorship," Sidney said. "And the only reason you are in the position in the first place is because Wallace Fields was found belly-up in the lake."

I winced at his crass and sadly too accurate description as to how I had found Wallace earlier that morning.

"Fine." Annette looked to me. "If you want to come, come. The meeting is Monday night at seven sharp at the Front Street Speakeasy above the Cherryland Boutique in Traverse City."

"I know where that is," I said and loosened my scarf.

Saying goodbye to Sidney and Annette, I picked up Huckleberry so he wouldn't get stepped on in the crowd as I wove down the busy path.

"Well, lookie here what the osprey dragged in," a high-pitched voice said.

I glanced over my shoulder and saw Hedy Strong leaning

against a pine tree on the banks of the lakeshore. She was wearing camouflage from the top of her head to the covers on her boots. Across her chest was the largest pair of binoculars I had ever seen. They probably seemed even larger than they actually were because of Hedy's size, as she was a very petite woman. Her brown hair had faded to gray, and she didn't care in the least about her appearance. As far as I knew, the only thing Hedy Strong cared about was birds. She cared *a lot* about birds.

During the summer, she'd almost single-handedly stopped a developer's campaign to put wind turbines in Cherry Glen for the sake of her beloved birds.

The Great Lakes and Michigan were a perfect place to harness wind power. The gusts coming south over Lake Michigan from Canada could knock a person clear off their feet. However, there was a problem: birds, or rather the migration of hundreds of thousands of birds over the Great Lakes every spring and fall. If the turbines were installed, thousands of birds might be killed by the spinning propellers.

Hedy wasn't completely against the clean energy; she just believed that the turbines needed to go in a spot less dangerous for her feathered friends.

"Someone told me that you were here," she said looking up at me. At five nine, I towered over her.

Hedy folded her arms. "I suspected you would be here when I heard the news."

"The news?" I wasn't sure what she was getting at, but I guessed it had something to do with Wallace Fields.

"Sure," she said in a matter-of-fact way. "I heard you have another murder on your hands."

I grimaced. *Here we go again…*

Chapter Eight

"Why do you think it's murder?" I hugged Huckleberry more closely to my chest. This couldn't be happening. Not again. Maybe I was cursed when it came to finding dead bodies. Why did they all have to be murders?

But I still held on to the hope that Hedy was wrong. Perhaps I was being a bit judgy, but I doubted Hedy and Wallace had known each other when he was alive. They didn't move in the same circles. I'd never seen her at the Fields Brewing Company. In fact, even though she supposedly lived in the Glen, I'd never seen her in town. The only place I'd ever seen her was out in the wild. And when I say wild, I meant the real thing with trees, plants, animals, and yes, of course, birds.

"I was walking up the lakeshore, making sure that everyone was being respectful to the birds in the area. You can never be too careful about that sort of thing. There are some people who only care about themselves, and you have to keep people like that in check." She took a breath. "When I saw the body lying there on the ice, I knew what got him, and it wasn't natural causes. I even went up to Milan and told him so, not that he wanted to talk to me about it. He had to do everything by protocol."

"You know Sheriff Penbrook?" I asked.

"The sheriff and I go way back. His father, Richard, is one of the foremost birders in Lansing. For three years running, Richard had the records for the most sightings in Michigan. I've beaten him many more times than that, but it doesn't make the losses sting any less."

"You can lose at birding?" I asked. This was an entire subculture I knew very little about, and what I did know came from Hedy. She lived, breathed, and slept birding. That was assuming that she slept. I wasn't sure that she did. It seemed that she was always out looking for birds, from the most common to the rarest of rare.

"Without a doubt," Hedy said with conviction. "And I hate losing."

"Why do you think he was killed?"

"Because I saw the telltale signs on his throat of where the garrote bit into his neck. His face was bloated too. It's not a pretty way to die, and it's something that doesn't happen to someone by accident. At least not in my experience. Sadly, it's something we do see with lakeshore birds from time to time, because they get caught up in fishing line and nets. That's why I'm here today. You better believe I'm keeping an eye on all these anglers to make sure they pick up every last piece of line, candy wrapper, bottle, or hook before they leave. Any one of those things can kill a shorebird or other wildlife too. And if that happens, they'll have to deal with me."

My head was spinning. I couldn't believe I was having

this conversation with her. Could what she'd said be true? I didn't see any reason to doubt her. Hedy was eccentric, but she'd never said anything that wasn't true, as far as I knew.

She put her hands on her hips. "So are you going to try to find out who did it?"

I shook my head. "Why would I do that?"

"Because you're nosy," she stated. "And you have a need to know. Milan is a nice man. He'll be much more pleasant to deal with than Chief Randy back in Cherry Glen. That being said, I'm not sure Milan will be thrilled over a civilian getting involved. I'd stay away from the whole thing if I were you. Milan is a good cop. He's almost as good at catching criminals as his father, Richard, is at spotting birds."

That was high praise coming from Hedy.

I shifted Huckleberry's weight in my arms. "I'm not getting involved."

"Uh-huh," she said with a knowing look.

I wondered what else Hedy had discovered about the current situation that I didn't yet know.

"Well, I need to make the rounds and ensure the numb-skulls out on the lake mind themselves. After this is all cleaned up, I can get a few hours' sleep before my owl walk tonight. It's promising to be a good one."

I didn't bother to ask Hedy what an owl walk was. The name seemed self-explanatory, and considering Hedy's pursuits, it couldn't be much else.

She stepped away from me, out onto the ice. Huckleberry and I watched as she moved surefooted across the surface in her sturdy boots.

"Huck, I really don't know why this murder stuff keeps happening to us, but we need to keep our noses clean and our heads held high."

He snuffled in agreement.

By this point, I had been away from the Cherry Glen booth for close to an hour. If Kristy knew about it, she wouldn't be happy. Scratch that, she'd be downright angry. I made it back to the booth without being stopped again, to find everything was safe and still in its place. However, there was one new addition. Sheriff Penbrook stood in front of the booth with crossed arms.

"I told you to let me know if you planned to leave."

"I didn't leave, Sheriff. I took my dog for a walk around the derby for a little exercise."

As if to help prove my point, Huckleberry marched in place. I could always count on that little pug to be on my side. I really couldn't have a better ally. He then seemed to remember he had the offending boots on and stopped marching. Instead, he started shaking his legs.

"He doesn't seem to like those boots," the sheriff said.

I sighed.

"All right. I'd like to go over your statement again."

"I thought one of your deputies was going to take my statement."

He studied me. "He was, but you were MIA when he came by."

I swallowed. "Oh right."

"Just tell me the story from the beginning like I'm hearing it for the very first time."

"Okay. Why don't you come back here and sit down? People will be less likely to overhear."

He nodded and sat in one of the two folding chairs behind the table inside the booth. I sat in the other. As quickly and concisely as I could, I told him about my day at the derby, from my arrival to the moment I found Wallace floating under the ice.

This time, he typed notes into his phone while I spoke. When my story was over, he thanked me.

"As Huckleberry and I were walking back to our booth, I ran into Hedy Strong." I let the name hang in the air.

"You know Hedy?" He sounded wary.

"Yes, I've had conversations with her about birds." I didn't add the reason for those conversations had been murder related.

"Do you bird?" he asked.

His use of the word "bird" as a verb made me smile. I knew from Hedy that birders called birdwatching birding. She told me once a real birder never said "birdwatching"— that was a sure giveaway that you were any amateur at the sport. Though I still wasn't sure what a person "won" at birding other than bragging rights.

I shook my head. "I mean, I love birds. We have a lot on our farm. I had thought to ask Hedy to stop by and identify many of them for me during fall migration. Do you bird?"

"Not really. There were too many times I was forced to go on hours-long bird walks when I was kid. It sort of takes the fun out of it. Birders like my dad and Hedy aren't just peeking out the kitchen window at their bird feeders. They're serious about it. My dad spends thousands of dollars on travel every year just with the hopes of seeing a rare bird. I'm not against his hobby. It's just…" He shook his head. "That's neither here nor there."

"Hedy told me Wallace was murdered."

He rubbed the back of his neck.

"Is that true?"

"It is," he said finally.

"And he was garroted." I touched my neck as if I could feel something biting into my own skin.

"Hedy shouldn't be talking about this," he muttered.

"So, it is true?"

He stood up. "It is. I don't think there is anything I can do to get Hedy to stop talking about it as much as she already has. She's never been one to follow the rules. I'm just sorry that she saw the body. We should have secured the area better. We had the crime scene well blocked from the direction of the ice fishing derby. We didn't expect someone to pop out of the trees."

"How awful. I wouldn't wish anyone to see it. It was bad enough seeing Wallace under the ice. It would be so much worse when he was pulled out." I got to my feet as well. "What was used for the garrote?" I asked.

He looked out onto the lake, where hundreds of anglers were leaning over twelve-inch circular holes in the ice. "That isn't a question I can answer."

"Was the murder weapon present on the body?"

"No, and you should keep in mind Hedy doesn't have the expertise or authority to have a theory on this matter.

The coroner is the best one to determine the cause of death." He cleared his throat. "I've spoken to the police chief, Chief Randy Killian, in Cherry Glen and told him what happened."

I grimaced. "Did you mention my name?"

"I did."

I sighed. "I'm sure he had some wonderful things to say about me."

"He said you've given him trouble during a past investigation. I'll remind you, Ms. Bellamy, this is the sheriff department's investigation. Do not get involved. Chief Randy might tolerate such behavior, but I will not." With that said, he left the booth.

When he was gone, I muttered to myself, "Chief Randy doesn't tolerate it either. And that's never stopped me before."

Chapter Nine

Traffic around the Cherry Glen booth was nonexistent at two thirty, so I decided to pack up. Thankfully, I was able to put the folding tables, chairs, and boxes of brochures in the bed of my father's truck. Huckleberry sat inside the truck cabin while I loaded up.

When everything was in the back and secure, I opened the passenger door. "Come on, let's go get Grandpa."

He whimpered. The pug had enough of the outside for the day. He was rarely out in the cold this long on the farm. He'd spend a few hours with Chesney—my farm assistant—and I while we worked outside in freezing temperatures, but he would soon either wander into the farmhouse to watch television with Dad or into the barn to snuggle with the barn cats.

We were still working on making him a proper farm dog. Though, I was beginning to have my doubts he would get there. Thousands of years ago in China, pugs had been bred to be companion dog to the wealthy. The plan had never been for them to herd chickens or ride on a tractor.

After one more snuffly sigh, Huckleberry hopped out of

the truck. He landed on his boots and shook out his legs in turn.

"We'll see if we can get you some new boots that are a bit more comfortable."

He snorted. In pug, that was a happy sound.

Fishermen and spectators were gathering to hear the end of the day announcements. I snapped on Huckleberry's leash. "Stay close," I told the pug. "I don't want you to get stepped on."

He shook out his left rear leg.

I led Huckleberry to the lakeshore. My boot slipped on the ice, but I kept my balance. Walking on ice was a skill that was taking me a little while to regain. I remembered coming to the lake as a teenager to ice-skate or just slide across the glassy surface on sleds or baking sheets. It had been so carefree until someone got hurt—and someone always did.

"What an amazing day we've had out on the ice!" a man standing on a crate and holding a microphone at the edge of the fishing area announced. "And this is just the first day. We hope that all of you anglers will be back tomorrow for the second day of the derby. The number of fish we are pulling in is outstanding. Let's announce our leaders in each division. Starting with the Silver Class, we have Sullivan Bellamy with nine pikes. Let's all clap for Sully!"

I clapped and cheered for my father. I spotted Dad standing with Hazel across the ice. The young girl jumped up and down. Dad waved to the crowd and gave Hazel a side hug next to his walker. I felt a twist in my heart. He hadn't celebrated with me. Grandma Bellamy had done that.

When my father emerged from his black hole after my mother's death, it had been too late. I was already a teenager and was closer to my grandmother than I ever would be with my father. He probably knew that, so, for better or worse, he didn't press trying to get close to me.

Hours of therapy in LA had told me I had father issues. Most women did, I supposed. There was something about a father-daughter bond that was different, special. My issues stemmed from not having a bond. I realized now—months after returning to Cherry Glen—that I'd come back here not just to save the farm, but also to have a chance at a relationship with my father before it was too late. There had been glimmers of hope since I'd returned, but no moments like those he so naturally shared with Hazel.

My LA therapist had worked with me a lot about accepting people for who they are. I'd tried to do that when it came to my relationship with my father, but it wasn't easy. It was especially hard whenever I was reminded how things could have been.

The leaders in the rest of the classes were announced. Hazel spotted me and Huckleberry across the ice and came running.

"Whoa!" I caught her just as she slid by on her boots. "This ice is slippery. You have to take it slow."

"Did you hear that Sully is in first place?" she asked excitedly. "He's going to crush it tomorrow and bring home the W."

"I don't doubt it for a second," I said as we walked over to where Dad and Quinn stood.

"Tomorrow morning, we're going to have to get here

earlier," Dad said. "If I want to clinch this win, I need my lines in the water by six. I can't just be setting up."

"Dad, I wasn't planning to come out tomorrow. Kristy doesn't need me for the booth." At least, as far as I knew she didn't need me. That might have changed since the death of Wallace Fields. I hadn't heard from her since she ran home to see Kent. I hoped that wasn't a bad sign.

"I have to be here at five, not a second later."

I held a breath. Tomorrow was Sunday. It really was the only day of the week I allowed myself to sleep in. And by sleep in, I meant wake up at seven. I let out a silent breath of air. I knew how important this competition was to my father, and he was very likely to win. I wanted to be there to see it. I just didn't necessarily want to spend another full day at the ice fishing derby. In any case, there was no way I could say no.

Just as I was going to agree to bring him back to the lake at five, Quinn spoke up. "I can give you a lift out here Sully."

"I'm coming too," Hazel said. "I want to be here when you win."

Dad grinned. "That's the spirit."

"If you guys are sure," I said.

"Of course, we'll just swing by your farm around four thirty and pick up Sully."

While Hazel and Dad spoke excitedly about all the fish they had caught that day, I pulled Quinn aside. "Are you sure that you can pick up my dad? I hate for you to have to get up any earlier just for that reason."

He laughed. "Hazel has been so excited about this derby; if I wake up earlier it will because she can't sleep. I think it will be even worse tonight because she is so pumped that Sully is leading his age division."

I let out a breath. "Okay."

He put a hand on my shoulder. "Hey, it will give you time to get your farm chores done without your dad looking over your shoulder, and you can come later to see how we are all doing."

I smiled up at him. "It sounds like a plan."

"We're good at making plans together, Shi." He walked away to join Dad and Hazel.

I really wished he would stop saying things like that. I was confused enough about how I felt about him as it was.

I rejoined our little group. "Are you ready to go home, Dad?" I asked.

"Sure am. I have everything packed up in the shanty."

"Why don't we put all your gear in my truck?" Quinn said. "That will give us less to do in the early morning."

"That's a fine idea," Dad said.

Dad, Huckleberry, and I were finally on the road home a little while later.

Dad leaned back in this seat with Huckleberry on his lap. "It's been quite a day. I didn't know I still had it in me to sit that long and fish. I'll be sitting on my heating pad when I get home and finishing the day with a hot toddy."

I glanced at him. "I'm glad it went so well for you."

"I heard it was an interesting day for you. You found another dead man. I never thought my daughter would find such things, but I suppose we must consider it some sort of habit for now."

"It's not a habit I want," I said.

"Many habits are unwanted, but that doesn't make them any less real."

"No, it doesn't," I agreed.

When we arrived back at the farm, I got Dad settled in the house with his heating pad, some chicken soup, and fresh bread. I gave some of the soup to Huckleberry too. While the pair of them enjoyed their dinner, I went outside and checked on the chickens and barn cats for the night. Esmeralda, Hazel's rescued Siamese mix, was usually lording over the barn cats if Huckleberry and I weren't around, but she wasn't in the barn with the other four cats.

I called her name, but she didn't come out from wherever she was hiding. Even though she was a diva, Esmeralda usually came running when she was called, probably because it was usually for dinner. That little cat didn't like to miss a meal.

I called again, but still, nothing. There was no sign of her.

I bit my lip. I didn't like any of the chickens or cats out at night, especially in winter. There were bobcats, coyotes, and other predators in the area that would see Esmeralda as a possible meal. And it was a bigger risk in the winter with prey more difficult to find.

I walked out of the barn, calling her name. The more she didn't come, the more I started to panic. First and foremost, I didn't want anything to happen to Esmeralda because I cared about the cat. Second, Hazel would never get over it.

Esmeralda was the queen of the farm. She hadn't grown up on the farm like the tabbies had. She'd led a sheltered life until she came to Bellamy Farm. At first, I hadn't known how this pampered cat would do around the chickens and other cats, but she had quickly fit right in. Basically, she'd strutted in and let them know she was the boss.

The sun was sinking low in the sky. The light would be completely gone in a few minutes.

"Esmeralda!" I cried as loud as I could.

Nothing.

I called her name again, and I heard a faint meow coming from the front of the house. I ran in that direction and found the little cat sitting on the step leading up to the front porch. Or more accurately, she was standing on the step that was leading up to what had been the front porch.

The farmhouse was in disrepair. More disrepair than I was able to financially contend with at the moment. It had been made all the more apparent when, just before Christmas, the front porch had fallen under the weight of a heavy snow.

As of yet, I hadn't been able to deal with the aftermath. Dad and I came and went from the back of the house; that door faced the barn and chicken coop anyway.

"Esmeralda, you scared me! You know I don't want you alone outside at night."

She meowed and pawed at the snow covering what was left of the porch.

I walked over and picked her up. I unzipped my coat and tucked her inside to warm her up. She snuggled against my chest. The little cat could snuggle when she wanted to, but it only happened on her own terms. In fact, when it came to Esmeralda, everything had to happen on her terms.

I started to walk back to the rear of the house when Esmeralda wriggled out of my grasp and jumped into the snow at my feet. She then leaped back onto the porch step.

"What are you doing? It's time for you to go in for the night. It's for your own good. You had a lot of wandering time around the farm today while Huckleberry and I were at the ice fishing derby."

I had always had conversations with my animals. As of yet, they'd never answered me back in English. When they started doing that was when I would get worried.

She pawed at a shingle that had once been on the porch roof.

"I know, I know, it's a mess. I'll get to it in the spring. It's too much work to dig it all out of the snow."

She hissed.

"Sheesh, you seem to have a very strong opinion on this."

I picked her up a second time and took her into the house.

Chapter Ten

I t had been a long and exhausting day, but I knew I needed to take the materials from the Cherry Glen booth to Kristy so she could give them to tomorrow's volunteers. I was worried about her too. Even though I'd texted and called several times to ask how she was throughout the day, I hadn't heard a peep from her in reply.

That was unusual. Kristy was a serial texter. I typically received dozens of texts from her on any given day. I used to feel obligated to reply to each one—even if my reply was just an emoji—but finally gave up. I knew if something was really important, she would call me. Many times, I didn't catch up on her text messages until I lay down for the night.

When Huckleberry and I rolled up to Kristy and Kent's cozy little ranch-style home thirty minutes later, I had a sinking feeling in my chest. There was an Antrim sheriff's department SUV in their driveway. A sheriff's vehicle in Kristy's driveway would always be alarming, but Cherry Glen was in Grand Traverse County, not Antrim. There was only one reason the sheriff from Antrim County would be there, and it had to do with Wallace Fields.

I hopped out of my father's truck and told Huckleberry to stay put. Just as I did, the front door opened, and Kent came outside, followed by a sheriff's deputy.

Kent spotted me and lowered his head. My heart sank. Why wouldn't he even look at me? Was he feeling guilty? Guilty of what? What had happened to Wallace? I felt like my stomach was being pulled in on itself with a dozen sharp fishing hooks.

Sheriff Penbrook came out the door next with Kristy close on his heels. Tears streamed down her face. I ran through the snowy yard to reach her. She didn't say anything, just threw herself into my arms and buried her head in my chest.

"What's going on?" I directed the question to the sheriff.

"Ms. Bellamy, I wish I could say I am surprised to find you here, but I'm not."

I ignored his comment. "Why are you here? Where are you taking Kent?"

"We're just taking Mr. Brown in for some questioning. At this point, he was the last person to see Wallace Fields alive, so we need to know every detail of those moments."

"Why can't you talk to him here?"

"We tried." He glanced at Kristy. "However, I believe it would be better to have a discussion without interruption."

I bit my lip. I believed he was telling me that Kristy had been trying to answer the questions for her husband instead of letting Kent speak. She was certainly the more talkative of the pair.

I cleared my throat. "Sheriff, Kent Brown is just the sweetest, hardest-working man on the planet."

"It's just questioning," Sheriff Penbrook said.

It may be "just questioning," but anything could happen in that situation. Kent could say something to make himself look worse, or he could appear like he was hiding information from Sheriff Penbrook, which could be just as bad.

The sheriff's face softened when he looked at Kristy. "We'll have him home as soon as we can."

Inside of the house, one of the babies began to cry, and Kristy took one last look at her husband—who was being helped into the back seat of the sheriff's SUV—before she went inside.

Sheriff Penbrook pressed his lips together and sighed. "I hate this part of my job." He then started toward his car.

I followed him. "Sheriff, you can't think Kent would kill another person. That would be like…like…accusing a koala of murder!"

He turned to look at me. "I've read koalas are actually very mean."

"Okay, then I chose the wrong species. You know what I meant. He's not the type to hurt someone."

"I never said he hurt anyone. Chief Randy has graciously offered his conference room in the municipal building here in Cherry Glen. Mr. Brown won't be gone that long. We will bring him back home as soon as we can." He nodded toward the house. "Go inside and see after your friend. Mrs. Brown has already told me how close the two of you are. She needs a friend like you right now." He patted my arm and walked to his vehicle where Kent and the deputy were waiting.

After they drove away, I collected Huckleberry and went into Kristy's house.

The moment you walked into Kristy's home, you knew little children lived there. A car seat was propped by the door, with an industrial-sized package of diapers next to it. All exits to the living-room-turned-playroom were blocked by mesh baby gates, and the middle of the floor was peppered with toys.

At the moment, the twins were happily sitting together on the floor playing with stuffed animals.

One of the girls chucked her teddy bear at her sister, and the other girl squealed. I couldn't tell if the squeal was of frustration or delight. To be honest, my interaction with babies was limited to the past few months around the twins. And even with all the time I spent with them, I couldn't tell them apart until I knew who was wearing which outfit that day.

Kristy sat on the couch looking at the girls. Tears gathered in the corners of her eyes. "Shi, this is bad. It's so much worse than I feared."

"The sheriff told me he's just taking him in for an interview. Kent will be back soon. He didn't do anything."

"That's the problem. He didn't do anything. If he had, Wallace Fields would still be alive."

"What do you mean?" I sat next to her on the couch. In the process, I sat on a pacifier, which I moved and set on the arm of the sofa.

She rubbed her face. "I don't want the girls to see me crying like this." She grabbed a baby wipe from the diaper bag on the floor and cleaned her face. "That's better."

"Now you smell like baby powder."

"Trust me, I could smell a whole lot worse having nine-month-old twins."

I'd have to take her word for that.

"Kent heard something that might have been related to the murder."

"What did he hear?"

"Hooting."

"Come again?"

"Hooting like an owl, but he thought it was a person pretending to be an owl. In any case, it was so late, and dark, and cold, that it freaked Kent out. He didn't wait for Wallace."

"Wallace wasn't there yet when he heard the hooting?"

"Not as far as he knew. He texted Wallace to say he'd found the spot where the brewery should have its booth and left."

"Did Wallace text him back?" I asked.

"Kent said he just wrote 'okay.' He took that to mean he could leave. It was the last text message Wallace received or sent. It's very possible my husband could have been the last person to communicate with him. The texts are how the police knew to come looking for Kent."

"They found Wallace's phone? I would've thought it'd be in bad condition if it went in the water with him."

"They haven't found his phone yet, but all of Wallace's text messages and voicemails were stored in the cloud."

I wondered how much information about myself was floating around in the cloud that I would rather not have people see if I were to die. I couldn't think of anything that'd get me in trouble, but I was certain there were some really bad photos of me up there somewhere.

"What was the time stamp on the text messages?" I asked.

"Kent's was 12:36, and Wallace replied at 12:41."

"It's possible Wallace wasn't even there yet. He could have still been on the way to the lake."

She shook her head. "Kent saw his truck in the parking lot. There was no one inside. He said it looked like it might have been there a little while longer than his because there was snow collected on the windshield. He said he was at the lake all of ten minutes before he heard the owl hooting and wanted to leave."

"So the time of death had to be sometime after Wallace's last text. I found the body at six thirty. That's a relatively small window. Not to mention that fisherman were allowed to arrive at three in the morning to set up their shanties and camps for the derby. I'm sure some of them were there earlier, just sitting in their trucks and vans waiting until three to claim a spot."

"That's what the sheriff thinks too. He and his deputies plan to talk to all the fishermen tomorrow to see if anyone saw anything between midnight and six. Kent said by the time he left, the parking lot was already getting crowded with fishermen waiting to go out on the ice. They get there so early with hopes of getting the best spot when they are finally allowed on the ice." She looked at me. "There was another sound Kent heard before he left…"

"What was that?"

"A big splash."

We both knew how noteworthy that was. The lake was frozen solid. A big splash would have been an unexpected sound.

"I keep thinking if Kent had investigated the hoot or the splash, he might have stopped whatever happened to Wallace." She hugged herself.

"You don't know that. You can't play the *if* game. There are just too many variables."

Even as I said it, I wondered if it was true. If Kent had investigated the noises would Wallace still be alive? Could Wallace have been pulled from the water and still been saved? There was no way to know, and it wasn't worth wondering about.

"At the same time, I'm glad he didn't investigate it. He could have been hurt or killed himself." She covered her eyes with her hands. "I don't know what I'm going to do. What if Kent gets arrested? I can't be a single parent. And think about how that would affect the twins!"

I watched the twins playing on the floor. I knew something about being raised by a single parent. It hadn't been easy for me. The twins' experience would be different, so much different, because Kristy was far more affectionate to her children than my father had ever been to me, but it would be hard on the girls. I didn't want that for them, for Kristy, or for Kent. It was hard for me to consider it was even a possibility, but from what Kristy had told me about the night that Wallace died, I knew that it was.

"What am I going to do?" my friend asked.

"You're going to take a deep breath and take all of it one

moment at a time. You need to be strong for your daughters and for your husband, just like you always have been."

She straightened her back. "You're right. There's no time for a pity party. Besides, you'll find the killer, and this will all go away."

I wished it was that simple. I really did.

Chapter Eleven

I stayed with Kristy until Kent came home. Kent was exhausted from his ordeal and didn't want to talk to me about it. I knew he was struggling with everything that had happened in the last twenty-four hours, but I couldn't help him if he didn't tell me his side of the story. Hearing it from Kristy secondhand wasn't the ideal way to get information. I had also been disappointed that a sheriff's deputy had brought Kent home. I'd wanted to ask the sheriff about the time of death.

When I'd broached the topic with the deputy, he'd just driven away.

After a long night, I woke up at six the next morning and was grateful Quinn had volunteered to take Dad to the fishing derby. At best I'd gotten an hour of fitful sleep. I couldn't stop thinking about how upset Kristy had been and how hurt, too, when Kent had refused to talk about what happened in the station. Perhaps he'd been so closemouthed because I was still there. I wanted to give him the benefit of the doubt. From what I knew of Kent, he was a private guy. Being scrutinized and questioned by a sheriff must have been difficult for him.

I got out of bed and both Huckleberry and Esmeralda beat me to the kitchen. I loved the kitchen in my little cabin, which sat back a half mile in the woods from the farmhouse and barn, because it reminded me the most of my grandmother. Other than giving it a thorough cleaning when I moved in, I had changed very little of it. It still had the linoleum flooring, white speckled Formica counter-top, and teal vintage appliances. I had even kept her white dishes with the tiny blue flowers on them. It made me feel close to her.

I fed the animals first and then made my coffee. I knew I wasn't going to be able to face this day without coffee.

After a few stops in town to see what I could learn about Wallace, I planned to head to the derby and ask the same questions the deputies would likely be asking. *Did you hear anything last night? Did you see anything?* I also hoped by going a bit later I wouldn't run into the deputies. I was certain Sheriff Penbrook didn't want me poking my nose into this. So it would be best to do it under the radar as much as much as possible.

Before I could do any of that, however, I had chores on the farm. By seven, it was first light and I went about my farm duties. My first stop was usually the farmhouse to see my father. Even though I knew he was supposed to be at the fishing derby with Quinn and Hazel, I had to check.

The house was empty. On the kitchen counter there was a note from Hazel. *Hope you can come to the derby today.* It was signed with a heart and her name. I smiled, folded the note, and stuck it in my jeans pocket. It warmed my heart that Hazel wanted to spend so much time with not only my father, but me too. She was a special kid.

I cleaned up my father's dinner and breakfast dishes and tidied up his house as much as possible. I folded his favorite blanket and laid it across the arm of his recliner. I wished there was more that I could do to improve my relationship with my father, but these little things were how I could show my love. Neither of us was great at telling the other how we felt.

Esmeralda met Huckleberry and I outside of the house and led the way to the barn. She liked a production of going into the barn and seeing her subjects, the barn cats. The barn cats were Esmeralda's servants. The chickens were more like her frenemies.

All four barn cats were asleep in the barn, curled up in a pile on a hay bale. Esmeralda meowed and the cats woke up, looking around like they'd done something wrong.

"I wish I could walk into a room and get that kind of respect," I said to Huckleberry.

Huckleberry looked at me as if to say, "Me too."

"I'm glad we're in this together, big guy."

The cats sat up and stood in a line on the hay bale. Esmeralda jumped up in front of them. She inspected each cat in turn and purred her approval. They each let out a sigh of relief. No one wanted to let Esmeralda down.

Now that Esmeralda had given the okay to go about their business, the cats curled up on the bale again and returned to their nap. *Oh, to be a cat.* I had thought that many times. I picked up an old horse blanket from a peg on the wall and gently set it over the sleeping pile of cats. They sighed happily.

I envied their peace and their ability to sleep. I wished I could go back to my cabin and get some rest, but I knew that wouldn't be possible, not when Kristy and Kent needed my help. I had promised myself I'd let this all go if or when I learned from the sheriff that Kent wasn't a suspect. There really was no other reason for me to be involved. I hadn't known Wallace, and he hadn't been in my little town when he was killed.

When I stepped out of the barn, I heard the crunch of tires on the snow-encrusted gravel driveway. I expected the newcomer to be Stacey or maybe even Chief Randy here to interrogate me over what had happened at the ice fishing derby.

It was neither. Instead, there was a shiny black pickup with temporary plates coming at me. It could only belong to one person: Tanner Birchwood.

"Hey, neighbor!" Tanner called in his usual cheerful way. He smiled from ear to ear, and it was a pretty smile. Tanner was a handsome man. In fact, he was the handsomest man I had ever met, and I used to cast male leads in Hollywood. He had movie star potential, but instead he had chosen to be a farmer.

It wasn't even a fair fight because he had a lot of something of which I had very little. Money. I reminded myself it wasn't Tanner's fault he was handsome, wealthy, and always cheerful. May we all be so unlucky.

I waved, doing my best to be neighborly. "Hi, Tanner."

Huckleberry hid behind my legs. He hadn't warmed up to Tanner yet. At this point, I was beginning to wonder if he ever would.

Tanner slammed his truck door closed. "I was just running into town and wanted to know if you needed anything while I was out."

"That's really nice of you, Tanner, but we're fine."

He shoved his bare hands in his coat pockets and rocked back on his heels. "It's the least I can do. I heard about your accident. You didn't say anything about it the other night at Fields." His tone was a tad accusatory.

"My accident?" I asked, and then I remembered sliding off the road into the ditch. How could I have forgotten that happened? It felt like I'd lived several lifetimes since Friday night.

"I wasn't hurt," I said. "The truck is fine too." I gestured at it to prove my point. As soon as I did, I regretted it. Compared to Tanner's new wheels, my dad's pickup looked like a rust bucket.

He glanced at Dad's pickup. "That's good to hear."

I cocked my head. "How did you hear about the accident?"

"I got a text yesterday from Jessa. She told me what happened and that I should stop by to check on you. I did stop by yesterday, but no one was home."

I bit the inside of my cheek.

Jessa was from Jessa's Place, the local diner in town. It was where every local ate and every local gossiped. I had been right. I had become the main topic of conversation. But I was sure by now I had been replaced on the roster by Wallace Fields's death.

Jessa also fancied herself a matchmaker. Tanner was single and handsome. He owned a large portion of my family's original farm. If we married, the land would be merged again, then Tanner and I would live and farm happily ever after. The end. It made sense...to her. It did not make sense to me.

"Yesterday, I took my father to the ice fishing derby on Lake Skegemog."

"I was there too." He frowned. "I got there and left again very early after I made the connections I was hoping for because I had to get back to the farm. There's so much to do, even in winter, especially when I'm making so many changes to the property." He studied me. "Were you able to make any connections while you were there?"

I knew at least one of those connections he'd wanted to make was with MOBA people. But I kept that to myself. I didn't want him to know I was interested in growing crops for organic beer until I weighed the pros and cons of the idea for myself. After the MOBA meeting Monday night, I would know more. My best option now was to change the subject completely.

"I was there to support my dad."

He pressed his lips together as if he didn't believe me but wasn't ready to come right out and say it.

"Well," I said. "If you see Jessa when you go into town, you can tell her I'm just fine. Quinn pulled my truck out of the ditch. I didn't even have to call AAA."

Tanner's brow furrowed. "Quinn helped you? How did that happen? Did you call him?"

I felt myself bristle. Who I did or did not call when I was in trouble was none of Tanner's concern. I had no reason to answer that question, but I heard myself say, "No, I didn't call him. He was on his way to pick up Hazel and just happened to be driving by at the right time. It was very fortunate for me."

"Oh, yeah, fortunate," Tanner said, seemingly mollified. He cleared his throat. "You know if you are ever in trouble, Shiloh, you can call me, day or night. I'll come running. It's important to me that you're safe, especially on these icy roads. You were in a California for a long time. Driving in these conditions takes some getting used to." His face flushed as if he thought he might have said too much.

I twisted my mouth to keep from saying anything I might regret. Tanner was from Chicago, and I knew Chicago got snow, but it wasn't like northern Michigan. I really didn't think that made him qualified to warn me about driving.

"That's very kind of you," I said neutrally.

"I mean it," he said, and then he cleared his throat again. "Well, I should get into town and back home so I can do some damage control around the farm before the next squall."

I nodded and watched as he climbed into his too-expensive truck and drove away.

Chapter Twelve

Owning a farm meant there was always, always something to do. This was an undeniable fact. Stalls needed to be mucked, fences needed to be painted, animals needed to be fed, equipment needed to be repaired, and on and on and on. It never stopped.

When I'd lived in LA, I'd thought I was busy, and I had been, to some extent. I was an in-demand producer. I wasn't a big blockbuster-level producer by any means, but when it came to true crime, cooking, or gardening shows on television or streaming, I was popular. I worked late into the night most days. Now, I had to do more on my family farm than I ever had in Hollywood. In LA, I could wrap a project, put it in the can, and walk away.

The farm would never be wrapped, canned, or left. The responsibility of it was constant. Something always wore out, broke down, or fell over. It was a daunting reality. So of course, instead of mucking, mending, or doing one of the dozen other chores, I decided to drive into town to see what I could find out about Wallace.

The best place to get a great meal—other than the

brewery, which was closed for the foreseeable future—and juiciest gossip was Jessa's Place. I could grab breakfast and learn what people were saying about Wallace Fields's death. I was no fool. I was certain that everyone in Cherry Glen knew by now what happened at the ice fishing derby yesterday.

As I drove into town it was hard to imagine I had found Wallace under the ice yesterday. The sun shone in a bright blue sky surrounded by huge fluffy clouds. Light sparkled on the freshly fallen snow and made the ice-covered tree limbs glisten. Winter could be beautiful when it wasn't being horrible.

Huckleberry seemed to enjoy the scenery too as he pressed his pug nose against the passenger-side window and watched the world go by.

Jessa's Place was at the very end of Michigan Street. It was the building everyone passed when they were on their way out of town headed to Traverse City.

It was the heart of town even though it didn't look like much as a nondescript building with a large sign on an old iron pole. The parking lot was usually gravel. Now it was mostly dirty snow and ice. And vehicles of every shape and size. The place was packed like always. It was nine o'clock, the time the farmers came in for their coffees and midmorning snacks.

I almost turned around. I wasn't one for the crowds, at least not crowds in Cherry Glen. I hadn't really minded them in LA because they had anonymity. However, in my hometown, everyone knew who I was, what I was doing. Gossip was a town pastime.

As much as I wanted to turn around and drive home, I didn't. The love of gossip at Jessa's Place might just be what I needed to find more suspects for Wallace Fields's murder. Because I knew without a doubt that Kent Brown was innocent, but until I heard Sheriff Penbrook say Kent was in the clear, I would keep pushing. Maybe if I made a big enough nuisance of myself, he would pronounce Kent innocent just to get rid of me. I was okay with that.

Huckleberry and I stepped into the diner, and the bell chimed over the door. Conversation stopped, and every head turned into our direction.

My pug looked at me with questions in his big brown eyes. "You all go back to your food and chatter. Do you have to stare at Shiloh Bellamy like she's from outer space every time she comes into the diner? Land sakes, she's been here for months now. Mind your own beeswax!" Jessa said as she scuttled through the crowded diner and took my hand.

She pointed at Huckleberry with her free hand. "You go wait by the rotating pie display; I will bring you a nice wedge of cheese just as soon as I get your momma settled."

Huckleberry lumbered over to the display case and lay down where he was told. He licked his chops. He really loved cheese, and who could blame him for that?

Jessa tugged on my hand. "Come on now, Shi. Let's get you to the back counter so we can chat while I work."

Jessa was a trim woman in her late fifties. She moved through the diner with more energy now than I had when I was ten. Her hair was naturally white, but she streaked it with bright colors that included anything from indigo, orange, yellow, green, and what she had today, which was neon pink. I guess the pink was in preparation for Valentine's Day in a few weeks. She typically chose her streak of colors based on the holiday calendar.

She had her long hair tied back with a rainbow scarf. She was cool and kind and probably the most well-liked person in town. And that wasn't even because she made the best coffee. However, the coffee was certainly a perk.

She let go of my arm, pointed at an empty stool in the middle of the counter, and scooted to the other side. As if she could read my mind, she flipped the mug in front of me over and filled it to the brim with black coffee. She slid the dishes of cream and sugar in my direction. "Just in case you want to use them this time."

I did want to use them, but I refrained. I had spent most of my life overweight. It wasn't until I moved to California that I finally got my health in check with diet and grueling exercise. I promised myself if I moved back to Michigan, I would be as disciplined as I had been in LA.

"How did you know I wanted coffee?" I asked.

"Because you always want coffee."

I guessed that was a good reason.

"And because," she went on as she topped off my mug, "I heard about yesterday."

"You already heard about that?"

She cocked her head as if she couldn't believe I'd asked the question. "It's *all* I've heard about today. Everyone is talking about Wallace Fields being murdered at the ice fishing derby."

I leaned over my black coffee. "What are they saying?"

She pressed her lips together and looked down the counter. There was an old farmer at the end milking a bowl of French onion soup. Perhaps some would say it was too early for such a meal, but I guessed he had been up since four, so it was lunchtime for him. He didn't look like he was listening to us, but you never knew. Jessa turned her back on him and said, "That Kent Brown is the killer because he was passed over for that promotion."

I blew out a long breath. It'd been just as I was afraid of.

"Chief Randy made it worse. He came in here—I'd say about an hour ago—and said the case would be closed soon because he already knew who the killer was. He was really upset that this isn't his case. He said it should be since it involves Cherry Glen citizens."

My eyes went wide. "Did he mention Kent by name?"

She shook he head. "No, but by that point everyone had been talking about it, so we all knew who he meant."

I rubbed my forehead. This was even worse than I thought it would be. Kristy was going to be furious, and when she was angry, she could be unpredictable. I worried she might do something she would regret, and also get her and Kent in a whole lot of trouble.

I sipped my coffee. "Have you heard of anyone who wanted to get Wallace out of the way? What would be the most likely motive?"

"Well, greed, of course. The man was rich. That brewery rakes in money and now that his beer is in grocery stores all over Michigan, I can't imagine how much he was worth."

"Who would be likely to inherit?"

"His son would be my guess."

The bell over the diner door rang.

"Speak of the devil…" Jessa nodded at the door.

I turned in my barstool to see a large man step into the diner. He had a trim goatee and wire-rimmed glasses. His plaid shirt stretched over his ample waist, and he wore jeans that I guessed were a couple hundred dollars from their perfect fit.

It was something I recognized because in LA it was commonplace for people's shoes and clothes to cost more than their monthly mortgage or rent.

Jessa pushed off from the counter and hurried to the front door, collecting the man just like she had done for me. She ushered him through the diner and sat him down on the stool right next to me. Subtle.

"I'll give Huckleberry his cheese and have to go take orders. Shiloh, can you get Spenser some coffee?" She scurried off.

I cleared my throat. "Would you like coffee?"

"I would." Spenser looked down at his empty hands.

I noticed that he was wearing a wedding ring.

I hopped off my stool and slipped behind the counter. Just like Jessa had done for me, I flipped over the plain white mug in front of him, filled it with black coffee, and scooted the cream and sugar in his direction.

Instead of drinking the coffee black like I had, he added enough cream and sugar to make the beverage almost white.

I stayed on the other side of the counter. It felt odd sitting next to Spenser on the stools, especially when I was looking at him as a prime suspect for his own father's murder. Now that I was looking directly at him, I could see he was young. I would guess no more that twenty-five. My heart went out to him. With his father dead, the weight of the brewery was on his shoulders.

"I'm really sorry about your father," I said.

He frowned. "What do you know about my father?"

"It's Cherry Glen," I said as if that was explanation enough.

Apparently it was, because his shoulders sagged in response. "I think the gossip will be the hardest part about coming back to this town. Everyone is always in each other's business." He looked up from the creamer. "Thank you for your condolences. It's come as a terrible shock. I just got married. This was supposed to be the best year, but it's only January and it's already ruined. I feel like every year starts out hopeful but quickly goes down the drain. It may not be worth being hopeful at all."

I bit my lip. That was a sad outlook on life. I didn't correct him though. The man was mourning. I hoped after he had grieved and accepted the loss of his father that he would gain a more positive perspective. It might take some time, lots of time. I knew that from painful personal experience.

"Did your wife come with you to Cherry Glen?" I asked.

He shook his head. "No, her final semester just started, and she has a study group. She wanted to come, but I didn't see the point of her missing her group meeting when I still didn't have a handle on what is going on here. She'll come over for the funeral, of course."

I nodded. "Have funeral arrangements been made?" I paused. "I know it's early yet."

"Not that I know of, but no one likes planning events as much as my stepmother, so she probably had the ball rolling before my father's body was cold."

I winced.

He dipped a spoon into his white coffee but hadn't yet taken a sip. "At least that's what my wife said. She and my stepmother don't get along. Larissa—that's my wife—is still mad at Chanel for trying to take over our wedding in December."

"Chanel is your stepmother?" I asked.

He nodded. "Yeah."

"How did she try to take over the wedding?"

"Larissa and I just wanted a simple church wedding with a cookie and cake reception. It's all we could afford. I graduated from college last May, but I do night-shift unloading at a warehouse, and then I'm working as a waiter in Lansing during the day. Larissa is a waitress at the same chain restaurant and doing night classes. We're making it work, but money is tight. It's always tight."

I wrinkled my brow.

He shook his head. "I know what you're thinking, how can we be so hard off if my father is so rich? Trust me. I've asked myself that so many times before. My father was a self-made millionaire, and he feels—felt—that it was essential I made it myself too. Even as a young boy, I knew he would never hand me something. I had to work for it."

I considered if this fit with what I'd known about Wallace

Fields, but I realized I knew very little about him. I'd only seen him in the brewery a few times while eating there or popping in to say hello to Kent when he was in the middle of a shift. I didn't believe I'd ever spoken to the man.

"Your father didn't include you in his business?" I asked.

"He wanted me to eventually take over the brewery business. Or so I was told, but I had to demonstrate my worth to my father. The problem was, Dad never told me exactly what I had to do to become worthy of him. It was a moving target. It's exhausting to be told your whole life that you're not good enough."

I knew something about proving yourself to a father, but Dad—as curmudgeonly as he was—had never been this harsh. I knew if I ever got in trouble, he would have helped me if he possibly could. The problem was that Dad always found himself in a tighter spot than me.

"So knowing that you had money issues, Chanel still wanted you to have a big wedding?"

He nodded. "I guess it was because she didn't think her daughter would ever marry."

"Lila Rae?" I ask, thinking of the girl with black hair I met the day before at the Fields's booth at the derby.

He nodded and didn't ask how I knew his stepsister's name. "Chanel said this was her last chance for a fairy-tale wedding. It didn't matter to her that was not what Larissa and I wanted. She canceled our little church wedding and reception and planned an elaborate affair at a fancy hotel in Traverse City. She made all the arrangements from the food to the decorations. She even found the officiant.

"Larissa and I were at the end of the semester, and I was taking a double course load so I could graduate a semester early in order to get a jump on our student loans. We just sort of allowed Chanel to take over. It wasn't what we wanted, but she's a force to be reckoned with. We never assumed for a moment that she would stick us with the bill."

"She asked you to pay for everything?"

"She didn't ask. She just sent us all the invoices. Along the way, all the contracts were in my name because I had to sign them as the groom, or so I was told by my stepmother. After the wedding when the bills came due, the vendors and venue came looking for me. I can't believe I was so stupid."

I wrinkled my brow. "But didn't you have to put down a down payment?" I asked. If he'd been asked to fork over an advance on the wedding, wouldn't it have been a red flag?

He pressed his lips together. "Yes, Larissa and I gave Chanel four thousand dollars for the wedding. It was all we had."

I picked up my coffee mug and sipped to hide my expression, but it seemed I wasn't fast enough, because Spenser said, "I know what you're thinking. We were stupid. You're right." He took a large slug of his coffee then, like he was throwing back a shot.

"Did you talk to your dad after you realized what Chanel did?"

"I tried, but he said he had done enough. He paid for the rehearsal dinner as is the tradition, but he refused to help with the wedding itself because he said it was the responsibility of Larissa's family. He was very traditional in that way.

The only problem was Larissa's parents have no money. They were farmers, and recently had to sell their land to pay their own debts. They now live in an apartment in Lansing not too far from Larissa and me. They're good people, but they can't financially help us. They can't even help themselves."

The idea of a family farm going under hit a little too close to home for me. I was determined it wouldn't happen to Bellamy Farm. Selling land wasn't an option. My father would never hear of it, and if I sold even one acre, I knew he would never forgive me. If I could find the treasure supposedly hidden somewhere in the heart of the farm—as my grandmother wrote in her last words to me before she died—that would be swell. Sadly, it didn't seem like Spenser had a hidden treasure to unearth. Although, I supposed that depended on the will…

"When Chanel left you holding the bill," I said slowly, "how did you pay for it?"

"We had to take out a personal loan. With that and our student loans… Well, suffice it to say, we're pretty far into debt. Debt like that makes Larissa nervous. She said we can't have children until we dig our way out. It'll take years, and all I ever wanted was to be a dad."

My heart went out to him, but I couldn't help thinking with his father now dead, his financial problems were solved. He could pay off all his debts and start the family he'd always dreamed of. That certainly was enough motivation for murder.

Chapter Thirteen

I left the diner and stepped out into the frigid air. I guessed the temperature had dropped at least three degrees in the time that I was inside of Jessa's Place. I wanted to walk to the brewery to see what I could learn there—assuming I could get in—but Huckleberry shivered at my feet.

"Okay, buddy," I said. "The good news is your jacket and boots are in the truck. The bad news is you hate wearing them."

He whimpered and I scooped him up. When we reached the truck, I grabbed Huckleberry's winter gear from the back seat. Who knew someday my Hollywood pug would need a ski jacket? Huckleberry allowed me to put on his ski jacket with little fuss. The matching boots were another story.

I made sure the elastic straps on his boots were secure and then set him on the ground. He kicked out his four legs one at a time, looking up at me with accusation in his round brown eyes the whole time. Apparently, having to wear the boots the entire day before at the derby had been too much.

"I'm sorry, Huck, but we can't take the risk of you getting

frostbite on your paws. We'll make it a short walk just to the brewery and back. I promise you'll get a nice nap by the fireplace back home later today."

He snuffled with irritation like only a pug could.

As we made our way down the sidewalk, Huckleberry kicked a leg out every third step. It was going to be a long one block walk to the brewery. When we reached the brewery, I saw a sign on the door saying the brewery was closed Sunday and would reopen Monday afternoon for the lunch hour. Typically, it wouldn't been open this early on a Sunday anyway, but I knew it had to be closed all day because of what'd happened to Wallace. I was surprised it was set to open Monday. It seemed to me the family would need more time before reopening.

Huckleberry shook his left front leg while I stood in front of the door wondering what my next step was to help Kristy and Kent.

When I'd come back to Cherry Glen after running away in my twenties, under stressful circumstances, Kristy and Kent were two of the few people who had welcomed me back with open arms, no questions asked. Kristy didn't care why I'd run away—she knew, of course—but she didn't give me a hard time about it. A lot of other townsfolk had. Because of that, I owed both my help and gratitude to her, and to Kent. And if I could help them at all I would. But in that moment—standing in front of the locked brewery—I wondered what I could honestly do.

A cacophony of barking interrupted my thoughts. Huckleberry stopped trying to shake off his boots and stared.

A woman in a long black wool coat and matching hat and scarf came up the sidewalk walking not one dog, not three dogs, but five dogs that ranged in size from a Pomeranian to a husky. The dogs tugged on their leashes trying to get to Huckleberry. Their tails wagged like propellers.

My cowardly pug ducked behind my legs.

"Silas! No! Settle!" the woman cried. "Junebug, calm down." Finally, she was able to get the dogs all to sit on the sidewalk. It was that moment that I realized the woman was Chanel Fields. She brushed a lock of blond hair out of her eye. "I'm very sorry about that. My crew is always ready to make new friends. Who is that shy little guy behind you?"

I gave a light tug on Huckleberry's leash, and he peeked around my leg. "This is Huckleberry."

Chanel's dogs wiggled with excitement but didn't move. She had them well trained.

Huckleberry stepped out a little more and then shook his leg. I smiled. He was comfortable enough to try to get his boots off once again.

The woman looked down at Huckleberry, who was alternating kicking out his rear feet one at a time. He looked like he was doing the canine version of the cancan…or having a seizure.

"I don't think you picked the right kind of dog for northwest Michigan. You need something bigger and with a lot more fur."

I noted that all five of her dogs had long hair.

"I adopted him in LA, and we just moved to Michigan

in the last year. I wasn't thinking of subzero temperatures in January when I adopted him."

"I would think not. I'm a dog lover myself, if you couldn't tell." She nodded at her canines. "But since I grew up in Minnesota, I have had huskies and chows my whole life. You really need a dog with an undercoat for these temperatures. The Midwestern summer wasn't the best for them. Usually, they stayed inside in the air conditioning. My guess the perfect dog for this climate would be a German shepherd or a poodle. I've been thinking of adding those to the family."

At that point she would have seven dogs. It boggled the mind. I could barely handle one.

"I'll keep that in mind for any future canine additions to the family," I said.

Huckleberry looked up at me again with those big brown eyes as if to say, "Yes, I don't belong here, and *what do you mean by canine additions*? I am the only dog in the world."

The truth of the matter was I didn't know if Huckleberry or I were meant for northwest Michigan. The move hadn't gone as easily as I'd hoped. Of course, I knew there would be challenges involved when I returned to my hometown, but I hadn't guessed it would also involve death and murder.

She glanced at the sign. "We're closed today. I'm the owner, Chanel Fields," she said matter-of-factly. There was no sadness in her voice over the death of her husband, and I found it interesting that she introduced herself as the owner.

"I was just reading the sign," I said.

"You look like you need a beer." The woman clicked her tongue. "Your little dog is freezing to death. Come inside with me and we will get him warmed up. My dogs need a break from the cold too."

"I don't need—" I started, but before I could even finish my sentence, she walked away from me toward the building.

She and her dogs disappeared around the corner just I picked up Huckleberry. I wasn't going to walk the dog on his leash when I had to hurry to keep up with the woman. Huckleberry would spend the whole time shaking out his feet.

I made it to the corner of the building as she unlocked a side door. The door itself looked like it was original to the granary and one swift kick would cave it in. The wood was worn and weathered. It was the type of door that might be found in a salvage yard in California and would cost a mint as designers clamored to keep up with the modern farmhouse craze. I was happy to see the door in its original location instead of in some pricey condo in Traverse City.

She pushed the door open and let her dogs inside. "Watch your step," Chanel warned. "The flooring is uneven here. I'm told that the granary was made in two phases, and this is where the two phases meet. My husband was very much into updating the granary only so far. He wanted to keep the original charm of the building. He said that the structure was a historical piece of the town and should be preserved. It was a point that I agreed on with him, probably the only one."

This was the first mention of her husband, but it was said with little emotion.

Huckleberry and I stepped inside.

She unhooked the leashes from the dogs. "It's all right to

let your dog off the leash. There is no one else here. My dogs will like making a new friend."

I studied the dogs for a second. They did appear to be a friendly and happy bunch. Whatever Chanel's relationship with her husband was, she had a great one with her dogs. I unsnapped Huckleberry's leash. He looked up at me and then shuffled over to the Pomeranian, probably because it was the dog closest to his size. They bumped noses and sniffed each other. The other dogs did the same. Huckleberry was accepted as one of the pack. I let out a sigh of relief.

"Wallace Fields was your husband?" I asked.

"You knew my husband?" she asked.

"Not really. I have a friend who works here as a bartender, so I saw Wallace a few times when I was in the building. However, I don't believe we ever formally met."

She removed her hand and fluffed her ash-blond hair and expensive highlights. I knew expensive highlights when I saw them. I used to have them too, when I first arrived in Cherry Glen. They'd grown out over time and were not a luxury I could afford any longer.

"You speak of my husband in past tense, so you must know he's dead." She waited as if challenging me when asking this.

I realized my appeal in the fact I had a cute dog was beginning to wane. However, I had the perfect save. "I just stopped by Jessa's Place for coffee," I said and let the comment hang in the air.

"Oh." She sighed. "I'm sure Wallace's death was all those old farmers were talking about. You couldn't pay me to go into that diner right now. I know they'll all look at me like I was the one who stabbed my husband in the throat."

I grimaced. She wasn't that far off the mark. When I'd been the suspect of a murder myself, the old guys at Jessa's Place had a field day talking about me.

"I'm sorry for your loss."

A strange expression crossed her face. "I'm sorry too. I certainly didn't expect to be a widow at my age."

I tried to keep my expression neutral, but I didn't know how well I did that. It seemed odd to me that she wasn't brokenhearted at her husband's death, just inconvenienced. I reminded myself that it could just be my perception on how she felt. It was impossible to know how she was processing her grief.

"Now, I have a funeral to plan," she said, which reminded me of what Spenser had said about how much his stepmother liked to plan big events. However, at the same time, it seemed weird that she would be enthusiastic over planning her husband's funeral, unless she was the one who killed her husband.

"What is your name? I should have asked before I let you in here. Wallace was always on me for taking my time with things. I always prefer to jump."

"I'm Shiloh Bellamy. My father and I own Bellamy Farm just outside of town. It's a little too cold today to do much around the place." I laughed. "Actually, that's not true. There's always something to do at the farm. Knowing my dedicated assistant, she's in the middle of a winter project right now even though it's Sunday and her day off."

Huckleberry kicked out his rear left leg. The husky barked at his boots. It seemed the other dogs agreed they were ridiculous.

"Get those boots off that poor pup. It is clear as day that he hates them."

As if he was determined to be even more pathetic in front of Chanel and his new canine pals, Huckleberry lay on the polished concrete floor on his side and slowly kicked his legs. He could be so dramatic when he wanted to. The Pomeranian hopped up in down and yipped as if sounding an alarm.

I knelt on the floor next to Huckleberry and plucked off all four boots. The boots were a fail. It seemed to me that I would have to carry the pug back to the diner when it was time to leave.

I tucked the tiny boots into my expansive winter coat pockets. I swore, I could carry an anvil in there and no one would even know. The puffy black coat hung all the way down to my knees. It wasn't the cutest look in the world, but it was warm, which was always the main objective in subzero temperatures.

"That's much better," Chanel said. "I hate to see animals uncomfortable."

"He wasn't in any pain," I said a bit defensively. I couldn't think of anything worse than someone accusing me of hurting Huckleberry. The snub-nosed pup was always my number one priority.

"I just hate to see animals uncomfortable even when it's for their own well-being. I especially feel this way when it comes to dogs. I've never met a dog that I didn't like. My daughter claims I like dogs more than people, and the truth of the matter is, she's right! I always have room for another dog in my life. People, not so much."

It was as if a light bulb went off over my head when she mentioned her daughter. The light bulb was emblazoned with the word "suspect."

"Does your daughter live close by?" I asked.

"I'd say that. She lives with Wallace and me. It was a source of tension. Lila Rae is twenty-nine, and Wallace didn't like the idea of her living at home. He was very much the kind of person who pushed his chicks out of the nest. If they didn't fly, oh well. Honestly, I didn't care for how he parented his son. The boy turned into a weakling, if you ask me, and is afraid of his own shadow. He certainly was afraid of his father. That was between the two of them, just like how I parented Lila Rae was between her and me. But that didn't matter to Wallace. He said she had to move out when she was thirty."

"When was she turning thirty?" I asked.

"Next week," she said. "But she'd already asked, and I agreed to let her stay a little while longer, until she could get her feet under her."

"She asked you this after your husband died?"

"Yes."

Interesting. While Spenser was getting loans to pay for a wedding he and his wife hadn't wanted, his stepsister was being coddled at home with his father's money. I guessed it was a difficult realization for him to make, and a bitter one at that. The double standard was glaring. I wanted to ask Chanel about it, but I couldn't see a way how without her figuring out I'd spoken to Spenser and Lila Rae already. I didn't think that was something I wanted to reveal to her just yet, if ever.

"Lila Rae is your only child?" I asked.

She nodded. "And Spenser—that's my stepson—was Wallace's only child too. I'm glad the family was small. When I agreed to marry Wallace I wasn't interested into some *Brady Bunch* sort of relationship. Kids really aren't my thing."

"You prefer dogs," I said.

"Always." She wasn't the least bit bashful about that admission, and I knew many people who were the same way. However, at the same time, they either had no children or claimed their children were the exception to the dogs-over-people rule. Chanel wasn't like that. I believed if I asked her, she would say she loved her dogs more than her own daughter.

"I can't be pushing my daughter out of the nest now. She's not making any money as long as the brewery is closed."

"Oh?" I asked.

"She was a bartender here. She has been since she moved in with us four years ago. Wallace gave her the job hoping it would be a sort of a springboard, but she seems perfectly happy living at home and taking a shift here or there. I do suppose I'll have to figure out what to do with her when all the business with my husband's funeral is over."

I shifted back and forth on my feet. The way Chanel spoke of her husband's death made me uncomfortable. She must have realized how callous she sounded, because she said, "I know I must sound awful, but I'm not the type of person who wallows. I see the problem and I take care of it. There is no time for tears. That's especially true now, when I have to get the brewery back open. This is my livelihood too. Everyone thinks Wallace built this from nothing, but he did it with my help. The best way I can start moving forward is by checking the schedule for tomorrow and making sure I have enough staff for all my shifts. We've been having issues with staffing lately."

"Why do you think that is?"

"Because my husband was a hard boss and wanted nothing less than perfection in every task. Not everyone can live up to those standards." She looked down at Huckleberry, who was sitting on my feet and watching the other dogs play. "Looks like he's ready to go."

It was a clever way of letting me know I was dismissed.

"Thank you for allowing us inside to warm up," I said and picked up my pug.

"I'd do anything for a dog. People? That's another story."

Chapter Fourteen

I'd only started working on the case a day ago, and I had more suspects than I knew what to do with. It all came down to who stood to profit the most from Wallace Fields's death. I thought if I could find that out, I would be able to solve the murder—or at least hand a few more suspects to Sheriff Penbrook so Kent Brown wouldn't be such an appealing scapegoat.

It was difficult for me to imagine how the sheriff could see Kent as the prime suspect. However, I wasn't surprised Chief Randy already had a suspect. I assumed that suspect was Kent as he was the last person to see Wallace alive, and he had a motive with not being chosen as the master brewer. I knew from personal experience that the chief tended to have tunnel vision. When he started to believe one theory, it was next to impossible for him to see any other possibility. I prayed Sheriff Penbrook wasn't like that as well.

I had to put Spenser Fields and his stepmother Chanel Fields on my list. I supposed Spenser's wife, Larissa, was a suspect too, as she had reportedly been so upset that her in-laws hadn't paid for hers and Spenser's wedding. I could see starting off married life with a huge amount of debt that you didn't know you were getting into would be cause for murder. If not murder, anger at the very least.

And I couldn't forget Chanel's daughter, Lila Rae, who could now stay at the Fields' home indefinitely because her stepfather wasn't there to kick her out.

And that was just the immediate family. I couldn't forget about the members of MOBA who were jealous of Wallace's success in what they viewed as a short period of time. I had only met two, Annette and Sidney, but there could be more who wanted Wallace out of the way. I hoped I would learn more about them that afternoon when I went back to the fishing derby.

I might have to do something about Huckleberry's boots before then. He would have to wear them on the frozen lake, or he would get frostbite for sure. Leaving him home at the farm with the cats and chickens might be the only option. He wasn't going to like that either, and to be honest, neither would I. I liked having my sidekick with me as much as possible.

I decided to make one more stop before going back home. I carried Huckleberry to the Michigan Theater. For now, I had given up the idea about putting the boots back on him. The pug nestled into my chest trying to gather as much warmth as possible.

The theater marquee advertised a showing of *The Wizard of Oz* that weekend on its new movie screen. In smaller letters it read, "Join us for dinner and movie to support the Michigan Street Theater." Stacey had diversified her business in the last few months. As the weather had grown colder, fewer and fewer tourists had made their way to western Michigan, so there weren't as many people to attend her productions. That hadn't slowed Stacey down. She'd put in a retractable movie screen and showed movies in the off-season. The license to show classic movies was less than new releases, and in a place where nostalgia was everywhere, it was a perfect fit.

I wondered if Hazel would want to go with me to see *The Wizard of Oz*. It would be a fun outing for us even though I didn't have fond childhood memories of the movie. And maybe her father too, as a friend. That was if I wasn't drafted to work at the theater that night, which, knowing my cousin, I probably would be.

To my surprise, the front door of the theater opened. Stacey stepped outside in skinny jeans and a formfitting sweater. She had a bucket of rock salt in her hands and was just about to toss it on the sidewalk in front of the building when she saw me standing there holding Huckleberry.

She jumped. "Good Lord, Shi, you scared me half to death. What are you doing in the middle of the sidewalk holding your dog like you're a lost orphan? I almost threw this salt on you." As if to make her point, she tossed some salt just a few inches from my boots.

"Sorry, I was stopping by to see you."

She arched her eyebrow and looked like she wanted to question me about that. I didn't blame her. Stacey and I had never been particularly close. She was ten years older than me, and while growing up, I was always the annoying younger cousin. By the time I was in high school, she'd been gone to Broadway for years. Before I'd returned to Cherry Glen, I guessed the last time I had seen her, I was twelve or thirteen. At that time, she'd come home for a visit.

"Come in and get out of the cold."

In the entryway of the theater, there was a black trash can that had "salt" precisely painted on its side. Stacey opened the lid and dropped the bucket inside of it. "I can't wait until winter is over. I need business to pick up again."

We went through the second set of glass doors into the lobby. To the right was the ticket booth where I'd worked on more than one occasion. When I say "worked," I didn't mean that I'd been paid. I was more of a guilt volunteer. However, Stacey had taken care of my father for several years before I came back home. I didn't mind helping her out at the theater when I could.

The floor was polished marble and overhead there were ornate carvings of cherries in the rafters. The lobby and the theater itself, Stacey had lovingly restored with the money she had made by selling her half of Bellamy Farm, the half that was now in Tanner Birchwood's possession.

Huckleberry's toenails clicked on the polished floor. He walked back and forth across it as if he liked the sound.

Stacey strode across the lobby and to the theater doors. She didn't ask me to follow or wait for me. I was immediately set back into the role as her kid cousin. It didn't matter how successful I had been in LA as a television producer. In Cherry Glen, I would always be Stacey's little cousin. That I was taller than her didn't seem to detract from this fact at all.

I caught the theater door just as Stacey went inside and

held it open for Huckleberry. The little pug dashed ahead, right at home in the theater. Stacey had let me bring him when I worked the ticket booth before.

The ceiling in the theater was painted like a sunny day over the lake with blue skies and fluffy white clouds. The seats were red velvet, and the stage floor was polished hardwood. At the moment, there wasn't a set on the stage.

Stacey walked up the steps and stood in the middle of the stage like an empress overseeing her dominion. She worked hard enough to earn that right. "There's just so much to do," she mused.

I understood that. I felt the same way whenever I looked out over the farm. At times, it was good to see the big picture and make grand plans, but other times, it became too overwhelming. Sometimes it was better to keep your head down and work on the task at hand.

"Is everything at the theater okay?"

"The theater is doing fine, but I'm always thinking of how I can take it to the next level. I don't just want to be a local theater with local actors. Eventually I want traveling Broadway-level productions to put the Michigan Theater on their list of tour stops."

"I thought groups like that only stopped in major cities."

"They only stop in places that have the amenities they need, and where they can make money. Professional sets, actors, producers, and orchestras all take money. They'll come here if they can make a profit. I just have to prove they will. It'll take a few years, but I'll get there."

I believed her. Stacey was nothing if not determined.

Everyone had thought she was foolish when she'd bought the condemned theater that had been closed for over forty years. When she'd said she wanted to fully restore it, they'd thought she was even more foolish. She'd proven everyone wrong, and the whole town of Cherry Glen had benefited from the theater being back in business.

"So why did you want to stop by? Is it something to do with Uncle Sully? Let me guess. He refuses to go to the doctor again."

"No, it's not that. I mean you're not wrong. Trying to get Dad to go to a doctor, dentist, and just about any appointment is close to impossible, but I'm actually here to ask you about Wallace Fields. I assume you heard about his death."

"Heard about it more than once. I think everyone in town has called about it. As for your question, Chief Randy beat you to that one. He asked me what I'd heard."

"And what did you tell him?"

"Not much, other than he died at the ice fishing derby. I was surprised to hear he'd go to such an event. He never struck me as outdoorsy."

"Did you know him well?" I asked.

"From the business community. And we worked together on events. We each owned one of the largest businesses downtown. Although his was much more financially successful than mine. I was hoping to capitalize on that, but now he's dead."

I wanted to ask her what she meant by "capitalize."

"Are you coming to the *Wizard of Oz* fundraiser? As family, I do expect you to be there. I need you to run the ticket booth. The theater needs the money. I was just working on the list of plays and musicals to produce for the upcoming fall and summer seasons. I already have spring locked down. We are doing *Death of a Salesman* and *The Music Man*. The people of Cherry Glen and the tourists who come to our town like the classics. I hope over time I can introduce them to more modern material. However, you have to build a following first, right?"

"I'll come. I planned to invite Hazel, but if you need me to work the booth, that's probably not a good idea. I won't have much time with her."

"You could invite her father to keep an eye on her while you're working," Stacy said.

I gave her a look.

She walked to the edge of the stage and sat down crossed legged. Huckleberry trotted up and down the rows of seats. I thought he might be looking for dropped bits of popcorn or candy. I could have told him it would be a waste of time. Stacey was meticulous about keeping the theater clean. As soon as a show was over, she had her crew in there making it look spic-and-span.

"Why are you so interested in Wallace anyway? Please don't tell me you got it into your head again that you should meddle in a police investigation," Stacey said.

I rocked back on my heels.

Stacey rolled her eyes. "You're ridiculous. Why on earth do you care? Did you even know Wallace?"

"I didn't know him, but Kristy's husband works for him. He's a bartender on weekends."

"Oh." Understanding dawned on her face. "And everyone in town is saying he's the killer."

This is what I had been afraid of.

"I got several calls this morning about it. Apparently, Kent was passed over for some big promotion." She folded her arms.

"That's not exactly what happened."

"Shiloh, I think you'd be a much better farmer if you spent less time playing detective and more time doing your actual job, which is saving the family farm."

I bit back a smart retort. Stacey could have chosen to save the family farm herself, but instead she'd decided to sell her half to live her dream. Because of that, the family legacy fell solely to me. No pressure.

"All I know is it's a hassle for the theater," Stacey said.

"Why?"

"Fields Brewing Company was going to start offering alcohol at the theater. They were the best business to partner with, since they're right down the street. It's a great chance to cross-promote. We were going to serve his new cherry beer when it was done too." She shook her head as if she couldn't believe her bad luck. "Eventually, I planned to add wine and harder stuff to the drinks menu, but I thought if I could start with local beer, it would draw in more tourists and those on beer tours throughout the state."

"Are you allowed to serve alcohol at the theater?"

"Beer? Sure," Stacey said. "Everything was in place. It was just a matter of signing the contract with Wallace and placing the first order. But there are other options."

"Do you have any reason to believe that Fields Brewing Company wouldn't want to work with you now that Wallace is dead? I would think they'd want some guaranteed business until they can get their feet under them again."

"What I've learned in this business is I have to always be looking for a backup plan."

I'd found the same in farming. If local brewers were also going organic, it could be a great partnership for me. "What is your backup plan?" I asked.

"I'll have to check with MOBA." Stacey unfolded her arms and dropped them to her sides.

"Wallace was a member of the group," I said. "From what I heard, his brewery was the most successful in MOBA. Not everyone was happy about that."

"I can see why they weren't happy," she said. "He hadn't been in the game as long as some of the others in the group, but he was a twice as successful."

I pressed my lips together in thought.

"Organic beer is a trend," my cousin said. "Trends draw people in, and I need to draw people to the theater. You have to stay in front of these things to be relevant. And if you really want to find out who killed Wallace, I'd go to that meeting."

"You think people there have a motive for murder?"

"Jealousy, greed, money, it's all there. All of that can be a motive," she said. "I really should go to the next MOBA meeting to find an alternative supplier."

"I was invited to the meeting."

She stared at me. "*You* were? Why would you be invited?"

"Because I can supply them with organic hops for their beers."

She looked dubious. From the beginning, Stacey had thought making Bellamy Farm an organic operation was a waste of time and money. She'd tried talking my father into selling the land numerous times and moving into town. He'd never do that, and now that the farm was in my name, I never would either. At least, I hoped I never reached a place where I would see that as the only way out. That's why a partnership with MOBA would be such a great thing for the farm.

"Take me as your plus-one."

I scowled. She insulted me and then wanted me to take her to the meeting. It was typical Stacey. "I don't know if I get a plus-one."

"Sure you do! Everyone gets a plus-one when invited to a party."

"It's a meeting, not a party."

"There will be alcohol there. It's a party."

I sighed. "Fine."

She grinned as if she'd just won, which in truth she had. She always did. "And I don't believe for one second that you want to go to this meeting just because you're an organic farmer."

"Well, if I could find the killer too, that would be a bonus."

Stacey snorted.

Chapter Fifteen

On the drive back to the farm, I was optimistic that by the end of the MOBA meeting I would have so many suspects for Wallace Fields's murder that the sheriff wouldn't look at Kent Brown a moment longer.

There was a beat-up SUV parked by the barn when I got home. A pang of guilt hit me. As I'd expected, my farm assistant, Chesney, was hard at work while I'd been in town drinking coffee and asking questions.

She came out of the barn with a smile on her face. Chesney was the happiest when she was working with her hands. She was in her midtwenties, tall, lanky, and more self-assured than I would ever be. She getting her master of agriculture science degree from the university in Traverse City. Today, she wore a blue stocking cap on her head that covered her shoulder-length brown hair. There was a pompom on the top of the hat the size of a softball.

I stepped out of the truck and held the door open so Huckleberry could hop down to the frozen driveway after me. When he landed on his paws, he looked up at me as if to say, "This is cold. Why is everything so cold all the time here?"

I put my hands on my hips. "That's why I bought you the boots."

Chesney waved. "Hey Shi, I was just working on cleaning out those three stalls to make room for sheep we're getting for me."

I smiled. We wouldn't be getting our new woolly staff members until late spring. In fact, they weren't even born yet.

In November, I'd placed an order with a sheep farmer a few counties over for Olde English Babydoll Southdown lambs. It was all part of my master plan for the farm. The sheep would help me control weeds and pests in the cherry orchard. Since they grew to be no more than two feet tall, they were perfect for keeping the weeds back but not tall enough to eat the cherries in the trees. Hundreds of years ago, sheep and goats had been used for such work before herbicides and large machinery were widely available. As Bellamy Farm was to be transformed into an organic farm, this was my first big step in that direction. It wasn't an inexpensive venture. Each lamb cost six hundred dollars, and some had cost more because of their pedigree. I had six sheep coming.

As much as I loved goats, sheep were much more docile than their hooved cousins, and I would be able to harvest their wool to sell at the local farmers' market. Babydoll sheep's wool felt like cashmere.

My purpose for the farm was to make it as multifaceted as I possibly could. The more diversity I had on the farm, the more chance it would have to thrive. It was a fail-safe too. If I had a season where the cherry orchard struggled because of too much rain or not enough, I could fall back on the sheep for wool or the bees that I already had in the orchard for honey for income.

However, the sheep weren't due to arrive until the end of April at the earliest. Chesney knew that, but she was a self-starter and was of the school of "why put off until tomorrow what can be done today?" I was grateful for that.

She removed her work gloves and shoved them into the back pocket of her jeans. "I'm just so glad you've finally agreed to have some real livestock here instead of just those hateful chickens."

"Diva and the girls are not hateful."

"Diva is the worst one of all. I swear she was sizing me up the other day and wondering if she could take me down. The truth of the matter is, she could!"

I almost said that Diva—the top hen in my flock—would never do that. However, she probably would. I had seen her attack on one or two occasions. She wasn't a chicken to be trifled with.

"Just give Diva a lot of space," I suggested.

"I always do."

"What are you doing here today, anyway? Sunday is your day off."

She chuckled. "I wanted to bring Huckleberry a surprise, and when you weren't here, I thought I'd wait for you to get back. One thing led to another, and I cleaned the barn."

I shook my head. "You say that like it makes complete sense, but it doesn't. Not even a little."

Huckleberry whimpered and looked down at his paws.

"Oh, poor Huck, his feet are freezing," Chesney said. "What happened to his new boots?"

I scooped up the pug and held him in the crook of my right arm. With my other hand, I removed one the boots from my coat pocket. "He won't wear them."

"I had a feeling those wouldn't be right for him, so I whipped up another set. That's the surprise I brought."

I tucked the little boot back into my pocket. "You *whipped up* another set?"

"I knitted some! It was fun. Hang on a second." She ran over to her SUV, threw open the passenger-side door, and got something out. A second later, she stood in front of Huckleberry holding four tiny orange booties out. "Ta-da!"

The booties looked like they were the perfect fit for Huckleberry, and the knit was precise and tight.

"You made those?"

"Sure! I had a few spare moments, so I looked up a dog bootie pattern on the internet and made them while listening to a lecture for my online class about irrigation. The irrigation class has really given me some great ideas of how we can improve the systems on the farm for both the fields and the cherry orchard. Between the changes to irrigation and the sheep, this is going to be the best growing season ever for Bellamy Farm!"

I wondered if I'd had that much energy when I was her age. Actually, I didn't have to wonder. I knew I hadn't.

She held up the booties. "I think he'll tolerate these better. They shouldn't feel as constraining, and with the cardboard and foam I put in the soles, his feet will be warm and dry."

Huckleberry whimpered. It didn't matter if these shoes were less constraining. They were still shoes, and he wasn't interested in wearing them.

Chesney stepped forward holding out the knitted booties. Huckleberry bucked in my arms to the point I couldn't hold him any longer without hurting him. I let him go, and he tore off into the barn with his tail flat. A sure sign a pug was upset was when his tail wasn't curled. Huckleberry wasn't going to be caught again in shoes.

"He really hates shoes, doesn't he?" she asked.

"He really does."

We followed Huckleberry in the barn. I marveled at how different the space looked from the day I'd arrived at the farm the past summer. A month ago, I had all the electrical wiring replaced in the barn from the breaker box to the light fixtures. It had cost more than I'd expected, but now, seeing the barn in bright light, I knew it'd been worth it. Without the new wiring, many of the other improvements would have been impossible. The cobwebs had been swept away, and the hay bales were now in orderly stacks along the south wall. All of the stalls—which at the moment didn't hold any livestock—had been raked and swept clean. Chesney had even taken a power washer to the concrete floor.

To be honest, it was lot cleaner than many of the production sets I'd been on. The stalls she'd prepared for our spring sheep were the cleanest of all. She'd even hung a welcome sign on the wall for our woolly additions.

"Chez, I seriously don't know how I would do any of this without you."

She grinned. "I'm happy to help. Working here at Bellamy Farm is a wonderful opportunity. Where else would I be able to see the revitalization of a family farm from the very beginning? This is an invaluable experience for me. I was hoping I could work it into my master's thesis."

"You should. And let me know how I can help." I scanned the barn. "Now, we have to find Huckleberry."

"I think I have a good idea where he is." She pointed to the opposite end of the barn where the horse stalls used to be. At Bellamy Farm's height of success, there'd been as many as six horses in this barn every night.

But there weren't any horses today, and it would be a long while before I added them to my growing menagerie. Horses needed a lot of care, and unless I was providing riding lessons or pony rides, there wasn't much reason to have them at the farm. That being said, there was a bit of status symbol among farms to have at least one horse. It made you seem legit. I bet Tanner had a horse by now. Probably two.

The horses were missing, but the four barn cats and Esmeralda meant the barn wasn't empty. Diva the chicken still wasn't too keen on Esmeralda, but the two of them gave each other a wide berth. I think both knew when they had met their match.

The five cats, including Esmeralda as the queen, sat in a semicircle around a horse blanket that had fallen—or had been pulled—to the floor. As Chesney and I drew closer, it was easy to see what they were looking at. Huckleberry's back end and his little curled tail stuck out from under the scratchy wool.

"Isn't a little bit creepy how the cats are sitting around him like that, perfectly spaced?" Chesney adjusted her glasses on the bridge of her nose as if she wanted to make sure she saw everything just right.

"I'm sure it was Esmeralda's idea," I said.

The Siamese looked over her shoulder at me and gave a very slow blink. I had read that a slow blink from a cat meant she was saying, "I love you." However, when it came to Esmeralda, I was certain it meant, "I am your queen. Sit down, peasant."

"Huckleberry?" I asked in a gentle voice.

The pug's visible back end shook even more. Slowly, I picked the horse blanket off my beloved pug. His paws covered his face, and his ears pressed against his head. He was in full turtle mode.

"Oh, that's just too adorable," Chesney said as she whipped her cell phone out of her coat pocket and took a picture of the cats and dog. "I'm going to post it. My followers will go wild."

"Post it?" I asked.

She looked at me. "You do know what social media is, don't you?"

"Chesney, I'm thirty-eight, not ninety-eight. Yes, I know what it is. It might shock you to hear this, but I even know how to use it." But I never used it much for my personal life. I had an aversion to it that stemmed from wanting to disappear from Cherry Glen after my fiancé, Logan, died suddenly and everyone in Cherry Glen thought I might have contributed to his death. I hadn't, but their suspicious had been enough to make me flee the farm and town where I grew up. Even though that had been over fifteen years ago, sometimes I was surprised I had the strength to come back, especially when some people like Quinn's mom, Doreen Killian, still wondered what part I played in Logan's death.

"You know, Shi, that's a missed opportunity for you. You need to have Bellamy Farm on social media. Do you have any idea how many farms are online? I can't believe I didn't think of this before. We need to get you on there. People will love to see the transformation story of the farm, and you can share organic and sustainable gardening tips like you do in the local paper too!" She shook with excitement. "Plus we can make Huckleberry a star!"

Esmeralda hissed.

"You too, Esmeralda," Chesney added quickly.

I wished I had Chesney's enthusiasm. "I just don't feel like I can take that on with everything else."

"You don't have to! I'll do it. Don't worry about a thing. I'll work up some ideas and present those to you for the types of posts we need and to keep everything on brand. Branding is very important."

"Are you sure you have time for that with school, work, and taking care of your sister? I don't want to put something else on you."

Chesney's parents died years ago, and she and her sister Whit lived in a small rental house in Cherry Glen. Whit was a college student studying theater production, and she worked for Stacey at the Michigan Street Theater.

"Shi, I'm Gen Z. I can use multiple pieces of technology

at once and hold down a conversation with the person right in front of me. This will be a piece of cake."

I'd never felt so old. "Okay. Go for it. Now, let's try these booties you made on Huckleberry before he finds another place to hide."

Chesney knelt by the dog. "Huck, I have a gift for you." She removed one of the booties from her coat pocket.

Huckleberry started to get up so he could back away, but two of the cats blocked his path. There was betrayal in his eyes as he looked at each cat in turn.

"You'll like them. They're so cozy," Chesney promised.

He sighed, as if he knew the only way he was getting out of the situation was to try on the booties. With eyes closed, he held out his right forepaw.

Stifling a chuckle, Chesney quickly put the booties on his feet and secured them in place with a Velcro strap.

Huckleberry opened his eyes and stared in the bug-eyed way that only a pug could. It was a mix between horror and wonder.

I bit the inside of my cheek to keep from laughing. Between his orange jacket and matching booties, my poor little pug looked like he was dressing up as a pumpkin for Halloween. I refrained from saying that though, because knowing Chesney, she would find a knitting pattern for a matching hat with a few taps on her phone screen.

When I was composed enough to speak, I said, "You look very handsome, and no one will miss you in the snow."

He looked up at her as if to ask, "You too? You're part of this humiliation?" He shook his right hind leg once as if testing it. He put it down. He shook his left hind leg next and then set that one down. He repeated the same move with each of his front paws. He placed all four paws on the ground and cocked his head back and forth as if he didn't know what was happening, and then he started walking around the barn like he didn't have a care in the world.

I stared in amazement. "He's not trying to kick them off."

"Of course he's not," Chesney said with the confidence that only someone in their twenties could. "I made them extra thick and cozy. My focus was comfort and practicality."

"Well, you've hit the mark. I'm relieved. It was going to be a long winter if Huckleberry wasn't going to abide by any footwear."

"No problem. So, what's the next project at the farm? I want to start framing out ideas."

I sighed. "I think we need to tackle the front porch. It's not actively snowing, so we might be able to assess what needs to be done."

Quinn had looked at it the week before said that most of the wood wasn't salvageable, but I would save what I could. It would be a big job that I'd been avoiding up until this point. However, it was something that needed to be addressed now. I couldn't have people coming to the farm and have the ruined porch be the first thing they saw. And as I went through the long and tedious process of certifying Bellamy Farm as an organic venture, the inspectors would not look kindly on the house in such a state.

She nodded. "I thought you were going to say that."

"Let's at least make a plan. We might have to just tear it off completely. I'll try to put together enough money by spring to replace it."

"It wouldn't be a bad idea to paint the exterior of the house at the same time."

I wrinkled my nose. "The only problem is the house was originally painted with lead paint. I'll have to hire that out, and it will be expensive."

"Everything we do is expensive."

"That's the truth." I flipped my hood up over my head, and we went outside. Huckleberry trotted behind us in his new boots like he'd been wearing them his whole life.

The front porch was worse than I remembered. All but one of the pillars had fallen down.

"You're lucky it didn't take the whole front of the house off," Chesney said.

In my mind's eye, I could see my grandmother sitting on the porch, removing the pits from cherries or shucking beans while chatting with a neighbor who stopped by. I could almost see the cherry juice that stained my hands all summer long. I hated that chore so much. My grandmother had pitted the cherries so she could make her tart cherry juice, which she swore had kept her in good health her whole life. She drank tea by the boatload all day long, but she drank an eight-ounce glass of tart cherry juice to help with inflammation and help her sleep just before bed every night. A thought tickled the back of my brain.

In the last six months, my ideas for Bellamy Farm had been all over the place. I was just fixing and mending what I could. The house was the last building that needed major work. However, it was time to focus. I needed to really sit down and decide what I wanted to plant in the spring and what my cash crops were going to be. True, it was January, but in reality, since I didn't have a plan just yet, I was behind. Most of the farmers in Grand Traverse County knew what they were doing in the spring. They might even have prepped their fields for certain crops before the snow.

"You okay?" Chesney asked.

I smiled at her. "I'm just thinking about what the next step is for the farm. Have you ever heard of MOBA?"

"Sure!"

I told her about the invitation to the upcoming meeting.

"MOBA would be a great business partner for Bellamy Farm," Chesney said.

"Let me guess. You've been following them on social media." I smiled.

"No." She gave a small frown. "I should check if they have an account. I know of them because one of their members came into one of my classes at the university and was talking about how brewers and agriculture work together to put out the very best beer possible." She sighed. "I wish I could go with you. I'd love to pick the brewers' brains about fermentation. I've always thought it was an interesting process. Who knows, maybe Bellamy Farm will be its own microbrewery someday."

I changed the subject. "Did you hear about Wallace Fields?"

"That he drowned in Lake Skegemog? Sure. Everyone is talking about it. Someone posted about it on Cherry Glen's Facebook group."

"Cherry Glen has a Facebook group?" I asked aghast.

"Shi, everyone has a Facebook group but you." She narrowed her eyes at me.

"And he didn't drown. He was murdered."

"Who told you that?"

"The Antrim County sheriff."

"You're not looking into his death, are you?"

I didn't say anything.

"Shi, come on. You're kidding!"

"I—well, Huckleberry actually—found the body."

She covered her mouth. "How awful."

I nodded.

"I still don't think you should get involved. Leave it to the authorities."

I didn't want to tell her I had to see it through because of Kent being accused. The fewer people who saw Kent as a suspect, the better.

She shook her head. "You need to figure out if you're a farmer or a detective. I'm not sure you can be both."

Chapter Sixteen

When Huckleberry and I made it back to the ice fishing derby later that afternoon, there was a new spring in his step. Every few feet he stopped and struck a pose until a bystander said something about how adorable he was in his orange ski coat and new matching booties.

By the fifth time he did this, it was getting old.

I tugged on his leash. "Everyone thinks you're cute. If you keep stopping, we'll never reach Grandpa."

Huckleberry snuffled but dutifully followed me onto the ice. It was a bit warmer than it had been the day before. The temperature hovered around twenty degrees. In my warm coat, snow pants, boots, hat, and gloves I was toasty warm. It was a nice change.

I spotted Dad first. He was sitting outside Quinn's fishing shanty on an overturned five-gallon bucket. He leaned over a twelve-inch circle hole in the ice like he was listening to the ice, waiting to hear his fortune.

"Dad, why are you sitting on that bucket when Quinn had a perfectly nice chair for you?"

"The chair hurt my fishing game. I've always fished on

an overturned bucket. I have to do what will bring in the most fish."

I didn't ask my father how a bucket would bring in fish because I knew he'd never be able to explain his superstitions to me.

Hazel came out of the shanty. "Shi! You came back. Sully said that you were coming today."

"I had a few things I needed to take care of before I could come out. Are you still having fun?"

"We're having the best time. I caught four fish. I would have to catch eleven more to win my division. It's okay if I don't win. This is my first time ice fishing."

"Would you do it again?"

"Sure. It's been a lot of fun hanging out with Dad and Sully all day. Sully has been telling us some funny stories from when you were a kid."

Great.

I glanced at Dad and he grinned.

"Sully is a lock to win his division. He has the most fish in his age-group."

"We don't know that for sure," Dad said. "We can't become complacent. I heard Merv Holiday was looking good today and already caught eight this morning. I have to keep my game face on and keep my lines in the water." As he said this his line jerked up and down.

"Hazel, get the net. I have another one."

Hazel grabbed the fishing net from its place against the shanty's outer wall.

"Hurry up," Dad called. "He's heavy."

Quinn came out of the fishing shanty. "Sully, you have another one? Do you need help?"

"No! No! I got it." Dad struggled to his feet, and Quinn stood behind him ready to catch him if he fell.

I bit my lower lip to stop myself from telling my father to sit down and give Quinn the line.

Hand over hand, Dad pulled the line up from the bottom of the lake.

Hazel grasped the handle of the fishing net like her life depended on it. "It's going to be a big one," she said.

"Hazel, I need the net," Dad said finally. "I can see the shadow coming up."

Hazel was ready with the net. The whole thing shook as she could barely contain her excitement.

"Here he comes!" Dad cried, but his cry quickly turned into a curse as he reeled in a boot.

An expensive black dress boot.

Dad threw the boot on the ice in disgust. "People throw anything into this lake. Don't they care about the fish? I need a moment." He grabbed his walker and hobbled into the shanty.

Hazel stood on the ice still holding the net. Her eyes were huge.

I rubbed her shoulder. "Sorry about that."

She looked at me. "Why are you sorry? You didn't throw the boot."

She had a point.

"I'll go check on him," I said.

I stepped into the fishing shanty. Dad sat by the battery-operated heater in a camp chair. "You okay?"

He grunted. "Yes, yes. I just hate it when people throw stuff in the lake. Can you help me up?"

I did, and he grasped his walker again. I followed him as he shuffled outside.

"Hazel, I'm sorry you had to see that," Dad said. "It wasn't good sportsmanship on my part."

Hazel held the boot in her hand. "It's okay. It's a really nice boot."

Dad grunted, sat back on his bucket and started to prepare another line to put into the water. He was nothing if not stubborn.

"Can I see that?" I asked.

She handed it to me. It was an expensive men's boot made of black leather. The strap had the designer's insignia on it, which was series of three gold circles. I had only seen a boot like this one other time, and it had been on Wallace Fields's foot floating under the ice. In the cold air, the soaked laces were already starting to freeze. Before too long the whole boot would be frozen solid like a leather ice cube.

"Shiloh, are you okay?" Quinn asked.

I blinked at him. "Oh, yeah, I'm fine. Umm, do you have a plastic bag—like a plastic grocery bag—I could put this in?"

"Sure," he said slowly. He went into the shanty and a moment later came out again with a white plastic grocery bag. He handed it to me.

"Thanks." I put the wet boot in the bag. "I'm going to walk around a bit and check on the Cherry Glen booth."

"What are you going to do with the boot?" he asked.

I glanced over at my dad and Hazel. Dad was showing

her how to put live bait on the hook. They were totally engrossed.

"I think this is Wallace Fields's boot," I said in a low voice. "I need to give it to the sheriff."

Quinn's eyes went wide. "Are you sure?"

"I'm pretty sure. He was missing a boot when they pulled him out of the water, and the one he was wearing looked much like this. I can't know for sure. When I saw the other boot, it was underwater."

"Yikes. I don't think the deputies will be able to get much evidence off it since it was in the freezing water for so long."

"Probably not," I agreed. "But I still have to turn it over."

"Right."

I started to leave, but then stopped. "Hey, thanks for looking after Dad these last two days. I haven't seen him this happy in a long time."

He grinned. "We don't mind. Hazel gets a kick out of him. She says he fishes like I watch football."

"So you have tantrums during football games?"

"All the time." He laughed.

Chapter Seventeen

When I reached the lakeshore, I removed my cell phone from my pocket with the intention of calling the sheriff. However, it seemed I didn't have to because he stood in front of a T-shirt and sweatshirt vendor, and the two were talking.

I took a deep breath and then walked over there.

"I didn't see anything," the vendor said. "I rolled in here about five that morning, and I was intent on getting all set up. I knew some people would forget to bring things to the derby. I have hats, gloves, and warm clothes for sale. I needed to be ready early."

The sheriff nodded. "All right. If you think back and remember anything—anything at all—that might help us, here's my card. My cell is on the bottom there. Call me day or night." The sheriff turned around and found me standing a few feet behind him. "Eavesdropping, Ms. Bellamy?"

"No, Sheriff. I need to talk to you."

"Let's go over here for some privacy," he said, seeming to understand the tension in my voice. He led me to a picnic bench between the lakeshore and the parking lot. We didn't sit on the bench. It was encrusted with ice.

He nodded at the bag in my hand. "What do you have there?"

"I think it's Wallace Fields's missing boot." I held the bag out to him.

"What?" He took the bag from my hand and peeked inside. "It does look like his boot. I can't think of anyone else in the area who would have boots like this."

"I can't either. And the insignia is pretty distinctive."

"Where did you find this? You should have brought me to the location. It would have been better that way because we could have searched the area for more evidence."

"It was at the bottom of the lake. My father is participating in the fishing derby and brought it up. He was very disappointed when it wasn't a large pike."

"Oh," the sheriff said. "Where is your father's fishing spot?"

I pointed at Quinn's shanty. "It's the one with the blue tarp over the roof."

Sheriff Penbrook shielded his eyes. "That's at least eight hundred feet from where Fields was located under the ice."

I nodded.

"The movement of the water could have made the boot travel that far."

"Or his body could have been the part that was traveling."

"Possibly. We're still looking for where he went into the water."

I stared at the frozen lake and shivered when I thought

of how it must have felt when Wallace hit the water. The icy depths would have been like a million knives in his skin. Even in my cozy winter gear, I felt a chill and rubbed my arms to warm myself up. "Was he alive when he went in?" I just had to know.

Sheriff Penbrook turned back to me, and his face softened. "No, the coroner didn't find any evidence of water in his lungs, so he was already dead when he hit the water."

"And was it a garrote like Hedy thought?"

"Yes," he said with a sigh. "The coroner believes it was fishing line, which makes this that much more challenging. There is a lot of fishing line around here right now."

I touched my neck, not sure knowing he'd been killed by a fishing line garrote was much better than drowning.

Sheriff Penbrook took the bag from my hand. "I imagine any other personal effects Mr. Fields had are also on the bottom of the lake."

"Like his phone?" I asked.

He nodded. "Not that there will be much hope of finding it. Thankfully, he had his phone backed up."

"Yes, Kristy told me that's how you made the connection to her husband, through their text messages in the cloud."

He made no comment on this. Instead, the sheriff held up the bag with the shoe. "I do appreciate you bringing this to me, but I hope it's the last part you play in all this. Please leave the investigation up to me and my deputies."

"Is Kent Brown still a suspect?" I asked.

His jaw tensed up. "I do not have to reveal to you who is and is not a suspect. You're not a member of law enforcement."

He didn't say this in a harsh way. The sheriff was only stating a fact I couldn't dispute, even though I wanted to.

"Because," I went on. "There are a lot of people to look at in this case."

He held the plastic bag loosely in his hand and cocked his head. "Oh really? And who are all these people?"

I bit my lip and tried not to take offense at his tone. "You probably already know about them, but I feel like I should tell you just in case."

He nodded at me to continue.

Huckleberry sat on my feet like he knew this was going to be a longer conversation. At least he wasn't trying to shake his booties off. I was starting to wonder if he would let me take them off when we got back home.

"There is his family. His son Spenser and daughter-in-law Larissa aren't happy with him over a dispute about paying for their wedding. His wife, Chanel, has to be a suspect too. He has a stepdaughter, Lila Rae, who he wanted to kick out of his house. Both his wife and stepdaughter weren't happy about that, and don't forget the MOBA members that were jealous of his success in such a relatively short amount of time. He's only been brewing for a few years, and he already sold his beers to retailers. That has to be infuriating. I would take a special look at Annette Woodhall, for one. Her husband used to work for Wallace as the master brewer but doesn't anymore. There seems to be some vagueness as to why." I took a breath.

"Was that all?" the sheriff asked.

"All that I know of right now, but I am getting the sense

that Wallace wasn't well-liked by his family or his indus-try. There might be others we don't even know about who wanted him gone."

"I'll agree with you that there are many suspects in this case. That is the very reason you need to leave the investiga-tion to me and the other law enforcement. At this point, it's impossible to know who to trust."

"What about the owl hooting that Kent heard?"

"Kent told you that?"

I wrinkled my nose. "Kristy did."

"I have a question for you, Ms. Bellamy."

"Sure." I wrapped Huckleberry's leash more tightly around my gloved hand even though the pug was quite clearly not going anywhere since he appeared to be quite comfortable sitting on my boot.

"Does Kent want you to do all of this?" He studied my face.

"What do you mean?" I pushed my winter hat up and it slipped down over my eyes again as I looked at him.

"Does Kent want your help finding the killer?"

"I think so. Kristy says that he does," I said with some hesitation.

"Kristy might be married to him, but she doesn't speak for him. He told me when we were at the station that he was upset you were involved."

My mouth fell open. "Then why didn't he just say that to me?"

He shrugged. "I guess you'll have to ask him that. But I want you to ask yourself, are you helping someone who wants to be helped, or are you just being nosy?"

I sucked in a breath. I'd thought I was doing this for Kent and for Kristy. They were my friends. But if Kent didn't want my help, then why was I spending all my time on this when I could be at home bringing the property back to life or searching for my grandmother's heart of the farm?

He held up the plastic bag I'd given him. "I have to go and get this into evidence. Think on what I said, Ms. Bellamy. It's for your own good."

Whenever I was told that something was "for my own good" I typically did the opposite, so he had chosen the worst thing to say.

Chapter Eighteen

When I'd gone to Jessa's Place earlier in the day, it had been with the intention of having a meal. However, when Spenser Fields had shown up, the thought of food had gone out of my mind. Now, my stomach was reminding me that I had eaten little more than a granola bar and coffee all day. It wasn't happy about it.

I looked down at my pug. "Huck, when you don't know what to do next, have a snack."

He gave a short bark as if he was in full agreement. Huckleberry truly thought a snack was the answer to all of life's ups and downs. His favorite snack was a piece of cheese. I didn't think I'd have any luck finding a block of cheese at the ice fishing derby, but it seemed to me I could buy just about anything else.

Vendors selling everything from T-shirts to popcorn balls lined the lakefront. Out on the ice, it looked like a city unto itself. It'd been a long two days, so I told myself it was fine to cheat on my diet a little bit. I bought a warm cherry scone and cherry cordial hot chocolate. I shared the scone with Huckleberry, but not the drink.

The pug licked his lips after the final bite. I dusted crumbs off my coat and threw my empty paper cup into the trash. "Back to investigating," I told the pug.

He gave a small bark.

"I know you're thinking, why should I do that if Kent doesn't want my help? Until Kent tells me that directly, I'm choosing not to believe it."

Huckleberry whimpered as if he thought that was a bad idea. Maybe it was, but Kristy was more my friend than Kent was. If she wanted my help, I was going to do what I could for her. She'd already done so much for me.

"Do you always talk to your dog like it's a person?" a voice asked.

I turned around and saw Sidney, who I had met the day before at the MOBA booth. He wore a plaid trapper hat with ear flaps.

"I talk to him more than I talk to most people. Huckleberry knows everything there is to know about me."

Sidney smiled. "I had a bloodhound for ten years. He passed on last year. He knew all of my secrets. He was a good guard dog too. Huron wouldn't hurt a fly, but he was big and slobbery, and the best dog I ever had."

"I'm sorry for your loss," I said dog person to dog person, and I really meant it.

"Thank you. Being in the booth keeps me busy."

"The members of MOBA didn't take turns in the booth?"

He grunted. "So many of them were selling beer here, they said they couldn't step away and help with the booth.

I think Annette and I were the only ones who weren't here for ourselves."

"You don't brew?"

"Oh, I do! It's my passion. I just don't have a storefront or restaurant, and I have no interest in one. It's such a headache, and I don't want to be managing people. People are not my thing. I'm happiest when I'm alone at home perfecting my recipes. Though I sure miss Huron at my side."

"You brew at home?"

"I've been home brewing for years. I hope to get my beer into grocery stores like Wallace was lucky enough to do. It was amazing to watch his star rise in the industry. I've never seen anything like it, and I've been a member of MOBA since the beginning."

"And how long was Wallace a member?" I asked.

"Maybe two years."

"Is she happy about that?" I asked.

He shrugged. "She seems as happy as Annette ever is about anything. However, I really do think she's pleased. She's a founding member like me and was hurt when the members voted Wallace for president over her. I felt for her too. There seems to be no loyalty to the group. Or at least not as much loyalty as is acceptable."

I wanted to ask him how he knew what level of loyalty was acceptable.

"You didn't tell us yesterday that you were the one who found Wallace under the ice," Sidney said.

"It didn't come up."

He cocked his head. "Seems strange since you were asking questions about him."

"The police didn't want me to speak about what I had found." In truth, Sheriff Penbrook had never said that specifically, but I guessed it was understood.

He nodded as if he liked this answer much better.

I brushed leftover scone crumbs from the front of my coat. "How did you hear that it was me that found him?"

"Hedy Strong came by our booth and told us."

"Hedy is interested in MOBA?" I asked.

He laughed. "No, she's interested in MOBA supporting her nonprofit bird group. If she had her way, everyone would give her money for her birds. She will hit up any and every organization for a donation to her cause. She is relentless."

She certainly was.

"Fundraising is hard work," I said, coming to Hedy's defense, even though she'd outed me with the MOBA people.

He eyed me. "Of course it is, but there is a way to do it. She can come on a little too strong at times."

I couldn't argue with him there.

"Is Hedy here today?" I asked.

"I haven't seen her, but I'm sure she's around. She's all up in arms over the owls."

"The owls?"

"Yeah. She said someone was making owl calls at night, and she's not happy about it."

"Why?" I asked.

He shrugged. "I had better get back to the booth," he said. "Annette will be wondering what's taking me so long. I just needed to walk around and stretch my legs. I feel like I've been sitting in that folding chair for days. I'm not used to staying in one place for so long."

"One more question. Did the sheriff or one of his deputies stop by your booth today?" I asked.

"Yes." He frowned. "How did you know?"

"I know they're planning to ask everyone if they saw anything about the time Wallace died. It would've been between midnight and six in the morning."

"The deputy did ask me, and I didn't have anything to tell him. I wasn't here until nine in the morning, when it was my turn to man the MOBA booth."

"The derby began at six. There would have been a lot of people."

"Oh, we didn't wait. Annette just said she could handle it herself before nine."

"She was alone in the booth for three hours?" I reminded myself it didn't mean she had anything to do with Wallace's death. Furthermore, I wasn't certain Annette would be strong enough to kill Wallace in the manner in which he had died. He'd have to have had a foot of height on her and outweighed her by sixty pounds. It would've been very difficult for her to kill Wallace that way, even if she'd somehow been standing above him.

"I don't know if you can really say she was alone. You said yourself, there were a lot of people around at that time."

"What time did she set up the booth?" I asked.

"You'll have to ask her. As far as I know, she set up the booth by herself since there wasn't much more to do than set up the table and put the literature on it. It wasn't rocket science."

I frowned.

He tugged on his earflap. "Why are you asking all these questions anyway? Are you a friend of Wallace's? Girlfriend?"

My face flushed red. "No! He was married."

"That doesn't stop everybody."

"It stops me." I scowled.

"Then why all the questions?"

"I found his body. Whether I like it or not, the image is burned into my brain. I want to make sense of what I saw."

He nodded. "Fair enough."

Without another word, he walked away.

I went over the list of people I wanted to talk to. Annette Woodhall and Hedy Strong were on the top of the list. However, I'd rather talk to Annette when Sidney wasn't in the booth. I knew it was where he was headed now. That left me tracking down Hedy. It turned out she wasn't all that difficult to find.

Chapter Nineteen

Hedy stood on a rock by the lakeshore. "You have to understand, making owl calls this time of year is detrimental to the owls. This is mating season. If you call them, they'll think they have a potential mate. When they don't find another owl, they get disheartened and may leave the area. Lake Skegemog, Torch Lake, and the surrounding area have a proud owl population. We have everything from screech owls to great gray owls, but these iconic raptors need to be protected."

Two of her under-birders—or whatever they might be called—handed out pamphlets about the Grand Traverse County Bird Society. A few spectators stood by and watched Hedy speak, but by and large, the people at the ice fishing derby just passed her by. This didn't go unnoticed.

"Take a minute out of your day to learn about the birds and raptors in this area," Hedy cried. "You wouldn't have a successful fishing derby without the diversity that this lake-shore provides."

"Ma'am, would you like a brochure?" One of the volunteers put a glossy brochure in my hand.

The heading read *Give a hoot. Protect our owls.*

Hedy jumped off the rock and collected the brochures from the volunteers. "Thanks, guys. I don't know what good it's doing. These people aren't paying attention to me. They care more about catching and killing fish than they do saving owls."

"A lot of people took the brochure," one volunteer said. "I think we're making a real difference."

"Not as much as I'd like to see." Hedy noticed me for the first time. "What do you want?"

I brushed off her brusque tone. "I wanted to talk to you." I paused. "About owls."

"Let's chat. You two take a break. Maybe go inside somewhere to get warm and be ready to advocate for the owls when you come out."

They nodded and left.

"They're good kids. It's heartening to see more younger people getting into birding. It's a sport that you can start anytime." She studied me. "You look like you'd make an excellent birder. How are you at hiking? There is a lot of hiking and walking in birding. You have to move with purpose and take it slow."

"I haven't hiked in a long time."

"Hmmm." Hedy pressed her lips together as if in thought. "We'd have to test you to see if you can keep up."

Was there an agility test for birding? Probably in Hedy's world there was. She took it so seriously. Before I'd met Hedy, all the birders I'd known had been backyard birders. They would put birdseed out and see what came to their feeders. Hedy was a little more professional than that.

"What can you tell me about the owls by the lake?"

Hedy's eyes sparkled as if I'd just told her she'd won a million dollars in the lottery. "The owls are being bothered by all this noise and commotion from the ice fishing derby. And I learned someone is trying to call them in. You just don't do that at this time of year."

"Are there other times you can do owl calls?" I asked.

"I never like to do owl calls, but many professional guides and birders do use calls to bring in all types of birds. In the olden days, they had to learn those calls. Now they just play them on their phones. You can find the call for every bird in the world on the internet."

"You said it confuses the owls," I said.

She nodded. "Almost all owl species have one mate through the entire breeding season. In some cases, they mate for life. By calling the owls in now, they are being confused. It's even possible they won't find a mate at all because they're distracted. Owls could teach people a thing or two about monogamy and being faithful."

"Were these calls made the night Wallace Fields died?"

She narrowed her eyes. "How did you know that?"

"A friend of mine was here and heard them too."

She scowled. "When I find the person who did this, he will be sorry. I haven't dedicated my whole life to protecting the birds of this region just to have some jokester ruin it."

"Do you think it was a joke?" I asked.

"Usually it's kids goofing around, or it could be some amateur birders who just want to get a good look at an owl.

You'd be surprised at the number of people who haven't seen an owl in the wild. It's shocking," she said, as if it were a major failing of our society.

"Did you hear the owl calls yourself?"

"Yes, just the end of them. One of my society members alerted me to what was going on, and I rushed over here as quickly as I could. It took me a bit to get here because I was hiking around the perimeter of the lake making sure no one was camping where they shouldn't have been."

"Isn't it the park rangers' jobs to do that sort of thing?"

"It is, but I severely doubt they'll ever take the time to do it. They're more concerned the fisherman don't get drunk and crash their ATVs on the lake."

"I would say that's a valid concern."

She harrumphed and sounded a whole lot like Huckleberry while doing it. "So when I came back to this side of the lake, I heard the hoot. I have a good ear and can pinpoint where a sound is coming from."

"Did you hear a splash?" I asked.

"A splash?"

"My friend said after the owl call, he heard a splash."

"A splash, like in the lake? I suppose one of the ice fishermen who were drilling holes with their augers could have dropped something into the water. I know they weren't supposed to be on the lake until three in the morning, but there are always cheaters out there wanting to get an early start."

"No, he said that it was a big splash." I swallowed. "Like a body falling into the water."

She tilted her head back and forth like a bird would. "I didn't hear anything like that, but I did see Kent Brown running out of the woods like his tail feathers were on fire."

Chapter Twenty

I felt ill. "You saw Kent?"

"Sure did. I tried to stop him too, but he didn't even hear me. He looked spooked. I couldn't believe he'd make the owl calls, so I let him go. I was intent on finding the culprit."

She was intent on finding the culprit for the owl calls, and I was intent on finding the culprit for the murder.

What she'd said about seeing Kent wasn't good. It wasn't good at all. Not when added to the fact he'd apparently told the sheriff he didn't want me investigating the murder.

At first, I'd thought he didn't want that because he was my friend, and it was for my safety. But now I wondered if it was actually to protect himself.

"How do you know Kent?" I asked.

"He's a science teacher at the high school in Cherry Glen. He has me visit his class every year when they study their bird unit. It's usually in the spring during migration. I talk to the kids and take them on a bird walk. My hope is to make lifelong birders of them all."

"Kent has just never mentioned you," I said. As soon as

I said the words, I wondered why I'd even made the comment. Kent and I rarely had a conversation that wasn't about Kristy or the girls, or just the kind of passing chitchat you would have with your friend's spouse. I was starting to realize I knew very little about Kristy's husband.

"I can show you where I saw Kent come out of the woods."

I stared at her. "You know where?"

She wrinkled her nose as if I'd accused her of misidentifying a bluebird. "Of course I do. I know every inch of these woods. I know them better than the rangers. I certainly spend more time here."

Hedy walked past the line of vendors. To my surprise, I saw Kristy at the Cherry Glen booth talking to a group of ladies about all the town had to offer. She didn't see me, and I didn't wave. I felt like I was betraying my friend by following Hedy into the woods.

I just had to understand what Hedy had seen that night and hear her out. It didn't mean Kent was in any way involved in the murder. Kristy had said he'd heard an owl hoot and a splash. It spooked him. He ran away. That could be the end of the story.

Beyond the vendors, we crossed a sidewalk leading to the park restrooms, which had to be closed in the winter. They were unheated, and the water was turned off for the season so the pipes didn't burst. For all the anglers and spectators at the event, there was a line of Porta-Potties in the parking lot.

Hedy hurried around the small building and stepped into a break in the woods.

I followed her, bare tree branches and evergreen bushes

catching on my coat and poking me in the sides. Hedy forged ahead. The brush didn't bother her in the least.

"Is this an actual path?" I asked.

"It's the spot where I saw Kent." She glanced over her shoulder. "I thought that's what you wanted to see."

"It is. I just don't want to be smacked in the face in the process."

"It's part of life in the woods."

I looked down at Huckleberry, who was strolling behind me. At least the pug was so close to the ground that he wasn't getting smacked with limbs.

After forcing our way through more undergrowth, we came to a small clearing by the edge of the lake. Just beyond the clearing, I could see a small fishing cabin among the trees.

Hedy dusted snow off her sleeve. "In the summer, you wouldn't have been able to get through there at all. The undergrowth would have been too thick, and you would have been eaten alive by bugs. You wouldn't be able to see that cabin either because of bushes and trees."

Sounded lovely. I made a mental note never to come to these woods in the summer.

I walked up to the edge of the lake to get my bearings. From where were stood, we were maybe half a mile from the derby. I hadn't realized we'd walked so far. I'd been so focused on not getting slapped in the face with bare branches and ensuring Huckleberry didn't sink into the snowdrifts to notice.

"You think this is the spot where Kent was?" I asked.

"I do. If you keep walking the woods just grow denser, especially when you go beyond that fishing cabin. I'd only go that deep in the woods for a rare warbler."

"Why would he be this far from the derby?" I asked. "His job that night was to find a spot for the Fields Brewing Company booth. No way it was going to be here."

She shrugged. "This is where the hoot came from. And like I said, when I headed this way to see what happened, he bolted out of the woods like he'd just robbed a bank."

I looked down at the lake surface and noticed a batch of ice maybe ten feet from the edge. The rest of the ice was blue. I remembered what I had learned about ice. The bluer and clearer it looked, the more frozen it was. This ice was frozen solid, but it had a milky quality.

"Does this look like new ice to you?" I asked.

Hedy leaned over and looked at the lake. She walked out on the ice and tapped the spot I'd pointed toward with her boot. "It's frozen solid, but it's not as solid as the ice around it. See how the other ice is clear and blue. That means it's thicker."

Apparently Hedy knew her ice too.

I looked around the area we stood for any sign this might have been the place where Wallace had gone into the lake. Other than the ice, I didn't see anything until I looked up. "Oh my."

"What?" Hedy said looking around. She had her binoculars on her eyes, scanning the treetops.

I pointed above me. In the trees—I guessed it was fifteen feet up—was a bit of fishing line.

Hedy dropped her binoculars. "This is the exact reason I am against these fishing derbies on the lake. People just throw their line anywhere. They don't think about how much it could hurt the birds, animals, and plants. You had better believe I'm going to send a scathing email to the state park service, the sheriff's office, and the organizers of this event!"

Hedy walked over to the tree and looked like she planned to climb it and retrieve the fishing line. I wouldn't have been surprised if she did, but I couldn't let her do that.

"Don't touch that," I said, peering up at the line. Small sticks had been tied at either end as if someone did that in order to have something to hold on to—not for fishing, but for murder.

"I can't leave it there," Hedy said. "It could hurt a bird."

"I'm not telling you to leave it here, but Sheriff Penbrook needs to be the one to remove it from the tree."

"Why?" she asked.

I stared up into the tree. "Because I think it's the murder weapon."

Chapter Twenty-One

A half hour later, the south end of the lake was crawling with deputies and crime scene technicians looking for anything to prove this was the spot where Wallace went into the water.

"Hedy, why didn't you tell me about this when I asked you yesterday?" Sheriff Penbrook asked.

"You didn't ask anything about the owls. The owls tied it together."

He rubbed his forehead. "You're just like my dad. It's always about the birds. I understand it's your passion, but it can be exhausting at times."

"Milan, you must admit that birders make the best witnesses. We don't miss anything."

He shook his head and looked up in the tree where I'd seen the fishing line. A crime scene tech was in the tree, carefully trying to untangle the fishing line from the branches. I knew the sheriff wanted as much of the line intact as possible so the coroner could compare it to the marks on Wallace's neck and gather any DNA evidence that might be on the line as well. I cringed at the thought.

Slowly, the technician unwound the line from the tree branches. When it was free, he tucked it into an evidence bag and tucked it into his pocket and then carefully climbed down the tree.

When he reached the ground, he handed the evidence bag to another tech. The second tech removed the line from the bag and held it out for Sheriff Penbrook to examine. The fishing line was about three feet long. Tied on each end were broken sticks, both close to four inches in length. In my mind's eye, I could see the killer holding either side of the fishing line, coming up behind Wallace, and wrapping the makeshift weapon tightly around his throat.

Hedy tapped me on the shoulder. "Are you okay?"

"Oh, I'm fine," I said, even though I felt a little woozy.

She narrowed her eyes at me. "You looked like you were about to pass out."

I had been close to it, but I didn't tell her that.

"Take it to the coroner's office for comparison," the sheriff said.

The tech nodded and walked over to his crime scene kit sitting on a tree stump in the snow.

"Do you think this is where he went into the water?" I asked the sheriff.

He looked down at the ice. "It's the most likely place, but the surrounding ice is rock solid here."

"It was so cold that night," Hedy said. "That the ice would freeze over quickly. If he went in around midnight, it would freeze over during the night. It would be like tossing him into a coffin and closing the lid. Where he actually went in, where the hole was cut into the ice, is only maybe few inches thick now. If you stepped on it, you'd fall straight into the water."

Sheriff Penbrook rubbed his forehead. "It's concerning."

"Isn't all murder concerning?" I asked.

"Yes, but this feels to me like it was premeditated. It would have taken a long while to break through ice to make a gap big enough for a man to fit into it."

"So you think the killer lured Wallace to this spot with the intention of killing him."

He gave the slightest nod.

"Then it couldn't have been Kent. He was tending the bar at the brewery party. He wasn't breaking a hole in the lake a half hour away."

The sheriff pressed his lips together. "The hole in the ice could have been cut well in advance. Like Hedy said, if you stepped on that spot even now, you could fall into the water."

I didn't take that to be a good sign for Kent.

"Hopefully we get something off the line that matches with the victim. I don't hold out hope for any evidence from the killer. It was so cold that night, he or she would've had to wear gloves just to keep from getting frostbite."

Hedy put her hands on her hips. "Well, I'm sure glad I could be of service to close this case."

"The case is not closed yet," the sheriff warned.

"It's close, though. The sooner the fishermen and your deputies are out of here, the better. The owls need their peace."

Sheriff Penbrook shook his head. "I think you like birds more than people."

"Of course I do. That was never a question." She cleared her throat. "How did your guys not see this line before?"

"We searched the area," the sheriff said. "Unfortunately, they didn't look up."

Hedy clicked her tongue. "Milan Penbrook, your father taught you better than that. He taught you to always look up. Always."

I bit my lip. Even though the murder weapon might have been found, it hadn't helped Kent. Hedy hadn't mentioned Kent yet, but I knew it was just a matter of time. I needed to warn Kristy.

"Do you still need us here?" I asked the sheriff.

He glanced at me in surprise. "No, I have your statement. Do you have somewhere you need to be?"

I made a point of looking at the time on my phone. "It's almost three, and the derby is coming to an end. My father was leading his age bracket. I want to be there when they announce the winner."

He nodded. "Go ahead. I have your contact information if I need to find you."

I hoped he wouldn't need me.

"I'm staying here to make sure no birds are bothered while you're searching the area." Hedy folded her arms, apparently to underscore the fact she meant business.

The sheriff sighed but didn't argue with her.

I scooped up Huckleberry and instead of going back the way Hedy had brought us to the crime scene, I walked along the edge of the frozen lake.

My heart was pounding. Huckleberry snuggled up against

my chest and looked up at me in concern. I kissed the top of his head. "I'm okay."

I made it back to the vendor area without having to force my way through the brush. My goal was to head straight for the Cherry Glen booth and tell Kristy everything, but that was not to be.

"Shiloh!" Hazel stood at the edge of the derby area and cupped her hands to shout my name. "Shiloh!"

I waved to her.

"Come on! They're going to announce the winner."

I glanced back at the vendor area. Everyone was packing up.

"Come on!" Hazel shouted.

I headed in her direction. When, I reached her, she grabbed my hand and pulled me to the award area. I held Huckleberry under my other arm, and his head bobbed up and down as we ran.

The master of ceremonies stood on his makeshift platform and was in the middle of a speech by the time Hazel led me to where Quinn and my father waited for the results.

"What a weekend we've had!" the MC said. "I want you all to give yourselves a round of applause for sticking with it through these cold temperatures. Michiganders are tough, and this is the proof."

Everyone clapped, but the clapping faded quickly as everyone was eager to hear the winners' names.

"We start with the eldest fishing class because elders should always go first. Am I right?" He laughed at his own joke.

"This guy is not funny," Hazel whispered to me.

I had to agree with her.

"In the sixty-five and older category with a whopping twenty-one fish caught, our winner is Sullivan Bellamy."

Hazel screamed so loud next to me I think she may have permanently damaged my hearing.

"Congratulations, Sully! You are an inspiration to us all. Hazel, can you come up and collect his prize so Sully can stay put?" the MC asked.

Hazel ran and skidded to the front to take the trophy and envelope from the MC's hands. She was back at my father's side before the next category was announced.

Dad opened the envelope. "Well, look at that. A check for five hundred dollars." His eyes twinkled. "I will be putting that to good use."

"I knew you could win," Hazel said. "You were so far ahead yesterday, you really couldn't have lost. Next year, I want to win my age bracket."

Dad nodded. "And you can. We'll just have to come out here a few more times while the lake is frozen so I can teach you all I've learned about fishing."

"Awesome," the twelve-year-old said.

I smiled. I didn't know many seventh graders like Hazel who wanted to spend their free time ice fishing with their elderly neighbor.

"Where have you been all this time?" Quinn asked.

I squinted into the sunlight.

"Shi?" Quinn asked.

"I was talking with Hedy Strong. Do you remember her?"

"The bird lady? Sure. Why were you with her?"

"She was telling me about the owls in the area. I'm trying to learn more about the wildlife. I want the farm to be sustainable and help the area, not harm it. Hedy knows a lot on that subject."

He squinted back at me but said nothing more. I felt like a shift had begun in our friendship. I was holding back from him, and he was holding back from me. I supposed this was always going to happen. The only thing that had drawn us together was Logan and now Hazel. A connection through a third party wasn't enough.

Chapter Twenty-Two

Kristy and the Cherry Glen booth were gone by the time I walked back to the vendor area. I called her, but she didn't pick up. I then shot her a text message asking her to call me as soon as she could. There was no response.

Short of driving to her house—which I didn't want to do for fear Kent would overhear our conversation—there wasn't much more I could do. Instead I helped Quinn and Hazel pack up the fishing shanty while Dad kept an eye on Huckleberry.

On the drive back to Bellamy Farm, Dad fell asleep with a snoozing Huckleberry on his lap. It had been a long weekend for all of us.

I got Dad into the house and settled in his favorite chair in front of the TV. Tomorrow would be a rough day for him as all the aches and pains of ice fishing the last couple of days would catch up with him. I put a heating pad under his back.

I went outside and secured the chickens in their coop and the cats in the barn. Esmeralda wasn't in the barn. Most likely, she was waiting by the door to my cabin. I swore that cat knew when I was coming home. She would be sitting on the cabin's doorstep, ready to snuggle in for the night.

Huckleberry and I walked down the snow-encrusted path to reach the cabin. As we walked, I heard the hooting of an owl.

I wasn't as versed in owls as Hedy, but I recognized the barred owl call. It was one I'd heard often when I was a child on the farm. I scanned the trees and finally saw the owl in the fading light.

It sat on a dead branch twenty feet from the ground and looked me right in the eye.

"Do you have any wisdom to share?"

The owl turned its head away, and I took that to mean no.

I thought that Huckleberry was too big for the owl to carry off, but I wasn't taking any chances, and I picked up the pug and carried him the rest of the way to the cabin. I hoped Esmeralda was all right. I knew the Siamese was wily, but it made me nervous when she tromped around the farm alone, especially at dusk.

Instead of seeing Hazel's cat on the doorstep, I spotted a man standing in my porch light. I sucked in a breath and was poised to turn and run back to the farmhouse. He must have heard me coming because he turned to face me. It was Kent Brown.

"What are you doing here? You almost gave me a heart attack." I set Huckleberry on the ground.

The pug waddled over to Kent and sniffed his boots.

"I need to talk to you." Kent's face was pale and drawn. "It's important."

I guessed it must have been if he'd come all this way to see me.

"Where's your truck?" I asked.

"I parked by the service drive at the cherry orchard."

"Why?" I asked. "You had to walk through the snow to get here."

"Because of the police." This was serious. "Can we go inside?" His voice was pleading.

I nodded and unlocked the cabin door. "Let's sit in the kitchen," I said, pointing to the right. "I'll make some tea. My grandmother believed tart cherry juice or tea could fix anything."

He took off his heavy coat and hung it over the back of his chair, then sat at the kitchen table. "I think I need a glass of both, because I need all the help I can get to fix the mess I'm in."

I filled the kettle with water and put it on the vintage stovetop. "Does Kristy know where you are?"

He shook his head. "She thinks I ran to the store to get diapers. If I'm gone too long, she'll know something is wrong."

"If you wanted to talk to me, why didn't you just call me?" I asked.

"This is easier in person. Plus, I can't get out of telling you when we're face-to-face. I need your help. I'm in a lot of trouble."

"The sheriff told me you didn't want my help."

He licked his chapped lips. "That's true. I did say that, but it was only because I thought if you meddled too much it would put more attention on me. Then, I realized all the attention I've received because of what happened two nights ago, I brought upon myself. Because I'm a coward. I need to take ownership and prove I'm not a coward any longer. I want the twins to know they have a strong father."

"The twins won't remember any of this."

"I know that, but they might hear stories someday. I want them to be proud of me for how I dealt with it all."

"All right. Kristy told me a lot of what you told her, but why don't you start at the beginning?"

He took a deep breath and repeated the story I'd heard from Kristy. After the brewery party, Wallace had asked him to go to the derby area to pick out a place for their booth. Kent had agreed, and they'd driven separately. When Kent had arrived, he'd claimed the spot quickly and then waited for Wallace, who never turned up.

Kent's Adam's apple bobbed up and down. "Then, I was about to leave, and I heard a hooting sound. I knew it wasn't a real owl, but then I heard an owl, a real owl, call back. I assumed there were birders doing an owl walk around the lake. I'd heard there was a great gray owl in the area and I wanted to see it, so I followed the sound. I walked maybe a half mile or so along the lake's edge." He swallowed again. "I never saw the owl, but when I came to a clearing, I could see open water that was maybe two-by-two feet wide. It was so cold that night and had been so cold for so long, it didn't make any sense that the water wouldn't be frozen solid."

I nodded, as I had thought the same thing.

"I went over to look at it because I thought it was odd. I teach biology, and any anomaly in nature can be a talking point with my students. However, when I got closer, I could tell it wasn't natural. The corners were too sharp and too clean. It was clearly done with a chainsaw."

"Did you see the chainsaw?"

He shook his head. "But I could tell from the cuts. I suppose it could have been a regular saw, but whoever did it would have to have the patience of a saint. It would've taken a very long time to cut by hand."

"Then what happened?"

"I started to leave. I still hadn't heard from Wallace, so I planned to go home. I texted him again to tell him I was leaving and got a text back that said, ok. I thought that meant I was free to go. I was exhausted from working the bar, and as you know, the night had not gone like Kristy and I had hoped it would." He took a breath.

I waited for him to continue.

"I was walking back through the woods when I heard noises behind me, like a large animal in the bush. I thought maybe it was a deer or a black bear. Then I heard the splash." His face turned bright red. "I—I just ran. All I could think is I wasn't going to find out what it was. I had a wife and daughters who needed me."

And that must have been when Hedy saw him.

The kettle whistled, and I used it as a chance to hide my face. Kristy had been right when she'd said her husband might have been able to save Wallace. That's something Kent would have to live with. It wasn't a crime but self-preservation. There was no way for him to know what made the noise in the woods.

"Kristy said you saw Wallace's truck."

"Yes, while I was leaving, but by that point, I had no intention of staying. I was spooked, and besides, Wallace said it was okay for me to leave in his text message."

"You have to tell the sheriff this," I said as I set a mug of tea in front of him.

He wrapped his hands around the steaming cup. "I can't. It makes me look bad."

"It might," I said. "But if you want to help Wallace's family, you need to tell the sheriff."

He looked into his mug. "I don't think his family much cares that he's dead. You should've heard him and his wife fight. It was so uncomfortable."

"They fought at the brewery?" I asked.

"All the time, but never when customers were there. When customers were inside the building, they were professional. But I would never say they were loving toward each other."

"What did they argue about?" I asked as I sat across from him at the table with my own mug of tea.

"All kinds of things from finances to personal stuff about Chanel's daughter, Lila Rae."

Esmeralda chose that moment to waltz into the kitchen. I let out a little sigh of relief. She must have come in the cat door at the back of the cabin. I usually had it latched closed when it was this cold out, but perhaps I forgot. It was also possible Esmeralda had figured out how to unlatch it herself. I reached down and petted her back. It was toasty warm. She hadn't just come in from the cold, she'd been in the cabin for a while. That was also a relief when I thought about the owl outside.

"What about Chanel's daughter?"

He looked at the tabletop like it was the most interesting piece of furniture he had ever seen.

"Kent, you've said this much, you might as well keep going."

"She's a bartender at the brewery, but not because she's good at it. I think Wallace just gave her a job to give her something to do. She rarely showed up for work, and the bar staff don't even bother to take her into account anymore when making the weekly shift schedule. She lived with Wallace and Chanel. Wallace wanted her out."

He was just confirming what I'd heard from Chanel.

"One night he told her to move out. Chanel wasn't there. I overheard Lila Rae tell Wallace he couldn't get rid of her because she knew too much. She said if he pressed the issue, she would tell her mother."

"What was she going to tell Chanel?"

He shook his head. "I don't know. Neither of them mentioned specifics."

"She was blackmailing him?"

"To stay in the house at least. I don't know if she was using it for anything else."

I sipped my tea and considered this.

Huckleberry walked across the kitchen to his water bowl. He was still wearing the booties Chesney made him. He'd let me remove the jacket, but it seemed he wanted to keep the booties on. He could be an odd little dog.

"Are you going to tell the police all of this?" I asked.

"I know I should."

"You have to. Hedy saw you run out of the woods. She and the sheriff are old friends. As far as I know, she hasn't mentioned your name yet, but there's no reason for her not to. You need to tell the sheriff first."

"Hedy's friends with the Antrim County sheriff?" he asked.

"Apparently Hedy and the sheriff's dad are both birders."

He didn't say anything.

"You think Wallace's family is behind this?" I asked.

"I don't know about that, but I'm telling you, it has to do with the beer."

"What do you mean?" I asked.

"The beer that won the contest wasn't the beer Jason entered. I don't know if he switched it out or not, but that wasn't Jason's beer. I tasted his a week ago and it was nothing like that. We were allowed to make tweaks before the finals, but his wasn't tweaked, it was brand new."

"Do you think Wallace knew he did that?"

"I don't know how he could have missed it. He tasted Jason's beer in the prelims too. If he knew and didn't disqualify Jason that wasn't fair to everyone who entered before we were narrowed down to the final two. If that was allowed, they should have been allowed to change their recipes too."

He had a point.

"All I know is what was served that night was not Jason's cherry beer from the first round of judging, not by a long shot."

"That's something else you need to tell the authorities." I stood up and took my empty mug to the sink.

Kent looked at his watch. "I have to go. Kristy will be getting worried. Getting diapers shouldn't take this long. Thank you for the tea."

He never took a sip of it, but I told him he was welcome in any case. He put on his coat, and I followed him to the door.

"Thank you for listening, Shiloh. You have been a good friend to Kristy and me."

I smiled at him. "And you two have been good friends to me."

I watched as he disappeared into the woods on the way to the service road by the cherry orchard. Now in the moonlight, I could see the prints that he made before when he walked to the cabin.

I prayed that Kent would do the right thing tomorrow morning and tell the sheriff what he knew. That way I wouldn't have to do it for him.

The barred owl hooted high in the trees.

Chapter Twenty-Three

My phone rang at four the next morning. These very early mornings were getting old even for me. In January, four a.m. might as well be in the middle of the night. I flailed about trying to reach the phone on my nightstand. Esmeralda hissed from the foot of the bed. She took her beauty sleep very seriously and didn't like to be shaken awake.

Huckleberry, on the other hand, walked up the bed and snorted at me as if to ask what was wrong.

I didn't know yet, but no one called at this time if it was good news.

Finally, I managed to get ahold of the phone and mumbled a hello.

"Shi, you have to go to the brewing company," Kristy said frantically in my ear.

"What?" I asked. "What's going on?"

"You have to go to the brewing company. Kent needs your help."

"What? Why?" I was still having trouble waking up.

"Shi, someone broke into the building last night, and Kent was there."

That got me awake.

"What? What was Kent doing there in the middle of the night?"

"Around nine or so, Chanel Fields texted Kent and told him to go there to make sure the bar was ready for reopening this afternoon."

"Why couldn't he have done it in the morning?"

"It's a Monday. He has to teach."

"So he's been there since nine?" I asked, still blinking at my bedroom clock that said four in the morning.

"Ten thirty. He left at ten thirty. He said he would only be an hour. I fell asleep and it wasn't until the girls woke me up at three that I realized he never came home. I tried to call and text him, but he wouldn't answer. It was a nightmare."

My chest tightened. "How did you find him?"

"The police called me. It seems Stacey called them because she noticed all the lights were on at the brewery and it was unusual at this time of night. They went over to check it out." She took a breath. "They found Kent behind the bar, knocked out cold."

It didn't surprise me that Stacey was up at that time. It was possible that she hadn't gone to bed yet. She always had been a night owl. I was certain that contributed to the fact she was happier in theater than farming.

"Oh, Kristy."

"They want to take him to the hospital, but Kent doesn't want to go. I can't go to talk him into it. Not with the girls. Can you go to the brewery to see what's going on?"

"Yes, yes, of course, I'll go." I jumped out of bed and started looking for my clothes. "Are you and the girls okay?"

"Yes, we're fine. I feel terrible that I can't go there, but I can't leave the girls. They both have colds, and I know if Ken or I are not here when they wake up, they will be hysterical. They only want us when they're sick."

"I understand. Kent will understand too. He'd want you to stay with your daughters."

"Thank you." Her voice tightened. "Shi, I'm scared."

I froze as I pulled socks out of dresser drawer. "I know. Kent will be okay. Did the police say he was okay?"

"He might have a concussion, but other than that he seems fine. The hospital will do a closer check if Kent will allow it. He hates going to the doctor, so I'm not completely surprised he's reluctant to go." Kristy took a breath. "But what if this is tied to Wallace Fields's murder? It seems like it would have to be. It will just embroil Kent more into all of this. I told him that I didn't want him to go tonight. I told him the Fields could figure out what the bar needed themselves, but he is so conscientious, he felt like he had to go."

"Everything will be okay," I said, but even to my own ears, my response sounded weak. Both Kristy and I knew from personal experience that a person could be blamed for murder for lesser reasons. Kent was the last person to communicate with Wallace, and after hearing those sounds in the woods, he didn't call the police. The authorities could claim he killed Wallace and then waited to report it or that he was an accomplice in some way.

I shook those dark thoughts from my head. "I'm leaving now."

"Call me as soon as you get there."

I promised I would.

It was going to take me some time to get to the brewery. I first had to go the half mile from my cabin to the farmhouse where my father's truck was parked. I quickly put on my ski coat, then I gathered up Huckleberry and went out the door.

I shook from the cold. It was frigid outside. I would guess the temperature was holding at ten below, but that was a generous guess.

My snowmobile was parked outside the cabin door. I set Huckleberry in his orange winter jacket in front of me on the seat and revved the engine. It sputtered to life. Like everything else on the farm, it was old and just a few minutes from completely breaking down.

"Come on, just work tonight," I urged the machine. I didn't use it often because it wasn't reliable and tended to stall out. I hoped just for the next ten minutes it would work.

And it did. I glided over the snow-covered trail between my cabin from the main farmhouse. Perhaps it would make sense to live in the farmhouse—especially in the harsher months of the year—but I couldn't do it. As much as I loved my dad, I couldn't live with him. He couldn't live with me either, which he had made abundantly clear more than once.

I stopped the snowmobile by the farmhouse. The walk I'd cleared between the back door and the driveway for my father was snow-covered again. I would have to clear it off before he tried to go outside with his walker. He was stubborn and might try to make it outside before I got a chance, but I couldn't stop and do it now. I was hoping after two days of the derby, he was fine with staying home for a bit.

I scooped up Huckleberry and went into the house. As I expected, the door wasn't locked. My father had it in his head that it was still the 1950s, and doors or cars could be left unlocked with no worries of intruders. It made no difference to him that now three murders had happened in the area over the last year.

"What are you doing barreling into the house at this hour?" My father poked his head out of his history room. It was an old walk-in pantry he'd built for my mother who had loved to cook. Now he used it to house his relics and collections from American and Michigan pioneer history. He had a lot. And when I said a lot, it was enough to fill two hundred square feet from wall to wall and from floor to ceiling.

I shook my head. Despite all he had done in the last two days at the fishing derby, he was still up at four like always.

"Can you keep Huckleberry until I get back?" I asked. "I have to run into town."

He blinked at me. "Sure. I know Old Huck would love to have some eggs and bacon for breakfast. That's what I was planning to have this morning. You interested, Pup?"

Huckleberry wiggled his back end, which was a sure sign he was in agreement.

My father grabbed his cane leaning on the wall outside of the collection room. "But why are you off to town so early? Nothing is open."

"Kristy needs my help."

"Women problems," he said, as if he knew exactly what that meant.

I bit the inside of my cheek. Right now wasn't the time to get into an argument with my father.

"Can you feed the chickens and the barn cats too?"

"Of course. Who do you think did it before you moved back home?" he said hotly.

I sighed. "Can you please call Quinn to clear the walk for you between here and the barn before you go out? I don't think he's working this morning, so he should be able to help."

My dad grunted. "Fine, I will. Maybe Hazel will want to come with him and help me collect eggs from the chickens." He brightened at the idea. He loved Hazel just as much as I did.

"Good," I said with relief. "Please stay on the shoveled path in the snow, and if for any reason Quinn can't come and help, the animals can wait. I'll feed them when I get home, or I'll call Stacey to stop by."

He grunted again. "You think I'm an invalid. Did I not just win the ice fishing derby? Or was that some other old man?"

"You won it," I admitted. "I just want to make sure you're all right."

He grunted in reply.

I said rushed goodbyes to Dad and to Huckleberry and then grabbed the keys to the truck from the hook by the kitchen cupboard.

As quickly as I wanted to reach the brewery, I remembered

my recent spill into the ditch. I didn't want a repeat of that this morning. It was unlikely Quinn would happen by at the perfect time again. I drove as quickly as I dared and firmly held the steering wheel at ten and two.

I made it to town without incident, but by this point it was well over an hour after Kristy had called and asked for my help. By this time, I doubted Kent was still at the brewery.

As soon as I reached my cousin Stacey's Michigan Street Theater, I could see the flashing lights of the police. Kristy had said Stacey sounded the alarm about something being off at the brewery, and I saw that she did have a clear view of the building from the theater.

At least I wasn't so late that the scene had been cleared.

Outside of the building I spotted Kent leaning against the police car. I parked the truck and jumped out. "Kent, are you okay?"

He blinked at me. He wasn't wearing a coat, hat, or gloves, and it was well below zero outside. He was going to get hypothermia if he stayed outside much longer, or at the very least frostbite on his ears and hands. He did have a blanket wrapped around him, but that didn't seem like nearly enough.

He stared at me. "Shiloh? What are you doing here?"

"Kristy called me. She told me to come here and make sure you were all right. You need to go back inside. You're going to freeze to death here."

He emphatically shook his head like a toddler on the verge of a tantrum. "I'm not going back in there. I can't. I don't ever want to go back in there again. I just have to think of a way to tell Kristy. I'll find another part-time job to help us make ends meet." He said this last part more to himself than to me.

Even so, I said, "Yes, you will. The brewery isn't the only restaurant in town."

"It's the only one with a bar, and I'm a bartender. That really limits what I can do."

"Okay," I said. "Then come sit with me in my truck so we can talk. I can blast the heat on you."

"All right."

I ushered him to the truck and slammed the passenger-side door closed after him. Then, I ran around the pickup and jumped onto the driver seat. I quickly started the engine and turned up the heat.

Kent held his palms in front of the vents. "Oh, thank you. I didn't realize how cold I really was."

"And that's the point when it gets dangerous." I reached behind him. "Let me see if my dad has a blanket or something in here." I rooted around behind the seat and came up with an old towel. I wasn't sure how clean it was, but it was the best I could do.

I wrapped it around his shoulders on top of the blanket he already had.

"It smells like mold."

"It's all I have."

He nodded and stared out through the windshield at the flashing lights.

"Kent, what happened? Kristy said you were hurt and going to the hospital."

"I told them I didn't want to go to the hospital, and they weren't able to take me without my permission. They made me sign a release form."

"Why wouldn't you go to the hospital?" I asked. "You could have a concussion."

"I just wanted to go home."

"I can take you home, but I think it would be better if we went to the hospital to get you checked out."

He shook his head and winced.

I frowned. "What happened in the brewery tonight? Can you tell me?"

"I don't know. I was behind the bar taking inventory like Chanel asked me to. The next thing I knew, Laurel Burger was standing over me."

I wrinkled my nose at the mention of Laurel Burger. She was an EMT and worked out of the same department as Quinn. As far as I knew, she was a good EMT but not a very nice person. I hoped I'd be able to avoid seeing her while I was here.

"Doesn't the bar have mirrors? You didn't even see anyone behind you just for a split second?"

"No." He touched his forehead. "I think I was so tired from the last few days I wasn't paying attention."

"How did you get into the building at this hour? Do you have a key?" I asked.

"I got in with the key code on the back door. Fields Brewing Company has so many employees, and most of us are part time, so we use that instead of keys."

"How many people know this code?" I asked.

"Dozens. It's never been changed, so people who don't work here any longer could still know it."

"A place like this would have video surveillance though, right?" There had to be in a place this large, with so many customers and employees.

He nodded. "Yes, there are cameras everywhere inside. The staff used to joke about the fact that Wallace didn't trust a single one of us. I suppose he had good reason, since now he's dead."

"You think it was an employee who killed him?"

"I—I don't know. I have no idea who would do such a thing." He winced.

"Do you know what you were hit with?"

"Chief Randy believes it was a beer bottle. There was one shattered on the floor next to me when I woke up. It was a bottle of Jason's cherry beer that won the competition." He said this last part like it added insult to injury. He touched the top of his head and gasped.

"I'm taking you to the hospital," I said. "I don't care if you signed a form with Laurel saying you didn't want to go. You didn't sign it with me."

He leaned back in his seat and didn't argue.

Chapter Twenty-Four

Rays of sunshine were starting to lighten the sky as I dragged myself out of the Grand Traverse Community Hospital, which was the closest medical center to Cherry Glen. Thankfully, the small hospital catered to farmers and high school athletes and was well versed in treating concussions. They planned to keep Kent for a few hours for observation. When I left, he was on the phone with Kristy telling her about his ordeal.

Even though Cherry Glen was only fifteen miles from the hospital, it took me forty minutes to drive back into town as another snow squall swept through western Michigan. I decided to wait until the wind calmed down before I continued on my way to the farm. Dad's truck had a high profile, and there weren't many trees between here and the farm to break the wind. After the last few days I'd had, I really didn't feel up to being rocked around in the pickup like I was riding a bucking bronco.

I parked on the street in front of my cousin's theater. The blowing snow made it hard even to see the brewery, but there was still one Cherry Glen police car parked in front of it. There was also the addition of an Antrim sheriff's department vehicle. I was willing to bet all the cinnamon rolls in Jessa's Place that Sheriff Penbrook himself was inside that building.

Someone knocked on the driver's-side door. I jumped and looked out the window. Standing there was a very angry-looking Chief Randy. His pug-like nose was wrinkled as he stared at me through the window. His luxurious black mustache twitched and was peppered with snowflakes. He wore a navy-blue stocking cap that matched his police coat, but I knew under the hat, his head was mostly bald with gray tufts of hair sticking out every which way.

I cranked down the window. This was reminiscent of when I'd had a similar encounter with his son three nights ago.

"Shiloh Bellamy." Chief Randy scowled at me. "What are you doing here?"

"I just dropped Kent Brown off at the hospital. Kristy called me and told me what happened."

He scowled. "He told us he wouldn't go to the hospital."

"Maybe he just didn't want to ride in the ambulance," I said. "He went for me."

The chief narrowed his eyes as if he wasn't buying the story, not one little bit. "I'm glad Kent got the help he needed, however he might have gotten there." He cleared his throat. "Now that you've done your Good Samaritan deed for the day, I suggest you head home."

"I was planning to do that," I said. "I'm just waiting out this weather."

As if to prove my point, a gust of icy wind blew off the

chief's hat. He snatched it out of the air before it could blow away completely. He clapped the hat back on his head and narrowed his eyes at me. "I hear that you and Milan Penbrook have become mighty cozy. He speaks highly of you."

Heat rushed up my neck, into my cheeks, and all the way to the top of my head. "I have only spoken to Sheriff Penbrook about the murder."

"A murder that you have nothing to do with."

I glared at him. "I found the body."

"People find bodies every day and don't make such a nuisance of themselves to law enforcement like you do."

I gritted my teeth.

"In any case, Milan seems to be quite impressed with you. Why exactly?" He studied my face.

"Maybe he respects my opinion."

The chief snorted as if that was the last possible answer. "If this was my case, I would make sure you stayed away from it."

"You're just upset it's not your case. Don't take that out on me."

He scowled at me. "Well, this break-in and attack on Kent Brown is my case, so I want you to stay away from it."

I didn't bother reply.

He straightened up and smacked the side of my car with his gloved hand. "Stay out of trouble, you hear?"

"I never get in trouble, Chief," I said with an LA smile. Mentally I added, "much."

After the chief got into his car and drove away, I put on my winter hat and turned the hood up on my coat before I slipped out of my father's truck. Since I was stuck in town for a little while longer, I wondered if I could get a peek into the brewery. Maybe seeing exactly where Kent fell, I'd get a better idea of what direction the attacker came from.

In the blowing snow, I walked the short distance from the theater to the brewery. While snowflakes stung my face, my brain mulled over what Chief Randy had said: "Milan seems quite impressed with you." What did that mean? What had the sheriff said to Chief Randy to give the police chief that impression, and was it even true? I would not put it past Chief Randy to be trying to confuse me and play with my emotions. He and wife Doreen had made it clear in no certain terms that they hated the idea of Quinn and me ever having a romantic relationship. They weren't even keen on the idea of us being friends. Logan had been Quinn's best friend since they were in diapers. After Logan died, Quinn had a rough time, and it led him to leave Cherry Glen a few years after I did. His parents blamed me for their son's difficulties and even more, they blamed me for causing him to leave because Logan had been coming to see me when he had been hit and killed by a drunk driver.

Even with Chief Randy gone, I doubted I would be able to go inside the brewery as there was a police officer stationed at the door.

"Shiloh Bellamy," the officer said. "Do you remember me?"

I grimaced. That question always seemed like some sort of trap. It seemed everyone in town remembered who I was, and I was expected to have remembered who they were these last fifteen years, even though there was just one of me to remember and hundreds of them.

"We went to school together." It was a shot in the dark, but the best one I had.

"You do remember me! I knew you couldn't forget your eighth-grade lab partner."

"Lab partner" was all I needed to clear the last of the cobwebs from my brain. "Of course, I wouldn't. I could never forget you, Jake," I said, even though I had thoroughly forgotten him for a decade plus.

I remembered him now. He had been a skinny kid and president of the chess team. I thought he'd won the state spelling bee in middle school. He was still very thin and seemed to be all arms and legs. I never would have guessed he'd end up being a cop.

"I haven't seen you in…what?" he asked.

"Fifteen years," I offered, because that was the exact amount of time I had been in LA working as a producer.

"Must be," the officer grinned from ear to ear. "I knew you were back, of course. Chief Randy grumbles about it all the time. He's afraid you're going to up and marry his son."

No chance of that happening, I thought. But I didn't say anything. It wasn't Jake's or anyone else's business.

"You know Kristy, don't you?" I asked. "She was Kristy Garcia in school."

"Yeah, of course. I can't believe what happened to Kent last night. How is she taking it? I remembered the two of you were close."

"We still are. She asked me to come here to find out any

information about who hurt Kent. She's a new mom of twins and can't leave her babies. Do you mind if I go inside and look around?"

His brow crinkled. "I don't think the chief would like it if I let you in there."

Drat.

Undaunted, I went on, "That's probably true. I'm just so worried about Kristy, and Kent is in the hospital. I don't think it's unreasonable that they want answers, do you?"

"Well, no," he said.

"So can I go in and take a look?" I flashed my Hollywood smile.

"Sorry, Shiloh, no can do. The chief said no one goes into the brewery without his authorization. You don't have authorization from Chief Randy, do you?"

My shoulders sagged. "I don't." I wasn't going to take the lie so far that I would be dumb enough to put words—words that surely would get back to him—into the police chief's mouth.

"Didn't think so." He shrugged. "Sorry."

"I understand," I said finally. It had been worth a shot.

He gave me a half smile. "Don't worry, Shiloh. No one can actually think Kent Brown could kill anyone. The guy is harmless. And now that he's been attacked himself, he should be in the clear."

I shivered as my brain played out the scene for me. I really didn't need to see that.

"Door!" someone on the other side of the brewery door shouted.

Jake snapped to attention and opened the door wide, while I jumped out of the way. Laurel Burger came out and was looking as disgruntled as ever. "Jake, can you grab the rest of my gear? It's just inside the door."

Jake jumped into action and ran around an SUV with Cherry Glen Safety emblazoned on the side of it. He disappeared from my view.

Laurel narrowed her eyes are me. "What are you doing here? Do you always have to turn up like a bad penny?"

She had called me so many worse names in high school, I wasn't even insulted. In fact, *bad penny* coming from her was almost like an endearment.

"Good morning to you too, Laurel," I said.

She scowled and marched way. Laurel disappeared around the other side of the ambulance, and I stood next to an open and unguarded door.

Before I could change my mind, I stepped inside the building.

But once I was inside the brewery, I really didn't know what I wanted to do. I had been so intent about making it inside that I had never thought about what would happen when I accomplished it.

Whatever you are going to do, I told myself, *make it quick.*

I soon found myself in the restaurant. It was a big, wide-open space with a high ceiling that showed off all the innards of the building. The furniture was masculine, made of metal and wood. The bar was at least twenty feet long and was made from reclaimed barn wood, polished to a high shine. Behind the bar, there was just about any kind of liquor or syrup you could think of. But at the forefront of every shelf, there was a bottle of Fields signature beer. No other beer was sold at Fields.

This was where Kent had been standing when he was struck. I stared at the bar. Why had the person bothered to hit him? This was a massive building; I guessed a person could have easily snuck around it without being detected. They could have come in and done whatever they wanted to do, and Kent would have never been the wiser. That made me think that maybe the person came to the brewery with the intention of hurting Kent.

But who could have known he was there, besides Chanel Fields and Kristy? Kristy wouldn't hit her own husband over the back of the head, and she had been home with the twins. That left Chanel. Chanel didn't strike me as a person who did her dirty work herself, and maybe I had a soft spot for her because she was a dog lover.

To my left, there was the glass wall separating the brewery from the dining portion of the building. All looked calm. The brewery was a large space going eighty or ninety feet back from the glass wall. The giant fermentation tank obscured most of my view.

At the end of the glass wall there was a set of double glass doors. They stood open. I had never seen them open before.

I was already in pretty deep here. If I got caught, Chief Randy or Sheriff Penbrook would have my head. I took a breath and walked quickly toward the door. In for a penny, in for a pound—at least that's what Grandma Bellamy used to say. And according to Laurel, I was a bad penny after all. She would know a thing or two about that.

It was cold inside the brewery. Not as cold as outside, but I was glad I had my coat and hat on. It was also a maze of tanks and daunting-looking equipment with levers, nozzles, and meters. Making beer looked complicated.

I realized I had no idea where to go in this massive space. I guess I had just wanted to see it because Kent believed the murder was about the beer at judging.

This was a bad idea. I started out the glass doors, but as I came through, the restaurant door opened. Chief Randy's voice carried clearly through the vast room. "What do you mean she disappeared? Shiloh Bellamy doesn't just disappear. She gets into trouble."

I covered my mouth. Without thinking, I scooted backward, farther into the brewery.

Chapter Twenty-Five

I knew there was a second exit out of the building because that's where Chanel had brought me and Huckleberry in with her dogs, but that exit was closer to the restaurant. I couldn't go back that way. A building so large would have multiple ways out. I just had to find another option. I ducked behind the tanks and ran in and around them to the very back of the room.

From there I could see the steel back door with the welcome red "exit" sign glowing over it.

"I bet she's in here. Darn it all!" Chief Randy's voice carried in over the massive tanks. "You can't take your eyes off her for one second."

I slipped out the back door, bracing myself for the sound of an alarm. Thankfully, none came. I found myself in the employee parking lot, and I was happy to see that it was covered with footprints in the snow. Mine would be difficult to detect. I hurried through the back of the parking lot and walked behind the neighboring shop to the right of the brewery. Now my boot prints were clearly visible. But it couldn't be helped.

I kept going until I was behind my cousin's theater. I walked around the entire building and came out the other side on the sidewalk. I let out a breath.

The advantage of growing up in Cherry Glen was I knew every nook and cranny of it. Even with the new businesses and shops on Michigan Street, the layout of the town was the same.

With my shoulders back, I returned to my truck like I didn't have a care in the world.

When I reached where I had left my truck, I walked toward the brewery door.

Chief Randy stomped out of the building. "Find her!" he shouted at Jake.

"Find who?" I asked.

The police chief spun around. "You! Where were you?"

"I went for a walk," I said. "I thought you went home, Chief."

His face was bright red. "I had to come back."

"Oh?"

His chest heaved up and down, and his mustache wiggled on his upper lip. He pointed at me. "Stay out of this, you hear me."

"I hear you," I said, but that didn't mean I was going to follow his directions. "I guess I'll go home then," I said and turned to walk back to my truck.

The chief called after me, "Don't make this more difficult than it has to be, Shiloh."

When did I ever do that?

As I climbed into my father's truck, I wondered where the sheriff had been all that time I was inside of the brewery. Had he really gone home?

I was exhausted, and all I wanted to do was return to my farm, hustle through my chores, and take a well-deserved nap. I drove straight home with a lot to think about. Who would want to kill Wallace Fields? Because I was certain that same person had hit Kent over the head. But why attack Kent when he was such a great scapegoat for the crime? Why didn't the attacker kill him? I rubbed my forehead. None of it made sense.

When I walked into the farmhouse a little while later, I found Huckleberry and my father watching cable news. The commenter on the screen shouted about the state of the country and blamed the president, congress, and his mail-man. It was amazing to me how much he was paid for being angry all the time. My father loved it.

"Tell it to him!" Dad shook his fist at the screen.

Huckleberry looked at me with wide pug eyes in alarm. To be honest, pugs looked alarmed the majority of the time. When they didn't, they were asleep.

"Dad?" I asked.

"Congress has to do something," my father said to the screen. "Bunch of cowards. What is this country becoming?"

"Dad?"

"The pioneers didn't live and die for this!"

"Dad?" I shouted this time.

"Wh-what? Shiloh? Why are you yelling?" He turned and looked at me standing in the doorway of the kitchen.

Huckleberry jumped off my dad's recliner and ran over to me. I leaned over and patted his head.

"I just wanted to let you know that I'm home."

"Oh well, did you have to interrupt my program for that?" He wanted to know.

I sighed and picked up my dog.

"Did you and Kristy settle your women's issues?" he asked.

I gritted my teeth. "If by women's issues you mean her husband being hit over the head with a beer bottle? Then no, no, we haven't."

He stared at me for a long moment and then his mouth opened and closed as if he had something to say but didn't know how to form the words. Finally, he said, "What did you say?"

I picked up the remote and turned off the TV. It was giving me a headache. It wasn't like my father was going to miss anything. The same man would be angry at the world tomorrow too.

"I had to rush to town because Kent was attacked at the brewery," I said.

"Is it related to the murder?"

"I think so."

"What are the police saying?" Dad asked.

"Chief Randy isn't saying anything."

"The police chief doesn't know anything about anything. Remember when he thought I was a killer? Me? On my walker?" He shook his head. "The whole world has gone crazy. You would know that if you watched the news."

I sighed. "I have chores to do and then I'm going to lie down."

Dad nodded and turned the TV back on. This time he turned the volume up to the sound barrier.

Huckleberry and I didn't need any further encouragement to leave. Outside, I checked on the chickens. Dad had fed them and collected the eggs as promised. I forgot to ask him if Hazel had been there to help, but someone had cleared the path between the barn and the chicken coup while I was gone. I assumed it was Quinn. If not Quinn, then it had to be my cousin Stacey.

I wrinkled my brow. Stacey had been the one who reported the lights on in the brewery at an odd time. It seemed like I was due for another conversation with my cousin.

Before I could face that, I needed a nap.

My phone rang, or I thought it rang. I was lying facedown on my bed like a sea lion on the beach. I pushed my hair out of my face. "What time is it?"

Esmeralda sat at the bottom of the bed, washing herself. She looked at me as if to ask why I was bothering her. It was a question the Siamese cat asked a lot.

"You were so sweet when you first moved to the farm. Your power went to your head," I told her.

She went back to grooming herself.

The phone rang again. It took me a moment to find it in the twisted pile of sheets and blankets. By the looks of it, I'd had a restless nap.

"It's about time you picked up the phone. What were you doing?" Stacey barked into my ear.

I rubbed my eyes. "Napping."

"Napping. What are you napping for? Don't you have work to do, or is the farm ready for the world to see it?"

"Stacey, I had a long night and was up early this morning."

"Well, you're in store for a long night again."

"I am? Why?" I asked.

"Did you really forget about the MOBA meeting tonight? The meeting you invited me to?"

I groaned. I had forgotten. "The meeting that you invited yourself to?" I corrected for the record.

Huckleberry whimpered on the floor, and then climbed up the set of benches and pillows I made for him to get up on the bed. Esmeralda watched him as if she could not believe he needed such help. It wasn't easy being a pug.

"I'll even do you a favor. I don't want to roll up in Traverse City in Uncle Sully's old truck. I have a reputation to uphold in the arts community in this county."

I rolled my eyes, but I was grateful she couldn't see me. I would never be dumb enough to do that directly in front of her.

"I'll drive," she said. "The meeting is at seven. I'll pick you up at five-thirty. That should give us plenty of time to find a parking spot."

"What time is now?" I still felt groggy.

"Three. Be ready."

Three? I couldn't believe I slept that long. Grandma Bellamy always said if a person slept like that, it was because they needed it. I did feel refreshed, but I wasn't ready to go to this meeting. Since moving to Cherry Glen, I had spent a good amount of time alone with just the animals or my dad—when he wasn't being a grump—for company. I found that I liked the change.

The last few days between the brewery and the ice fishing derby had just been too people-y for me, and now, I had to attended an association meeting. It sounded horrible.

I flopped back down on the bed.

Chapter Twenty-Six

Stacey was never late. Instead, she was always early. Which to be honest was an annoying habit of hers, and she usually caught me unprepared. That evening was no different. I rushed through my chores on the farm and got ready for the meeting. And even though I made it to the farmhouse with twenty minutes to spare, she was already inside.

I found my cousin sitting in the kitchen chatting with my father. Dad had one of his old Michigan history books in front of him and was examining the page with a magnifying glass. The pair of them looked so comfortable with each other. Far more comfortable than I ever felt around my dad. I reminded myself that Stacey—who had lived on the other half of Bellamy Farm, which was now Tanner Birchwood's Organic Acres—had spent more time with him than I had in the past fifteen years, and he was her uncle, not her father. As his niece, she had some distance from his grumpiness that I never had.

Stacey looked like she was ready to go on a date. Her blond hair was curled and teased. Her nails were painted red, and she wore jeans, knee-high leather boots, and a form-fitting sweater.

I, on the other hand, looked like I was going to an association meeting. I had brushed my hair—this was noteworthy because since becoming a full-time farmer I was hit or miss with the brush and usually wore my hair in a messy bun—and wore a blazer with slacks left over from my other life. At least they were a nice blazer and slacks.

"There you are," Stacey said, making a point of checking her phone for the time.

I didn't bother to tell her I was early. There wasn't much point to having the argument, and I was going to be trapped in a car with her for next thirty minutes. It was best to make that experience as painless as possible.

"I was just telling Uncle Sully about the Michigan Organic Brewers Association meeting we're going to." She eyed me. "He said you hadn't mentioned it."

With everything else going on, I wasn't up for another lecture of him telling me why changing Bellamy Farm into an organic venture wasn't going to work. This was a case where I had to believe in my vision and not my father's opinion.

"It must have slipped my mind," I said. "Dad, can I leave Huckleberry with you?"

"Sure, sure," Dad said. "He likes to watch cable news with me."

Huckleberry looked up at me and whimpered. He did not enjoy cable news.

I squatted and scratched his ears. "Grandpa will give you lots of treats."

He licked my face. The treats would make up for the assault on his ears by the television.

"Where's Esmeralda?" Dad asked.

"She opted to stay back in the cabin." I shrugged. "I guess she needs alone time."

"She's a very peculiar cat."

I agreed.

Stacey stood up, grabbed her winter coat off the back of the chair, and put it on. "I expect both of you are coming to the showing of *The Wizard of Oz* on Tuesday? And Shiloh, I need you to help."

I gritted my teeth. Stacey never asked me to pitch in at the theater, she just told me I needed to help. The truth was I didn't mind helping. I loved that she had brought the historic gem back to the community, but it would be nice to be *asked* to help and not told.

She hugged my dad and went out the door.

"I'll stop by and pick up Huckleberry when I get home."

Dad nodded and went back to examining the book in front of him with a magnifying glass.

When Stacey and I were in her SUV, she started the engine. "Uncle Sully looks like he's exhausted. I can't believe you let him spend two full days outside at the ice fishing derby like that."

I gritted my teeth and looked out the window. "It's what he wanted to do. He wasn't alone. Hazel and Quinn were with him the whole time, and Quinn is an EMT."

"That may be true, but he's going to be stiff for days from fishing. I was just telling him that he should start up physical therapy again for his back."

"And how did that go?" I asked, even though I already knew the answer. My father hated physical therapy.

"He told me he'd think about it."

He'd think about it because Stacey had mentioned it. But I knew he had no intention of going. If I had asked, it would've been a straight *no*.

I pushed my irritation down. For a long time, Stacey had looked after my dad while I was in LA. As irritating as she could be at times, I couldn't lose sight of everything she'd done for us.

"Thank you for talking to him about it. He listens to you," I said.

"As he should," she said.

I kept looking out the window so she couldn't see my face.

Relief swept through me when we pulled into Traverse City. Growing up, I had always thought it was the perfect size city. It was big enough to have all the amenities a person would need, but modest enough to still feel like a friendly small town. That feeling was reiterated when I moved to LA, an enormous city that was completely overwhelming in all it had to offer.

Maybe I liked limited choices. During the winter in Traverse City, those choices were narrowed down to outside winter activities, and cherries. But who really knew what they would do in that situation when fear takes over? A person couldn't know prior to the event.

Right on time, I received a text message from Chesney. Talking points for MOBA meeting. I smiled. She never disappointed. Her list read: cherry production, crop in most need, timetable of supplies, and new flavors. It was brief and to the point.

Even on a Monday evening, the city was busy. It was the middle of ski season, and an ice sculpture contest was taking place at the lakefront along Lake Michigan all week. The whirl of chainsaws broke through the night and muffled the laughter of the onlookers.

The bay water hit the ice along the lakeshore and sent spray as far as the parking lot on the other side of the street. The ice sculptors and spectators didn't seem to mind. These were hardy Michiganders. Freezing water would never chase them away.

I hopped out of the SUV, grateful to make it here without getting into an argument with my cousin. She carefully stepped out in her platform boots. Her footwear had good tread. If you grew up in northern Michigan, you knew tread came before fashion. But Stacey's platform soles were so high, they were still a bit precarious to walk around on. As she navigated the icy and salt-sprinkled parking lot, she reminded me of a newborn calf finding her legs.

The sidewalk was much clearer, and I gave a small sigh of relief when we walked up the hill on from the waterfront to Front Street.

Along the block, there were still remnants of Christmas as twinkle lights glistened in all the trees and pine garland wrapped its way up the lampposts. There was a fresh dusting of snow on everything, but the street and sidewalk were both treated vigorously with deicer.

In the winter around here, deicing was a full-time job.

"The meeting is above the Cherryland Boutique," I said as we walked down Front Street.

"I know where it is," my cousin said. "It's right there on the corner. I've been to the speakeasy on a few dates before."

This was news to me. Stacey never talked about her dating life. She had been so focused on the theater lately; I hadn't even considered she might be seeing someone.

I was curious. I was her little cousin after all, but I pushed any questions about her social life away. They would not be well received.

The Cherryland Boutique was closed for the night. Through the storefront window, I could see anything and everything I could imagine that was made with cherries: cherry pop, cherry candy, cherry syrup, cherry bread, cherry ice cream. The list went on and on.

A lit metal arrow pointed to the right around the corner of the building.

I was glad I was with Stacey because she followed the arrow as if it made perfect sense. There was a set of metal steps on the side of the building that led to a metal door on the second floor. There was no signage to indicate there was anything of interest at the top.

Stacey started up the stairs. "Be careful," she warned. "The stairs are slippery. This is a death trap waiting to happen."

I didn't find her caution encouraging.

We reached the top, and Stacey knocked three times on the door. *Knock, knock, knock.* The knocks were perfectly spaced out and purposeful.

An eye slot opened, and I could just see the nose and eyes of a man. "What do you want?"

"A Shirley Temple, sir," Stacey replied, as if it was the most logical answer in the world.

The eye slot closed and the door opened.

We stepped inside the room and found ourselves in a dance hall of sorts. There was a buffet table with appetizers on one side and a table with local beers on the other. There was no bar and no drinks other than beer, but I supposed that made sense considering the business everyone in the room was in.

I removed my coat and hung it over my arm. "I'm not sure I would have gotten in if you hadn't been here. I didn't know you had to have a password."

Stacey glanced at me. "I've been to this building before. The password is always the same. They didn't tell you? Maybe they didn't really want you to come."

I sighed.

A man called my name. I turned and saw Tanner Birchwood walking toward me. He had a big smile on his face and a beer in his hand.

Next to me, my cousin fluffed her hair and smiled prettily at my neighbor. It could be she had a crush on him. This was good news for me. Stacey could distract him while I made my escape to do what I really came here to do, which was learn how my farm could be a supplier to this association. And oh, find a killer too. No big deal on either assignment.

"Hi, Tanner."

His smile wavered. "How did you hear about this meeting?"

"I was invited by some of the members."

"Oh," he said. "That is so funny. I was too. I know they're looking for suppliers. I thought I was the only one who was asked."

I shrugged. "Just a little healthy competition."

"Yes, right." He forced a smile.

Across the room, I spotted Sidney, who I'd met at the ice fishing derby. "Tanner, why don't you tell Stacey your plans for Organic Acres?" I said. "After all, it was her home for so many years. I'm sure she's interested."

Stacey brushed her hair over her shoulder. "I am. I would love to hear about your plans for my family farm."

Tanner smiled from ear to ear. He held his arm out to Stacey. "Let's get you a drink and we can talk."

As they moved across the room, I noted they were a very handsome couple. In my mind, they were a perfect fit. Also, I had the added bonus that if they were together, they would leave me alone. Although that last part might be wishful thinking.

I hung up my coat in the small closet in the corner of the room, and then went to find Sidney. He was no longer near the podium where I'd spotted him earlier. Frowning, I scanned the room and saw Annette standing in the corner. To my surprise she was talking to Spenser Fields, Wallace's son. I hadn't expected him to be there.

"Are you looking for someone?" a deep voice asked.

I turned and found myself looking up at Sheriff Milan Penbrook.

Chapter Twenty-Seven

※

My guess is you are," I said.

"It's part of the job," the sheriff said.

I smiled. "I just arrived and was taking everything in before the meeting."

I noted that the sheriff was out of uniform. The corners of his eyes wrinkled as if he doubted my answer. "Why are you here? Do you brew beer?"

"No, but I have an organic farm. At the ice fishing derby, the members invited me to the meeting to see how we could partner with each other. It would be quite a feather in any brewer's cap if they were able to say their beer was organic and made with local ingredients."

"I can see that." He paused. "So you're not here because of the murder?"

"Just because Wallace was the incoming president of this group and not very well-liked among the membership doesn't mean I can't be coming here out of my own interests that have nothing to do with him."

"Right." He drew out the word.

"Attention. Attention everyone." Annette tapped a

gavel on the podium. "Please take your seats so we can get started."

I slipped into a row of chairs near the back of the room, and to my surprise, the sheriff sat right next to me.

I tensed and said nothing. He just pointed straight ahead as if to tell me to concentrate on the meeting.

Annette tapped the podium again. "Good evening. Thank you all for coming here, especially after such a busy weekend at the derby on Lake Skegemog. I personally think our presence at the event was well received. Not only was it a great opportunity for the brewers to share their beers with a wide audience, but it got the news out about our group. The hope is we will attract more members and be able to cast a wider net throughout the state." She cleared her throat. "As encouraging as the weekend was, we were saddened by the news of our president-elect Wallace Fields's passing. He was a strong voice in the organization, and we send our condolences to his family. His son, Spenser, is here this evening to say a few words."

Spenser fidgeted with his collar as he stepped up to the podium. "Thank you, Annette, and I want to thank everyone here for your ongoing support of my father."

"No one here supported Wallace," someone muttered behind me.

I went to turn my head to see who it was, but Sheriff Penbrook grabbed my hand and squeezed it, stopping me. I felt like I'd been zapped with an electric current.

"Don't turn around," he whispered. "He's more likely to say more." He let go of my hand.

I dropped my hand into my lap.

"My father loved working with this group, and he understood the importance of organic beers. Consumers deserve
to know where their beer is coming from. He felt strongly
about this, and he felt strongly about supporting microbrews
across the state. Please know that Fields Brewing Company
will still advocate and be active in the MOBA community
even though my father is gone. My stepmother, Chanel, and
I will work together to make sure that happens."

"He wanted to steal our recipes and shut us down," the
same irritable voice as before said.

Oh, how I wanted to turn around and see who was speaking. His voice dripped with animosity. The killer could be
right behind us, but would he be so stupid to publicly criti-
cize Wallace after killing him? It wasn't the smartest way to
get away with murder.

"I'm not only here to share my gratitude for your support
of my father, but I would like to invite you to his celebration
of life party at Fields Brewing Company tomorrow evening.
The funeral will be a small, private affair, but my stepmother
and I felt my father deserved one last party. He loved a celebration. We do hope that you will all attend and share your
memories of my father, Wallace Fields." Spenser thanked the
audience and then stepped back from the podium.

Conversion sprouted up around us. "The only reason I
would go to that charade is because Chanel Fields knows
how to throw a party. The food will be great. She never dis-
appoints on the spread."

"I'd go to see what a disaster it's going to be. You know

Spenser and Chanel will be arguing over the brewery. I overheard Wallace say once that his wife and son didn't get along" a woman replied. "It's ridiculous to even think they would share it. There are going to be lawyers involved, mark my words."

The first voice snorted. "It's more likely that Chanel will have her boyfriend run the business with her."

I tensed up at the mention of a boyfriend, and Sheriff Penbrook put a hand on my arm.

I was wound as tight as an electric fence for the rest of the meeting. I was desperate to see who was behind us. It was hard to concentrate on what the members were saying about upcoming events and budgets. To be honest, it was all rather boring.

After the formal part of the meeting, there was an opportunity for networking and tasting of the beers made by different members of the group. The audience stood up and began to mill around the large space. The volume went up as well.

Sheriff Penbrook stood, and so did I. At that point, I looked behind us, but whoever had been sitting there complaining about Wallace had moved.

I turned back to the sheriff. "Didn't you want to know who was speaking?"

He smiled. "I already knew who was speaking. I was just letting him dig a deeper hole for himself."

I looked around the room. "Who was it?"

"I have a feeling if I tell you that you'll march right up to the person and ask him if he killed Wallace."

"Don't be ridiculous. I would stop and get a drink first."

He laughed, and I found myself smiling too. However, my smile was short-lived as I thought about what the man had said. I lowered my voice. "Did you know that Chanel had a boyfriend on the side?"

He nodded. "She's not made it much of a secret since her husband died."

"And?" I looked up at him.

"He's a bartender at the brewing company. Jason is his name."

I gasped. "Jason Brennan? The hipster bartender who beat Kent for the master brewer job?"

"One and the same."

"Did Wallace know?" I asked.

"Chanel said he did."

"Then why were they still together? Why didn't he divorce her?"

"That's a very good question. One I have asked but never got an answer to."

"Why would Wallace give that position to someone having an affair with his wife? It makes zero sense. There had to be more going on there. Jason is looking like a serious suspect to me. And Chanel too."

The sheriff walked across the floor and spoke to Spenser. It wouldn't surprise me if Wallace's son was on his list. I took this as my chance to thank Sidney for inviting me to the meeting.

A man older man raised his glass at Sidney. "It's not right that we are treated like second-class citizens in this group because we don't have a storefront or restaurant. Home brewers are important too. That's how beer started. It's the genesis of all of this."

My eyes went wide as I recognized the man's voice as the heckler. "It seemed that Sheriff Penbrook didn't have to tell me who the heckler was after all."

"I agree with you, Reg, but what do you suggest that we do?" Sidney asked calmly. "Make our own group?"

"Yes, yes, that's what I think we should do." He raised his hand, and liquid sloshed out of the glass onto the floor.

Sidney took a small step back from him. "That will never work because we just don't have the clout that the large brewers do. We are being invited to more places like the ice fishing derby because of them and because we are with them."

Reg folded his arms. "Well, I hope things change now that Wallace is out of the picture. He was the worst of them, belittling us and what we do."

"Wallace just didn't understand making beer. He was a businessman first and foremost. He didn't understand the science. He didn't have to be good at brewing. Where he beat people like you and I was with his business savvy." Sidney glanced over his shoulder. "Oh, Shiloh, I didn't know you were there."

I smiled. "I'm sorry to interrupt. I just wanted to thank you for inviting me to the meeting tonight. It's been great to learn about MOBA and what you all do." I nodded at Reg to include him in my comment.

Sidney made introductions. "This is Reg Pipe. He's a home brewer like me."

I held my hand out to Reg, and he shook it half-heartedly. "Shiloh Bellamy. I'm an organic farmer from Cherry Glen and am looking into growing organic hops and other ingredients for your recipes."

"Cherry Glen?" Reg wrinkled his nose. "You're friends with Wallace Fields then, aren't you?"

"No, not at all," I said quickly. "I knew who he was, of course. Cherry Glen is a small town, but we never spoke."

He seemed somewhat pacified by this. "I'm glad to hear it. Wallace Fields was the worst. I bet half the people in this room are glad he is dead. The brewer competition in this area and in the whole state really is fierce. They don't want some upstart like Wallace coming in and making a splash."

"An upstart?" I asked.

"Oh yeah," Reg said. "He's only been brewing for four years, and he's already the most popular microbrewer in Grand Traverse County. He seemed to come out of nowhere. People still don't know his recipe for success."

"It's because he hired the best people in the business," Sidney says. "He didn't care if that meant he had to recruit or steal talented employees from his competitors. He would do that. Wallace always just said *all's fair in love and beer.*"

"He was a cheat." Spittle flew from Reg's mouth. "I'm trying to do it the right way, from home, like beer was meant to be made. I can barely pay for my supplies. He was making money hand over fist, and his family will continue to do so while they know nothing about what it takes to make beer from scratch"

I wondered if Reg was also angry at the large corporations

that made beer and made money doing it. It was a billion-dollar industry.

"He should never have been chosen as the cherry festival official brewer," Reg went on. "That's just a slap in the face for those of us who have been working tirelessly for years, if not decades, for that honor! He just waltzed in and charmed the committee and flashed his wallet at them."

"He did have really good beer," Sidney said.

"He didn't make it," Reg snapped. "It was his master brewer that he killed who put him on the map."

I stared at him. "What did you say?"

Reg looked at me. "He killed his master brewer. Drove him into an early grave from what I heard."

"Bastian had a heart condition, Reg. Everyone knew that." Sidney sipped his beer.

"And Wallace knew it too. He was hard on Bastian anyway and drove the man to a heart attack. Just ask his wife. She'll tell you the same."

"Annette didn't blame Wallace."

"Bastian was Annette Woodhall's husband?" I glanced around the room. I spotted Annette speaking with Sheriff Penbrook. She was a person that he needed to speak to? Was it because she was a suspect?

"Yes, but Bastian's heart attack was two years ago now," Sidney said. "I don't know what it has to do with anything that happened recently."

"I'm just illustrating what an awful person Wallace was. Everyone is whispering about how terrible he was. I'm the only one who will come right out and say it. His wife and son won't have anything kind to say about him either."

Sidney shook his head.

"Bastian's death was why Wallace was looking for a master brewer?" I asked.

Sidney nodded. "That's right. He had a few people here and there to take the job over the last year and half, but no one could work for Wallace for long. He's too demanding. From what I heard that is why he made the competition for his staff. He thought if he hired someone for the job who could already handle his high standards that the person would stick around longer. It's a great disruption to replace the master brewer every few months. He was losing consistency in his product by doing that."

"He's a tyrant," Reg said.

"Did his wife find him to be a tyrant?" I asked. I still thought Chanel, who was having an open affair, was a solid suspect. Maybe her husband refused to divorce her, and she needed him out of the way so she could be with hipster bartender Jason.

Reg snorted. "She didn't care as long as he was paying the bills and she had her boyfriend on the side."

"Jason Brennan? I heard rumors..." I didn't say that I had just heard the rumors at the meeting from Reg.

"That's right," Reg said.

"Why didn't they just get a divorce?" I asked.

"They had a prenup," Reg said. "Chanel was Wallace's second wife. His first wife took him to the cleaners when she divorced her. He wasn't going to let that happen again with Chanel. If they divorced for any reason, she got nothing."

I raised my brow. "Nothing?"

"Nothing. The prenup was explicit. That's not to say that some attorney wouldn't be able to challenge it."

"Couldn't he have divorced her for her infidelity?"

"That's the million-dollar question," Sidney said. "No one knew why he didn't divorce her. He had an ironclad prenup or as close as you can get to one." He shrugged. "I think he was too busy building his empire to go to the trouble. Maybe he was going to divorce her after the cherry festival. I can't believe he liked the fact that his wife was stepping out on him. It must have been embarrassing. Everyone in MOBA knew about it. Jason wasn't quiet about it either."

"Jason is a member of MOBA?" I asked.

Sidney nodded. "He's not here tonight though. Maybe he knew Wallace's son was coming, and it would have been a bad idea to show up."

I left the men after that, and my head was spinning. I wanted to talk to Annette, but a brewer from Ballden stopped me. He was interested in my cherry orchard for his recipes. Even though I was torn between helping my business and solving the murder, I spoke to him. By the time we finished the conversation—and I had a feeling Bellamy Farm would be a good supplier for him—Annette was nowhere to be seen.

I was wandering around the room when Stacey walked up and handed me my coat. "Let's go. I'm tired. I've done enough schmoozing for one night. I want to go back to my empty theater and decompress."

"Where's Tanner?" I asked.

"He already left. He has an early morning." She blushed ever so slightly.

I was shocked to see it. I didn't think I had ever seen my cousin blush unless it was on stage for the role she was playing.

"I have work to do too. The *Wizard of Oz* event is at the theater tomorrow night. Everything has to be perfect." She narrowed her eyes at me. "I expect you to be there at eight sharp. It starts at eight thirty."

"Wallace's celebration of life party is at six."

"That's fine. All the mourners can come down and watch Dorothy and Toto after."

I grimaced. As I put on my coat, I found myself looking around the room for Sheriff Penbrook so that I could say goodbye. When I couldn't find him I felt just the slightest pang of disappointment.

Chapter Twenty-Eight

T he next day, Huckleberry bounded around me in the front yard in his new orange booties. I would have to ask Chesney to make him a second pair because he never wanted to take them off and I would need to wash them eventually.

When we reached the barn, I let Diva and the chickens out of their coop as the weather was milder, and they now looked on with disdain.

I decided to put off any more investigating until Wallace's celebration of life party that evening and spend the day concentrating on the farm while the weather cooperated.

Chesney wasn't going to be at the farm until ten o'clock because she had to take her sister to the university. Money was tight for the sisters, so they shared one car. I thought I could make a plan of attack to deal with the broken-down front porch while I waited for her.

My phone rang in my pocket. I unzipped my snowsuit and pulled it out of an inside pocket. It was Kristy. A wave of relief washed over me. I had sent a dozen texts and made just as many phone calls to her over the last day to see if she was okay. She had been very shaken up over Kent being attacked at the brewery.

I answered the call.

"I'm glad you picked up," she said.

"Did you think I wouldn't?" I brushed snow from the bench under the willow and sat down.

"I wouldn't have been surprised, considering the numerous times you called me and I didn't pick up. I'm sorry that I've been blowing you off."

"It's okay," I said. "I know you have a lot going on."

She barked a laugh. "That's a diplomatic way to put it. I was so upset over what happened to Kent. It's just been so frightening. I couldn't think straight."

"I can understand that. You needed time."

"Yes, that's what I needed," she said.

"How's Kent?" I asked.

"He's all right. He has a slight concussion, so there are some limitations on what he can do right now. But he's home, and that's what matters." Kristy took a deep breath. "I do have some encouraging news. Sheriff Penbrook told us that it's not an open-and-shut case, and he's looking at multiple suspects. It's not the same as clearing Kent's name completely, but it's something for me to hold on to. I need that."

I nodded. "I understand."

"Kent and I had a long talk too. He's going to quit working at Fields. He never enjoyed it and did it only for the money. We can make things work on both of our salaries for now. In the spring, he'll look for something for the summer months when he's not teaching."

"I'm glad to hear that. Kent is hard worker. He'll have no trouble finding seasonal work. I'd hire him to work for me if I could afford it."

"Thanks, Shi," Kristy said. "I don't know what I'd do right now if I didn't have a friend like you. You came back to Cherry Glen at the perfect time for everyone."

"Thank you," I said.

"You can stop looking into the case now. I truly believe that Kent will be cleared."

I frowned. "Stop?"

"Yes, there's no other reason for you to be involved."

"I…"

"Shi, promise me you'll drop it. Kent was seriously hurt. I don't want something like that happening to you. I'll feel awful if it does because I was the one who asked you to get involved."

I knew what she'd said made sense, and she was saying it because she cared about me. However, I couldn't give up now. Last night at the MOBA meeting, I felt I like I made real progress in the case. I learned so much about Wallace and his family relationships. I had to see this through. Wallace was killed in one of the most violent ways I could imagine. Despite the kind of person Wallace had been, he didn't deserve that. I had to see this to the bitter end.

I changed the subject. "Is Kent going to the celebration of life service?"

She sighed. "He is. It's his last shift at the bar. Chanel needed him, so he agreed to do it when he resigned."

"I'll be there too," I said.

"I kind of figured that you would."

We ended the call, and I started shoveling the snow off the front porch.

After Chesney arrived and all the snow was cleared away, she and I took a better look at the damage. She pushed her glasses up her nose. "It's worse than I thought. Most of the boards are rotten."

"We'll throw out anything rotted through, but if any of the wood is salvageable, let's save it. We can use it for something else later or even sell it."

She tossed a rotten board into the front lawn and laughed. "You sound like a true farmer now. Farmers save everything."

"I know. I still remember what the barn looked like a few months ago."

"You can get good money for old boards like this at a flea market or salvage yard. People used them for paneling in their homes or to make furniture. There won't be a huge amount of money in it, but every little bit helps."

She was very right about that. Every little bit helped.

We worked on dismantling the front porch into the afternoon. Chesney and I piled the boards worth saving in one spot and the rotten boards in another. We made a third pile of boards that we might be able to salvage. The time passed quickly, and I felt a release from working with my hands. I didn't feel the cold from the wind or the muscle pain from moving heavy board after heavy board. I just felt like I was accomplishing something and moving forward. I never got the same feeling when I was working in film and TV or investigating a murder.

We took a break at one for lunch, and I went inside to check on my dad. He was parked in front of the TV with a ham sandwich in his hand. Seeing he was seemingly content, I tiptoed back outside.

When we got back to work, I wedged the end of a crowbar under one of the boards. As I pushed down on the bar, the rusted nails in the wood screeched and squealed. They had been in the same place for decades. They weren't giving up without a fight.

"What are you guys doing?" Hazel ran down the driveway with Esmeralda on her tail.

When Esmeralda appeared, Diva flapped her wings. The Siamese cat hissed at her. Those two really didn't care for each other.

I checked my watch; I couldn't believe it was almost four o'clock. Chesney and I had been working for hours, but it only felt like minutes. On Tuesday, Hazel came to my house after school until her dad could pick her up. I hadn't even heard the bus. Even though the house was far away from the road, I could usually still faintly hear Hazel's school bus rumbling down the road in the stillness of winter.

Chesney threw a board on the keep pile. "We're tearing down the old front porch so we can rebuild it."

"Awesome! Can I help?" She threw her backpack in the snow.

"You can help if you're careful, but first, take your school bag inside and change into your farm clothes. This is a dirty job. I don't want your grandma getting after me because you ruined another nice outfit here."

Without a word, she scooped up her bag and ran around the house to the back door. A minute later, she was back outside in winter coveralls and an old winter coat. My dad's Michigan State stocking cap was on her head. She clapped her hands. "Let's do this!"

"You know, Shi," Chesney said. "You think I have a lot of enthusiasm, but Hazel has me beat."

"For sure," I agreed. I told Hazel to walk around the outside porch and look for any smaller pieces of wood or nails that might have fallen in the snow.

Ignoring my request, Hazel climbed onto the porch.

I tossed another board behind me. "Hazel, get off there. We don't know how sturdy it is."

"It's sturdy!" She jumped up and down.

"Hazel, please get down from there."

"Oh, okay." She took a step forward and, with a cry, crashed through the wood.

Chapter Twenty-Nine

❦

C hesney and I ran onto the porch. Hazel had fallen through up to her waist.

I looked her over, but it didn't look like she was hurt, although we wouldn't know for sure until we got her inside and looked for lacerations and bruises.

"Are you okay?" My heart raced.

Hazel let out a breath. "I'm okay. More surprised than anything. The ground under my feet is frozen solid." She looked down. "I can move my feet around."

"Don't kick around in there. We don't know what's under the porch and don't want you to get hurt."

Esmeralda yowled at me as if to ask how I could let this happen to her girl.

"I already feel bad enough," I told the cat.

Huckleberry ran over and barked.

"Shi, I'm not hurt," Hazel said. She wiggled around some more. "There's something down here."

"What do you mean there's something down there?" Chesney asked. "Like an animal?"

"No, like something hard."

"Whatever it is, it's been under there for decades. Just leave it."

Hazel wrinkled her nose like she didn't like that idea. She wriggled her right arm down next to her in the hole. "I can feel it. It's a box!"

Suddenly, all the cold that had been held at bay all these hours swept over me. The images of my grandmother sitting on this very porch for hours on end, reading, knitting, and talking to neighbors. It was the heart of the farm!

Hazel knew about my grandmother's letter, but Chesney did not.

Calmly as I could, I said, "Okay, you climb out of there, and I'll reach in and grab the box."

"Deal," Hazel said.

Slowly, we pulled her from the hole, taking care not to scrape her on the broken wood. Thank goodness she had so many layers on.

When she was out and safely standing on the lawn, she said, "It's to the right."

I removed the small flashlight I kept in my pocket whenever I was working on the farm and shone it in the hole. All I saw was frozen dirt.

"To the right," Hazel said again.

I shone my light in that direction and it reflected on something metal. Lying on my stomach, I stuck my head, arms, and chest into the hole. I still couldn't reach it. I wriggled in a bit more to my waist, reached, and grabbed the metal box.

"I got it. Pull me out!"

I felt Chesney tugging on my legs. Splinters bit into my

stomach, but finally, I was out. I rolled over and lay on my back in the middle of the rotting porch with the metal box on my chest.

"What in the world is that?" Chesney asked.

I sat up.

Hazel's eyes were huge. "It's the heart of the farm!"

"The what?" Chesney asked.

I scrambled to my feet. "It's an old cookie tin. Let's go open it in the barn to see if anything is inside."

Hazel, Esmeralda, and Huckleberry ran ahead of us to the barn.

"Are you going to tell me what's going on here?" Chesney asked as we walked to the barn.

"Let just see what's in here," I said. I set the box on the worktable in one corner of the barn. The three of us gathered around and looked at the cookie tin. It appeared to be old, but it wasn't that old. It had a barcode on it. According to the can, it once held gingersnaps made by a local cookie company, Lakemore Cookies, which had long gone out of business. I blinked back tears, which came unexpectedly to my eyes. My grandmother had loved gingersnaps, and Lakemore made her favorites. I remember her having them with her tea every day when I was a little girl. Lakemore had been in business from the 1960s to the 1990s. That and the barcode were enough clues that can had not been under the porch since the house was built more than one hundred years ago.

"It's been dipped in wax," Chesney said and grabbed a utility knife from the toolbox at the end of the table. "We can use this to break the seal."

She handed me the knife and I ran it along the seam on all four sides. I used the side of the blade to scrape wax from the hinges. Because of the wax, the tin was surprisingly free from rust.

Chesney gave me a flathead screwdriver. "This should work. I feel like I'm assisting in surgery."

Finally, after several minutes, the lid flipped open. Inside there was a manila envelope, and that was all.

I opened the envelope and stared at the papers inside. They were certificates, and each one had my grandmother's name on it.

Chesney gasped. "Those are stocks. Paper stock certificates." She looked closer. "They are all for Fortune 500 companies. Look at those names and the figures too. These are serious stocks bought before the companies really took off."

My heart was pounding and my hands shook. "We don't know if they are still worth anything."

Chesney tapped on her phone. "It says here that you need to find a broker and have them verified, but if they are legit, they can be worth a lot of money. I mean *a lot* of money."

"It's the heart of the farm, just like Grandma Bellamy promised!" Hazel fist pumped the air.

"Will someone tell me about that?" Chesney asked.

Hazel quickly told her about the letter my grandmother had left for me in the cabin.

I closed my eyes for a moment. "I'm not going to get my hopes up. They could be out of date or have been cashed in and she just still had the documents for some reason."

Chesney opened the envelope again. "There's a letter in here." She pulled it out. "Shi, it's addressed to you."

I took the letter from her hands and walked a few feet away. My grandmother's distinctive slanted handwriting blurred in front of my eyes. I wiped away tears and started to read.

Dearest Shiloh,

If you found this letter, you have found the stocks I have left behind in your care for the benefit of the farm. Your grandfather and your daddy are two peas in a pod. They are great at working the land but terrible at managing the wallet. My husband, God rest his soul, knew that about himself. Over time, I squirreled money away. I learned what I could about stocks from books at the library and from tape sets. I would read the financial pages every day. I always tucked them inside of the comics, so your grandfather didn't know.

For a man of that time, it was hard for him to admit that his wife was better with money than he was. It would have been very hurtful for my Horace if it got out. In fact, he's probably rolling over in his grave at this very moment.

You have always had a good head on your shoulders and have made good decisions. I don't know if you married Logan. I know you were set on doing it. He's a good boy. If you married him, I trust he will be a great help to you as to what to do with these. He is a wise boy.

Tears came to my eyes again. Marrying or not marrying Logan had never been a choice for me. That choice had been taken away.

But I do know that my girl is successful in whatever she does. You will take these stocks and do the right thing with them. I do love the farm and all that it could be, but I was never one to back someone into a corner. Where you are in time when you find these will let you know what you should do. I trust you and love you. You don't need my guidance.

She was wrong. I needed her guidance, so much of her guidance.

There were so many things I wished I could ask her about the farm or ask her about life. I thought at thirty-eight I had it all figured out. Maybe I'd had my life in Hollywood figured out, but not Cherry Glen. It was so much more complicated back home than it ever had been in California. Who knew I would wish for the simpler days when I lived in a big city and worked for a demanding studio that only cared about the bottom line? At least then I knew what to expect. I knew how to play the game. Here in this place that I loved but didn't fully understand, I didn't even know the rules.

I folded the letter again and tucked it back inside the envelope. I could feel Chesney and Hazel watching me.

"What does it say?" Hazel blurted out.

Chesney wrapped her arm around Hazel's shoulder.

I swallowed. "That I should save the farm."

Chapter Thirty

Quinn came to pick up Hazel not long after we closed the box and Chesney went home for the day.

When he drove up, I was outside trying to convince Diva and her hens to go back into the henhouse. Hazel was inside the farmhouse with my dad. Huckleberry ran around the yard barking and was no help at all, but he knew better than to take on Diva. She played dirty.

I ran after Diva, and she galloped in front of me like it was no challenge out all to hop out of my reach. "Diva, come on! It's time to go to bed. Do you want a coyote to get you?"

She bawked at me.

I didn't bother to chase the other chickens because I knew if I could get Diva to run into the henhouse, the others would follow.

Quinn got out of his truck and leaned against it. "Having some trouble there?"

Thinking I had Diva trapped, I took the chance to glance at him, and of course in that split second, she ran away. "A little," I groaned. "Maybe more than a little. I wished we had better-behaved hens."

"I'm pretty sure that all hens are ornery now and again." He walked over to me. "I'll help."

Between the two of us, we cornered Diva again by the barn, and this time, she had nowhere to go.

By her squawking, she wasn't happy about it, nor did I expect her to be. I lunged forward and caught her by her legs. It was the best way to grab a chicken. I then flipped her upright, cradled her in my arms, and put her in the henhouse.

All the other chickens ran after me and went through the open door with little fuss.

After the last chicken was inside, I latched the door closed. "Phew! Thanks for your help. She was in a mood tonight. Had I known, I would have asked Chesney to help me get her into the coop before she left. She has a way with chickens."

Quinn laughed and glanced back at the house.

"Hazel is with Dad. Do you want me to go get her?"

I started for the farmhouse, and Quinn grabbed my hand, stopping me. "No, not yet. I was wondering if you and I could talk."

I felt my heart rate pick up. "Sure." I hoped that my answer came out a lot calmer than it sounded to my ears.

He looked over at the farmhouse again. "I feel like since we had that conversation last year things have been off between us."

I didn't have to ask him what "that conversation" was. I knew. It was the conversation about him not wanting to have a relationship with me.

"I don't want that. I want us to be friends. You're important to Hazel, and you're important to me."

"As a friend," I said.

"I wish it could be more than that, but I'm just not ready. It's not you. It's me."

I swallowed and couldn't help but think his "it's not you, it's me" speech was so very LA.

"I'm not asking you for anything more than friendship, Quinn," I said.

"I know. I'm just asking you to be patient."

I felt a twisting in my chest. "You're asking me to wait until you're ready."

"Maybe. Can you?" he asked.

Before I could answer, the back door of the farmhouse flew open and Hazel ran out with her winter coat and backpack trailing behind her. "Dad, I didn't know you were here!" She ran over and gave him a giant hug.

I blinked. "You guys better get home. Hazel worked so hard on the farm today, she didn't start her homework."

"Ugh!" Hazel cried. "I just have math and a little bit of science."

Quinn looked at me one last time, and I forced a smile.

He walked to his truck with his daughter, and I went to my cabin to get ready for Wallace Fields's celebration of life party.

After hiding the cookie tin with the letter and stocks in my sock drawer, I tried to put it out of my head. I wasn't saying that it was easy to do, but I had to set it aside to get through this evening.

Like I usually did when I went to an event where bringing your pug might be frowned upon, I left Huckleberry with

Dad. This time Esmeralda joined the pair, and three of them were settled in to watch a game show rerun with grilled cheese sandwiches and tomato soup when I left. The game show was a big step up from cable news. There was a lot less shouting both from the people on the television and from my father.

I parked in the lot behind the brewery and noted that both Chief Randy and Sheriff Penbrook's vehicles were there. I sensed a jurisdiction turf war stirring, and I certainly didn't want to find myself in the middle of it.

The place was already busy when I arrived. The celebration of life party was just that: a party. Near the entrance there was a large portrait of Wallace Fields with his birth year and death year under the image, but that was it. When I entered the restaurant side of the building, all references to the deceased owner were gone.

I spotted Kent behind the bar. He looked more relaxed than he had in a long time. Even from here, I could see the sizable goose egg on the back of his head. Thank heavens it hadn't been worse than that.

Chanel stood on the stage where her husband had stood less than a week before. "I just want to thank each and every one of you for coming here tonight to celebrate the life of my beloved husband, Wallace Fields. Wallace would be as touched by this turnout as I am. Wallace's death has left a giant hole in our lives."

Someone behind me snorted. Sheriff Penbrook wasn't there to stop me, so I looked over my shoulder and spotted Lila Rae, Chanel's daughter, leaning against a support beam in the middle of the restaurant.

"I know all of you will greatly miss him, as I do, and—"

"Liar!" someone cried, and a young woman jumped on the stage. She had long brown hair and wore a black bodysuit and heels. She pointed at Chanel. "Liar. You didn't care about Wallace. You were having an affair behind his back."

The crowd gasped.

Spenser stepped on the stage. "Larissa, sweetheart, please."

So this was Spenser's wife.

"And now that he's dead you get everything. You have cut my husband, his son, out. How dare you?" She shook with fury. "You're the worst kind of woman. You marry someone for his money and then make a fool of him by sleeping with his assistant. You should be ashamed of yourself."

Spenser was on the stage now and looked like he was teetering between passing out and crying. He was clearly at a loss as to what to do. He reached for his wife, touching her arm. She hastily pushed him away.

Chanel looked down her nose, which was no small feat since Larissa had a good six inches on her. "I can't control what Wallace's will says. If he chose to leave everything to me, that was his right to do. Clearly, he had his reasons for doing that, but he's not here to tell you what they are." She stood a little straighter. "Could it be that he was disappointed in his son's bride?"

The crowd gasped.

Larissa launched herself at Chanel, and Chanel screamed. Spenser ran forward and tried to pull his wife off his stepmother, but Larissa threw him off like he weighed little more than a mouse. Chief Randy and two other men ran onto the stage and were able to break the two women apart.

Chanel's hair was tangled, and her chest heaved up and down. "Chief Randy, I want you to arrest this woman and press charges for assault."

Chief Randy led Larissa—who was now crying hysterically—away and handed her off to one of his officers. Spenser followed the pair out the door.

Behind me someone was laughing, and I saw that it was Lila Rae again. It seemed she enjoyed witnessing this mess.

I turned to her. "What's so funny?"

"It's just shows how messed up my family is. This is a fitting end to Wallace's life. I couldn't think of a better one." She fiddled with a vape pen in her hands and was dressed in black from head to toe. The only color she wore was her bright red lipstick. However, I thought it had more to do with her personal style than the fact she was in mourning over her stepfather's passing.

"That seems a bit harsh," I said.

She shrugged and put the vape pen to her mouth. She took a long drag. It smelled sickly sweet. Lila Rae blew smoke out the side of her mouth. "Mom will be nursing whatever injury, or supposed injury, that Larissa gave her for a good long time. She takes being a martyr very seriously. Now Mom will just dig her heels in more to make sure they don't get any of the money from the brewery. I'm pretty sure Spenser and Larissa won't be invited to Thanksgiving, if you know what I mean."

Laurel Burger walked into the restaurant carrying her

medical kit. It seemed that someone called for an EMT. I was relieved Quinn was off duty tonight. Laurel walked over to where Chanel was and started to ask her questions.

"Do you really think she'll press charges against Larissa?" I asked.

"For sure. She won't stand for being attacked like that, and it gives her more ammo against Spenser and Larissa if they do contest the will. As entertaining as it was, it was a dumb move on Larissa's part."

I had to agree with her there.

"I had heard before that your mother was having an affair." I didn't say where I had heard it. "Is there truth to that?"

Lila Rae shrugged. "Sure, it's true. It was never a secret. Mom and Jason have been an item for years. Everyone working at the brewery knew it. They made a laughingstock of Wallace, and there was nothing that he could do about it."

"Couldn't he just divorce her?" I asked.

"Well, he could if Wallace was willing for her to ruin his reputation." She put the pen to her mouth again.

"Ruin his reputation how?"

"He was a thief, and she threatened to tell everyone who listened. As soon as that got out, he would never sell anything again. People would lose their trust in him, and the business would go under. He wouldn't make any money, and making money was Wallace's number one goal in life."

I blinked. "What did he steal?"

"He stole recipes. He would take recipes from other brewers and repackage them as his own. He didn't know anything about making beer, but he knew how to swindle.

He was a master of that. It was one thing, the only thing, I admired about him."

"You admire that?" I asked.

She studied me. "Sure. If I could figure out a way to make money like that I would. I think most people would; they just don't want to admit it."

Before I could argue with her, she took another drag from her pen and walked away.

There was one person in this case that I hadn't had a real conversation with, and that was Jason Brennan. In some ways, he seemed to be at the center of all this. He had been awarded the job of master brewer for a suspect cherry beer, and he was having an open affair with Wallace's wife, Chanel. It just seemed to me if I was looking for suspects, he was as good as any of them.

I wove through the party. As I went, a waiter pressed a bottle of beer into my hand. I looked at the label and saw it was Jason's—or more correctly—Fields Brewing Company's new cherry-flavored beer that they planned to serve at the cherry festival. I was certain Chanel wasn't going to give up on the opportunity to be the official brewer of such a major event in Michigan.

I circled the room twice and didn't see Jason.

Behind the bar, I noticed a swinging door that led to the kitchen. On a whim, I went through it. I found myself in a hallway. I could hear the clatter of dishes and pots and pans from the cooks and waitstaff. To my left was another hallway. From my understanding of the building, that hallway would go behind the brewery.

I was in this deep; I might as well keep going. I walked down the hallway. On either side of me the walls were brick, and I could tell by the color and the lack of uniformity in the bricks that they had been made by hand, which meant they were very old. My guess was this was part of the original granary.

I was still holding that beer. I didn't know why I kept carrying it. Maybe I thought it would give me a good cover as a partygoer who became lost in the bowels of the old granary.

There were three doors to my right, and I felt a little like Alice, unsure which one would lead me to Wonderland.

I tried the knob on the first door. It was locked. It was the same result for door two. However, the third doorknob turned.

I pushed it open and was deafened by a string of loud barks as a fluffy Pomeranian jumped into my arms.

Chapter Thirty-One

L ancelot, get down. You too, Moneypenny!" a man cried.

Chanel Fields's five dogs jumped excitedly all around me. It wasn't until I set down the Pomeranian—Lancelot, I guessed—that I realized that he'd knocked my beer onto the floor and it had spilled all over the carpet. I bent down to pick it up, but the damage was done.

"I'm so sorry," I said. When I looked up, I saw Jason Brennan standing across the room from me. Chanel's dogs lay down all around the room. They certainly were well trained. I wondered how she had been able to do that with so many different breeds.

"What are you doing here?" Jason wanted to know.

"I—I was at the party and must have taken a wrong turn looking for the bathroom."

He stared at me like he didn't believe it for a second. He stepped behind the desk in the middle of the room and sat in the leather captain's chair like it had been made for him. The room was modern and clean. All the colors were white and ivory. The desk had a clear glass top with no clutter at all, not even a stray paper clip. It was at that moment I realized we were in Wallace's office.

Jason was acting very much like it was his office.

He leaned back in the chair. "The restrooms are on the other side of the building, but I am pretty sure that you already know that, don't you? I've heard about what you have been up to the last several days."

"Me?" I asked. "I just came to the party to pay my respects to Wallace."

He cocked his head. "And why is that? Because he was a great friend of yours?"

"Because I found him in the lake."

He nodded. "Yes, I heard about that."

This guy's Dr. Evil impression was starting to get a little old.

"You can stop the act," I said. "I know you're in here because Chanel wanted you to watch her dogs. You thought when Wallace died that you'd be able to take over everything at the brewery. Instead you learned that she was the boss. Must be tough to be promoted to master brewer only to be demoted to dog watcher. That must make your relationship a challenge."

What I said to him was just a guess, but I had met men like Jason in LA. They were all show and no real power. They were too busy trying to look the part that they didn't bother to do the work to get the part.

He jumped out of his seat. "I am the master brewer. Chanel promised she would keep me in that job."

"Isn't part of that job knowing how to brew beer, and you don't?"

He paled.

"How did you get an entry in the competition if you don't brew it yourself?" I asked. "Did you take it from someone else?"

"No, Wallace did." He covered his mouth as he realized what he was admitting.

But it was too late. He couldn't take it back.

The Dalmatian yawned. It seemed the dogs were growing bored with the conversation. They really were very well-behaved.

"Who did Wallace steal the beer from?"

"I don't know. I didn't care either. I just wanted to be given the position. It was Chanel's idea in the first place that I try to get the job," Jason said.

"Why would Wallace do that for you when you are with his wife?"

"Because it wasn't the first time. He had done it many times before. That's what made him successful. He took other people's beers and recipes and made them his."

"Stealing ideas is hard to prove," I said.

"It can be, but just the talk about it would ruin his reputation. The beer community, organic or otherwise, is very small in Michigan. Everyone would hear about it. It had the potential to destroy his business."

"How did he do that?" I asked. "Did he know how to make beer himself?"

This made Jason laugh. "Not at all."

"Then if he just stole, or let's say borrowed idea or recipes, how did he make them?"

"Well, Bastian did that until he died. He was truly a master brewer and was able to mimic any flavor that Wallace gave him. Most of the time, the beers he made were better than the originals that Wallace borrowed."

This was news. "Some people blamed Wallace for Bastian's death."

Jason snorted. "No way. Wallace loved that man and what he did for the brewery. He was very aware that the brewery would be in trouble if Bastian ever left. But he did something worse than leaving. He died."

Someone stepped in the doorway behind me, and all the dogs jumped up and wagged their tails. Their mistress was here.

"Settle, settle. Down," Chanel said.

All the dogs lay down on the floor in one collective motion. It was sight to behold. This woman was really good with dogs.

Chanel's hair was still mussed from her fight with her stepdaughter-in-law. "What are you doing here?"

I thought about using the same bathroom excuse that I had used with Jason. However, it hadn't worked with him, and I had a feeling that Chanel was the sharper of the two in the relationship.

"I was just asking Jason about how it was being the master brewer." I smiled.

She frowned at me.

"Do you still plan to be the brewer at the cherry festival?" I asked.

"I don't see any reason why not," Chanel said and picked up Lancelot the Pomeranian.

The little dog bared his teeth at me.

"I think it's time for you to leave," Chanel said coldly.

One of the dogs growled, and I took that as my cue to slip out the door. I might have even run down the hallway.

I let out a breath when I was back in the restaurant. It seemed to me that Jason and Chanel were a perfect couple, and I didn't mean that in a good way.

I had been there long enough. It was time to head over to my cousin's theater for *The Wizard of Oz*. Maybe the Scarecrow and the Cowardly Lion could get my mind off Wallace's murder.

Someone tapped me on the shoulder, and I looked down to see Hedy Strong standing next to me. I couldn't hide my surprise. I had never seen Hedy indoors before. In fact, I suspected she slept in a tent somewhere. It would be where she was most happy. "You showed a lot of interest in owls the other day. I was impressed by that. It's not often that someone who isn't a birder would ask me that many questions about a species."

"Well, I was—"

"I'm having an owl walk tomorrow night at seven at Lake Skegemog. You should come. If you want to learn about owls, the best way to do it is out in the woods on a bird walk. We are on the lookout for a great gray owl that is reportedly in the area."

"I'd like to, but you see I have a lot going on, and—"

"Leave your dog at home. Dogs and birding don't mix, and that little pug is not up for the hike I'm about take you on," she said and walked away.

"What just happened?" I murmured.

"You got Hedied," a deep voice said beside me.

I turned to see Sheriff Penbrook. My face flushed. "I hadn't realized that I spoke aloud. And I guess I'm going on an owl walk tomorrow night. I wasn't given a choice. What happens if I don't show up?"

He shrugged. "She'll send an owl to haunt you in your dreams."

My eyes went wide.

He chuckled at my reaction. "I'd just go. If you don't, she will just pester you until you do. She got me too, so looks like I'll be there," he said. "I haven't been on an owl walk for a long while, and it will be a good way to clear my head."

"What about the murder case?"

He pressed his lips together. "Unfortunately, it will still be there. Most of my prime suspects have alibis, so I'm back to square one."

"Kent?" I asked.

"He's still under consideration, but with the attack on him, I see him as a long shot."

I gave a sigh of relief. Kristy had essentially told me the same thing, but it was nice to hear it straight from the sheriff. "Chanel and Jason?" I asked, thinking of the conversation I'd had with them only a few minutes ago.

"They are each other's alibi, but it is confirmed from a hotel in Traverse City. Apparently, they went there after the party. They were in the hotel bar the time that Wallace died. The bartender and other patrons at the bar vouched for Jason and Chanel."

I grimaced. "Chanel's daughter just told me that Wallace built his career by stealing recipes from other brewers."

The sheriff nodded. "I heard the same. It would have hurt his reputation if it got out, but it's not necessarily illegal. Ideas can't be trademarked or copyrighted, and the list of ingredients in recipes can't be copyrighted either. It's unethical but won't send a man to jail."

I nodded and looked down at my watch. "I have to go. I promised to run the ticket booth at my cousin's theater. Doors open in thirty minutes. If I'm late, she will kill me."

"Hey," the sheriff said nonchalantly. "Why don't I pick you up tomorrow evening for the owl walk? I know the birding ropes and can tell you about it on the way."

"How do you know where I live?"

"I have your address from your statement."

I blinked. "Oh right. Umm." I looked down at my watch again. "Sure. That would be fine. It would be nice not to do something related to murder for once."

"I agree." He smiled. "I'll be there at six. Just like your cousin, Hedy will kill us if we are late."

Chapter Thirty-Two

Stacey paced back and forth in front of the ticket booth when I slid into the theater a few minutes later. "You are late," she barked at me.

I looked at my watch. "No, I'm not late. It's seven thirty on the dot."

"In my book that means you're late."

Her book was annoying.

"Just be ready for people to arrive. I have stuff to do." She marched away.

I rolled my eyes at her back and set up my ticket booth. When I was done, I stepped out from behind the booth and looked at the lobby. There were high-top tables set up, covered with black cloths and decorated with emerald-green candles. The candles were a nice touch considering the movie was *The Wizard of Oz*. The waiters—who actually were interns at the theater—leaned against the wall until it was time to walk around with trays of appetizers. At the top of the steps, guests could pick up their dinners before going in. It seemed Stacey had thought of everything.

To my surprise, craft beer was being sold in the concessions area. Instead of someone from Fields Brewing Company down the street, Sidney from MOBA was behind the bar.

I had a few minutes before the door opened, so I walked over there. "Hi."

"You seem to pop up everywhere," he said.

I shrugged. "This is my cousin's theater. I'm helping her out by selling and checking tickets."

He cleaned a glass with a white cloth. "Very good."

On the counter were five different beers. They all had a label on them that said Skegemog Ale. An owl with huge eyes perched on a bare tree in front of a cabin on a lake.

"That really looks like Lake Skegemog," I said, pointing at the label.

He nodded. "That was the idea. I had a local artist draw it up. It came out nice."

"Are these your beers?"

"They sure are," he said. "I have five offerings here tonight. I'm sure everyone will find something they like."

Unless they didn't like beer, then they were out of luck.

"If you don't mind me asking, why are you here and not Fields? I thought that was the plan."

"With Wallace's party tonight, Chanel told Stacey she couldn't do it. Between you and me, I don't think she wanted to do it at all. She doesn't need a small event like this to get word out about Fields Brewing Company. Not like someone with an operation my size might. I met Stacey at the MOBA meeting and gave her my card. She called me this morning saying she was in a bind and the rest is history. I'm happy to help out for the free publicity."

"Is it your goal to have a place like Fields?"

"Oh no." He laughed like that was the most ridiculous thing he had ever heard. "I'm just a home brewer. What I want is for my beer to be available in local specialty and grocery stores. I don't want an operation like Fields. There are too many employees and too many things that could go wrong. I just want to brew and sell what I make. I have no interest in the rest of it."

I could understand that. A restaurant and brewery like Fields Brewing Company would be a tremendous amount of work. Sometimes I wondered if I was up to having a little farm-to-table bakery at Bellamy Farm. It might be a lot to manage on top of the farm work. Chesney would help me, of course, but Chesney wouldn't be at my side forever. She was going to graduate from grad school in a couple of years and would want to venture out on her own. What would I do then?

"Shi! The doors are opening," Stacey cried. "Get back to your post."

I ran back across the floor to the ticket booth.

The doors opened and people began to pour into the theater. I was checking tickets as fast as I could. After they passed me, they went to the tables and found their boxed dinners, which had been donated by Jessa's Place. Jessa was a saint with all she donated to the other businesses in the community, Bellamy Farm included. Jessa and her cook stood behind the table passing out food. Each meal came with a bottle of water, but if guests chose, they could buy a local beer from Sidney. Based on the length of the line, many of them made the choice to do that.

After collecting their food and drink, they headed into the theater to eat while watching the movie. Stacey fluttered around the lobby with a proud smile on her face. She had a reason to be proud. The evening was a hit.

After I checked everyone in who had prepaid tickets, I sold another twenty. The last person in the line to buy a ticket from me was a surprise. It was Annette Woodhall.

"Oh," I said, unable to hide my surprise. "Would you like a ticket?"

"Yes, I would." Her voice was clipped. It was clear to me that she didn't want to chat, but that didn't mean I wouldn't try. It might be my only chance to speak to her alone.

"That will be twenty-five dollars," I said. "It includes a boxed dinner. You have your choice of chicken salad, brie, or roast beef on a crescent roll. It comes with chips, grapes, dessert, and a water bottle. If you would like to purchase a beer you can do that from Sidney at the counter there."

"Sidney?" she asked as she handed over her money. She frowned. "I suppose that's why he wasn't at Wallace's party. He didn't tell me he was doing this."

"Would he have normally told you?"

Her eyes slid in my direction. "I would hope so when there is an opportunity to advertise MOBA. More people need to know about it. Michigan is a big beer-drinking state, but people need to set that mass produced garbage aside and support local, organic beers. Had I known that he would be here, I would have given him some literature about MOBA to pass out." She pressed her lips together in a thin line.

"Well, we are glad that you are here tonight for *The*

Wizard of Oz. The Michigan Street Theater appreciates your support."

"*The Wizard of Oz* is my favorite movie. I thought I would come here to get the bad taste out of my mouth after Wallace's party," Annette said. "Actually, I needed something to get the bad taste out of my mouth from this last week." She plucked the ticket from my hand and walked away.

I frowned. That was a missed opportunity there. When else would I have a chance to ask her about her husband, Bastian, who was Wallace's master brewer and died of a heart attack?

To my surprise, Annette gathered up her boxed dinner and went into the theater without a glance in Sidney's direction, but he had to know she was there.

Stacey pranced over to me in her too-high heels. "The movie is starting, and everyone is settling in with their meal. How many tickets did we sell?"

"Ninety-two."

She frowned. "I was hoping for at least one hundred."

"This was the first event like this. When everyone who came tells their friends about how much fun it was and how good Jessa's boxed dinner was, it's going to be a hit. You might want to think about doing something like this for Valentine's Day, like a dessert event and show *Casablanca* or another timeless romance."

My cousin studied me as if to check if I was being serious. I was completely serious. I never for a moment doubted Stacey's business sense. She wasn't the best cousin in the world, but she made this theater into something great, and I knew it would just get better and better over the years.

"That's not a bad idea," she mused. "I will see if we can make it happen."

Across the lobby, Jessa and her cook were packing the meals that hadn't been sold. Knowing Jessa, she would drive them to a soup kitchen in Traverse City to pass out to people in need.

"I'm going to go speak to Jessa now about that idea. I'm sure she has some stellar desserts that she can serve." She hurried away as fast as she could in her heels.

I wanted to say hello to Jessa too. However, before I spoke to her, I wanted to chat with Sidney again. However, when I looked in the direction of the beer counter, he was gone. If I knew Stacey, she wouldn't like that. She would have wanted Sidney to stay at his post in case anyone came out of the theater during the movie and wanted to buy another drink.

I counted up the tickets again. Ninety-two. I organized the cash and receipts and locked them in the cash register. At the end of the night, Stacey would come and collect the money. My job for the evening was finished. I could go home or I could sneak in the back of the theater to watch the movie.

Stacey said something more to Jessa and then flounced away.

I walked over to see my friend. Tonight her hair was tinted emerald green. It was fitting.

The cook pushed a cart of boxed dinner and supplies out of the lobby, heading for the exit at the back of the theater that opened on the parking lot.

"I swear your cousin is the only person in the town who can walk in shoes like those and not break her neck. It's quite a talent," Jessa said as she folded the ruby red tablecloth that had been draped over the folding table in front of her.

"One she's been practicing for years. I remember her wearing heels around the farm when I was a little girl. Our grandmother was always shouting at her about that. It was clear from the beginning that Stacey wasn't going to be a farmer forever."

"No one would consider that woman farmer potential," she said with a laugh.

"I know that she appreciates you being here today, sharing your time and food. That was really nice of you."

Her ever-present smile widened. "It's what I do." She set the folded tablecloth into a crate on the table. "I noticed you speaking to Annette Woodhall for a little while there."

My brow went up. "Do you know her?"

"Of course I do. She and her husband lived in Cherry Glen for ten or twelve years. She moved when he died."

"I heard it was a heart attack." I paused. "Some said it was brought on by Wallace Fields's demands."

She cocked her head and her white and green ponytail fell over her shoulder. "I don't know about that. Wallace was hard to work for. I'm guessing that Kent Brown can vouch for that, but Bastian Woodhall also knew he had a heart condition and he still ate like a college football player. If it was fried and fatty, he was buying it. There were many times I shooed him away from my diner because I didn't want him to keel over into his fried chicken."

This was news to me. "Did Annette blame Wallace for her husband's death?"

"Not that I ever heard. Maybe Wallace pushed him too hard, but ultimately, Bastian refused to take care of himself. That's what got him in the end."

"I think in the future when I have a question about someone, I'm just going to come to you first. You seem to know everything about anyone who lives or lived in this town."

She grinned and picked up her crate. "It wouldn't be a bad way to go about an investigation."

Chapter Thirty-Three

Like Annette, *The Wizard of Oz* had been my grand-mother's favorite movie. I remembered she had me watch it when I was five, and I had been so terrified of the flying monkeys that I threw up. After that Grandma Bellamy was very careful of what movies she let me watch. Over time, I grew less frightened of the movie, but I believed that some of that childhood fear stuck with me, so I opted to skip the movie and go home. Before I did, I wanted to find Stacey so she wouldn't reprimand me for bailing.

I knew this was a risky endeavor, because when I found her, it was very possible she would have another assignment for me about the theater. She enjoyed barking orders and if they were at me, all the better. If I didn't find her outside the screening room, I would leave and say that I gave it my best shot.

I walked up the wide staircase that led to the theater doors. Through the three sets of double doors, I could hear Dorothy talking to the Tin Man for the first time, but in the waiting area, there was no sign of my cousin. I went back downstairs to the lobby and looked in the ticket booth and concessions area. No Stacey. No one at all, in fact. Sidney had never come back to his post.

He must be in the building, though. His bottles of beer were still lined up on the counter. I picked up one of the bottles again and studied the picture on the label. I noticed a large owl drawn on the label. It seemed like I was seeing or hearing about owls everywhere I went now. Maybe I had owls on the brain because of the owl walk I was going on the next night with Hedy...and Sheriff Penbrook. In the background of the label, there was a fishing cabin in the drawing.

"Listen to me. If you want to stay in MOBA, you have to follow the rules," a woman's voice said, coming from the restroom area.

"You don't make the rules, Annette," I heard Sidney say.

Instinctively, I ducked behind the counter where Sidney had been serving beer and crawled behind a four-foot stack of beer crates. However, I can't say it hid me completely.

"My husband founded this organization," Annette went on. "If it weren't for him, you'd still be in the woods making beer that no one drinks. He found you. He helped you get established. You would be nothing without him. You wouldn't have labels or bottles without his help. He taught you everything about the business. All you knew was how to brew."

I couldn't hear what Sidney said in return but heard footsteps coming in my direction.

I covered my mouth when Sidney's legs appeared behind the counter. If he looked down, he would surely see me, but he was too busy angrily packing his beer from the counter.

My legs were starting to twitch from squatting for so long. I inched a couple of frog steps back away from the beer crates.

"Are you listening to me?" Annette asked.

"How can't I listen to you? You followed me across the theater and have continued to speak when I have made it abundantly clear I have no interest in what you have to say." He folded his arms.

I took another frog step back. I was glad I was able to do it without toppling over. I had to give credit to the animal workout that my friend Briar forced me to take back in LA. I only went once. It was trendy and not my thing, but I did learn to walk like a bear, frog, and penguin. Who knew that one of those skills would be so useful?

"You're being ungrateful," Annette said.

"You may be right that Bastian did all those things for me, but it was him that I owed. Not you. I don't owe you anything," Sidney shot back.

The rubber sole of my boot squeaked on the marble floor just as I was frog walking around the corner.

Sidney's head snapped in my direction. *Busted.*

"What are you doing down there?" he demanded.

I hopped to my feet like a jack-in-box. "Oh, hey, Sidney." I nodded to Annette, who stood on the other side of the counter with her mouth hanging open. "Hi, Annette. I was just making sure the counter was secure. We—we've had complaints from some of the kids that were working the concessions stand that it seemed to have loosened from the floor." I grabbed the edge of the counter and shook it. "But as you can see, it's rock solid. Kids." I shrugged.

Both Annette and Sidney stared at me as if I just told them the Loch Ness monster now lived in Lake Michigan.

"Annette, how are you enjoying the movie?" I asked.

She shook her head. "I'm leaving. This whole thing is a joke." She stomped out of the building.

I grimaced at Sidney. "She seemed upset."

"You think?" He started packing up his beer and supplies again.

"Do you need help?" I asked. It seemed like the only right thing to do since I was caught eavesdropping red-handed.

"You are a very nosy person. Do you know that?"

"I've been told that a time or two." I noticed he had a canvas wagon beside him. I set a case of beer inside of it.

He shook his head.

"How did you do tonight?"

"All right." He studied me as if gauging my actual interest in his answer. "I didn't sell as much as I hoped, but everyone who bought seemed to like it. It's about word of mouth in this business."

"It seems like a lot of businesses are like that, even movies and television."

He eyed me. "What would you know about that?"

"I was a producer in LA once upon a time."

"Huh," he said as if he couldn't quite believe it.

I can't say I would blame him; the transition from producer to farmer was quite a leap.

"If you don't mind my asking, what was all that Annette was saying about her husband helping you?"

He frowned and set a second case on top of the one that

I had already placed in the wagon. "I do mind you asking, because it's none of your business."

"She just seemed to think you owed her something."

He added a third case to the wagon and turned to face me. "She thinks I owe her loyalty and need to convince the other members of MOBA that they should be loyal too."

"Why does she need loyalty? I thought no one was going to try to take her place as the next president of MOBA."

"I thought that too. You couldn't pay me to take it, but it seems some people just want to be in a position of power. Wallace's widow is asking to be appointed her husband's place. The group will either just give it to her or have a runoff election between Chanel and Annette. I have to tell you Chanel is the more charming of the two, and charm wins campaigns. That's why Annette is upset."

"What does that have to do with you?"

"I was one of the first members of the group when Bastian Woodhall formed it. It's true that Bastian helped me a lot when I was trying to get my start. He taught me a lot about business. Before he worked for Wallace, he had been the master brewer at two other places. He had over thirty years' experience in the industry. No one knew more about micro-brewing in the state. Why else do you think Wallace Fields snapped him up when he opened Fields Brewing Company? He knew Bastian was an asset."

"If he did all that for you, and you and Annette seem to be friendly, if not friends, why don't you help her?" I asked.

"Because this is a business. I can't have someone with so much power in the organic beer brewing world angry at me.

Even if she doesn't become MOBA's president, Chanel still has a lot of influence. I can't take the risk."

I frowned. I could see his point, but I could see Annette's too. There didn't seem to be an easy answer for either of them.

He set the last case on the wagon and put on his winter coat. "I overheard Hedy Strong talking about an owl walk tomorrow night by Lake Skegemog."

I nodded. "I think it's supposed to be near the spot where the ice fishing derby was."

"Are you going?" he asked.

"I think so. I haven't completely decided yet."

"You should," he said and nodded to the owl logo on the side of his beer cases. "I love owls, and there are some good ones in those woods. I'm glad Hedy is there to protect him. She is fierce."

"She is," I said. "Are you going? You seem interested."

He shook his head. "Oh no. I have brewing to do."

He pulled the wagon out from behind the counter and rolled it away.

I wondered what else was brewing in MOBA…and if some of it had led to murder.

Chapter Thirty-Four

The next day at the farm, Chesney and I spent another day tearing apart the porch. We got it completely dismantled and didn't find any other cookie tins of valuables underneath it. However, there was clear evidence that a family of raccoons had once made a home there. I supposed I should be happy that the raccoons didn't break into the cookie tin. It must have been tempting for them.

A little after three, Hazel showed up after getting off the bus, but after the incident the day before, I wouldn't let her help us dismantle the porch. Instead, she used my snowshoes and tromped around the front yard with Esmeralda and Huckleberry on her heels. Huckleberry kept barking at the snowshoes as if he couldn't understand how her feet had grown so big.

Quinn was set to pick Hazel up at about the same time Sheriff Penbrook was coming to get me. Hazel and I went back to my cabin so I could get ready. She watched as I looked in my closet for my warmest clothes. It was going to be freezing on the lake, and I was regretting that I'd agreed to go. I'd much rather be curled up on the couch with a cup of tea, searching my phone for brokers who could authenticate the stocks in my sock drawer.

"Where are you going tonight?" she asked.

I pulled on my warmest pair of wool socks. "On an owl walk with Hedy Strong."

"Oh wow, can I go?" She sat up on my bed.

"Maybe another time. It's a school night, and I would like to go first to see what it's like."

She sighed. "It's always a school night."

"It does seem that way, doesn't it?"

When Hazel and I walked up the path from the cabin with Huckleberry and Esmeralda on our heels, we found Quinn and Sheriff Penbrook standing outside of their respective trucks talking to each other.

My heart rate kicked up. Why did that make me so nervous?

"Who's that?" Hazel asked.

"Sheriff Penbrook," I said. "He's a birder and is giving me a ride to the owl walk."

She frowned as if she thought there was something more to it than that. There wasn't. At least, I didn't think there was. There definitely wasn't, I assured myself.

Though I couldn't help but notice how nice the sheriff looked in his snow pants and long winter coat. How on earth did he make that look good? I appeared thirty pounds heavier than I was because I was dressed for an Arctic expedition, and here he was looking so darn handsome and warm without resembling a polar bear. It just wasn't fair.

"Hi," I squeaked. "You two have met."

"We've known each other for a long time," Sheriff Penbrook said. "Quinn's team has helped Antrim County on a fire call now and again. We do appreciate the help."

"No problem," Quinn said. "Are you ready to go, Hazel?"

"Yeah, but I wish I could go on the owl walk," Hazel said.

"Maybe next time," the sheriff said. "I have a feeling that if Hedy can make a birder out of Shiloh, she will be inviting her on a lot more bird walks and owl walks. Perhaps you can go on one of those."

My heart fluttered. It was the first time he called me Shiloh. I didn't know why that was such a big deal. I ordered my inner self to chill out.

"Maybe," Quinn said, but his tone said it wasn't going to happen. He glanced from me to the sheriff and back again. "Why are the two of you going together?"

Sheriff Penbrook scowled. "Hedy invited us both tonight, and I thought it would make more sense if we rode together," the sheriff answered. "I live closer to Bellamy Farm than the lake; I figured I'd pick her up on the way."

"Uh-huh," Quinn said.

I bit the inside of my lip, and my palms were sweating inside of my gloves. I gave Hazel a hug before she climbed into her dad's truck, and then I turned to two men. "Sheriff, would you mind waiting a second while I take the animals in the house and check on my dad?"

He smiled at me. "No problem."

When I got inside it felt like a furnace, and not just because Dad was always cold and kept the temperature over seventy-five, but because I was wearing four layers of clothes.

I left the animals with Dad, made sure he had dinner (microwaved macaroni and cheese was on the menu), and ran out of the house before I melted. The cold outside air came as a relief.

What wasn't a relief was the look on the sheriff's face. Whatever Quinn was saying, Sheriff Milan Penbrook wasn't happy to hear it.

Sheriff Penbrook and I waited for Quinn and Hazel to leave before we got into his truck. I was dying to ask the sheriff what he and Quinn had been talking about, but instead, I brought up the subject of murder.

"I had an interesting conversation last night with Sidney Tucker," I said.

He glanced at me. "Is that so? What about?"

I told him about Annette, Annette's husband, and the politics and power struggle for MOBA.

He nodded. "I have been told the same thing."

"I still think Chanel Fields is a really good suspect. Perhaps she killed her husband. She had an affair but couldn't divorce her husband for fear of losing all her money and the privileges that money could bring. He dies. She can be with Jason, inherit the brewery, and take his place in MOBA. She gets everything that she wants."

"You're forgetting," Sheriff Penbrook said. "Wallace was killed with a garrote. Chanel is considerably smaller than her late husband. Most likely, he would have been able to fend her off even if she caught him by surprise. Also, how did she get him into the water? It would have been extremely difficult for her to move him."

"She had Jason do it?" I suggested. "You said that they were each other's alibis. He could have done it for her." I leaned back in my seat with a sigh. "But they have an alibi from the hotel they were staying at. That's unfortunate."

He chuckled. "It can be disheartening when theories don't come together. I will give you that."

I rubbed my forehead. "I don't know what to think about any of it anymore."

"What I want to know is why you are still thinking about it all." He took his eyes off the road to look at me just for a second.

"I, well, you see…"

"Because I told Kent Brown he's no longer a suspect. You told me that was your reason for asking questions in the first place. If he's no longer a suspect, you should no longer be worried about it."

"That's true in theory," I said. "But the truth of the matter is I feel bad for Wallace."

He raised his brow. "How so? I haven't met many people in this investigation who feel bad for Wallace Fields."

"I feel bad for him for that very reason. The man is dead, and it seems to me that more people are celebrating his death or jockeying for position to take advantage of it than mourning than man who died. I'm not saying he was a good guy. It is clear that no one in his family thought he was, but it is upsetting that no one is sad he's dead."

We had reached Ballden by now, and the sheriff stopped at a red light, the only red light in the town, and looked at me. "That's a very good reason to want to be involved. You want justice for the person who died because he was a human being and deserves that as a human right."

I nodded, and a lump caught in my throat. The sheriff was looking deep into my eyes. I wanted to turn away but just couldn't make myself do it.

The light turned green, and he turned his attention back to the road. "But that's not your job. It's mine."

Chapter Thirty-Five

D o you hear that?" Hedy cupped her ear. She was dressed from head to toe in camouflage again. Even her binoculars had a camouflage wrap on them. I was glad I was wearing black. I had feeling bright colors in this group would have been greatly frowned upon.

"That's a great gray owl," Hedy said in a hushed tone. "What a find! Stay back and be quiet," she hissed. "If I hear so much as a whisper, I'm leaving you behind."

I didn't think that was an idle threat.

Hedy led a group of eight down a snowy path in the woods. Everyone around me seemed to be serious birders. Even Sheriff Penbrook had a camera with a night vision lens.

He and I were at the end of the line.

"Are you cold?" the sheriff asked.

"In this outfit? Are you kidding? I'm toasty."

"You do have a lot of layers on," he said.

"I don't mess with being cold, Sheriff."

"No talking," Hedy hissed. "I *will* leave you behind."

The sheriff smiled and put a finger to his lips. I nodded and had to push back a giggle. I realized as Hedy led us farther and farther into the woods that we were headed in the direction of the cabin where Hedy had discovered the hole in the ice, which was the mostly likely spot where Wallace's body went into the water. I tensed up as I thought of finding Wallace's body just a few days ago.

Sheriff Penbrook must have sensed my nerves because he put his hand on my back—or at least I thought that he did. It was hard to tell through all the clothes.

Hedy held up her hand, signaling for us to stop. She pointed up at a dead limb overlooking the lake with a magnificent bird perched in the middle of it. The owl looked down at us with big round eyes. My breath caught. It was huge. Even from where we were on the ground it was clear the owl was almost two feet tall.

"Wow," I breathed.

The sheriff smiled at me and whispered, "When I see sights like this, I understand why my dad is into this birding stuff. I probably didn't appreciate it as much as I should have when I was a kid."

It flapped its massive wings and took off. The rapid sound of shutters going off overtook the forest as all the birders took pictures of the owl in flight.

After it had disappeared into the distance, Hedy turned and faced the group. "Now, I want you to break off into groups of twos and threes and look for owls. If anyone finds anything, send me a text and I'll alert the group. We'll meet back in here fifteen minutes."

"Want to be my partner?" the sheriff asked.

I laughed. "Sure."

He and I went down a snowy path.

"Do you mind if we walk over to…"

"To the spot you found Wallace." He said this like he already knew what I was going to ask.

I nodded. "It just seems odd to be so close to it and not pay some respect. I can't say that his celebration of life was very respectful."

"You're right about that."

As we walked in that direction, I blurted out, "Sheriff, what were you and Quinn talking about when I was in the house?" I couldn't believe that I had gathered up the courage to ask, but it could be the cold had gotten to my brain.

"First of all, you don't have call me Sheriff when we're birding. I'm just Milan right now."

"And I'm just Shiloh." I smiled.

"Right."

"So what did you talk about?"

Milan kicked a tuft of snow. "Oh, he was just telling me that you were off-limits."

I stopped in my tracks, and I suddenly felt hot. "Off-limits?"

"He thought we were on a date, and he didn't like that idea." He shrugged.

I laughed. "This isn't a date."

"Not officially," he said.

I turned around and continued walking so he couldn't see my surprise, and I was glad I was so bundled up from the cold that he couldn't see how red the back of my neck was.

We had almost reached the spot when a gunshot went off. Milan grabbed my arm.

Another shot went off.

"It's not hunting season," he said in a harsh whisper. "Stay here. I'm going to check it out."

"I'll go with you." I started to follow him.

"No." He didn't wait for my answer and melted into the woods.

I sat on a log next to the lake and worried about Milan and the other birders. I wondered if I should walk back to the parking lot, but if I did would Milan know where to find me? Cell reception here was iffy. I had half a bar. Who knew what he had?

I decided I would walk just a bit down the lakeshore to the spot where Hedy and I found the fishing line. When I got there, I was surprised to see a square hole in the ice again, clearly made by a chainsaw just a few inches from the spot where Wallace likely went into the water. I inched out on the ice for a better look.

"Hello, Shiloh. How is your owl walk going?"

I turned around and saw Sidney standing a few feet from me, holding a gun. I gasped and stepped back farther on the frozen lake. I took care not to go anywhere near the hole.

"You didn't tell me at the *Wizard of Oz* event that you were bringing the sheriff with you. That's an unfortunate wrinkle I did not expect. The two of you walked off on your own to look for my cabin."

"That's your cabin?" I pointed to the small cabin at the edge of the lake, and as I stared at it in the moonlight, I gasped. The cabin, the location on the water's edge, even the dead tree in front of it was all illustrated on the label of his beer bottles. Something about that label had struck a chord with me, and now I knew why.

"Don't pretend you don't know that. It's been in my family for four generations. Why else do you think I asked Wallace to meet me there that night?" His voice was sharp.

"You killed Wallace?" I had a light bulb moment.

"He was quite surprised when I came up behind him with the fishing line."

Instinctively, my hand went to my throat. "He stole your recipe and gave it to Jason to submit."

"I spent years on my cherry beer recipe. I found the right ingredients, the best ingredients. I was patient. Perfecting the fermentation takes time. I didn't rush a single step. I worked on it day and night for years in my family's fishing cabin. I knew that I would have one shot at this. It had to be perfect. I was going to submit it to the cherry festival, but Wallace beat me to it. Before I could submit, he already had, and I was disqualified because it was too similar to another entry: Fields Brewing Company's entry."

I could run away from him. The frozen lake was behind me. There was nothing stopping me from running and not looking back.

He guessed what I was thinking. "If you run across the lake, I'll shoot you in the back."

"Sidney, listen to me. The sheriff is here with me. You should be the one to run before he comes back and finds you."

He laughed. "He's too busy investigating those shots I let off. Now, what I want you to do is to hop into that open water there."

"Why would I do that? I would die anyway."

"You might have a shot at survival, who knows? Your choice."

I thought I had a better chance with the gun than I did with the lake, but before I could make up my mind, Sidney lunged at me and pushed me into the water.

The cold and wet seeped through all of my layers of clothing. The soaked cloth pulled me down.

I remembered what I was taught as a child on the ice and what my father had told Hazel. I controlled my breathing and kicked to the edge of the ice. I tried to pull myself out like I was swimming on the top of the ice.

"No, no, no!" Sidney said. He stomped on my fingers.

I cried out in pain, and he pushed me back into the water. This time, my head was submerged.

Don't lose sight of the hole in the ice, my brain told me. I reached up and somehow grabbed the edge with fingers I could no longer feel. My head and neck were out of the water. I wanted to rest there, but I knew I didn't have time.

I heard the crack of a gun. Had I been shot, but I didn't feel it because I was so cold? I closed my eyes for a second. *Keep kicking*, I told myself.

Milan yanked me out of the frozen lake. I saw his face before I passed out.

Epilogue

The next week, an austere man sat across from me behind a massive desk in a well-appointed office. The name plate on the desk read, "Janus McComber."

"Miss Bellamy, I'm glad you were able to come in and meet with me today," Mr. McComber said.

I smiled and sat in the chair across from him. For this meeting, I wore one of the last remnants of my life in LA, a black pencil skirt and royal blue silk blouse. After so many months in jeans, T-shirts, and flannel, the clothing felt odd. It was as if I had put on old skin that I had long ago discarded.

"I have to say this has been a very interesting project, looking into these stock certificates. I haven't seen ones this old, well, ever. In fact, no one has actual paper certificates any longer. From a purely academic perspective, this has been exciting for me."

I folded my hands on my lap and waited. There were so many questions I wanted to ask him. Every last one of them was on the tip of my tongue. I was afraid if I started asking questions, however, I wouldn't be able to stop.

"I know you have been waiting for my analysis, and I

am happy to tell you the certificates are valid and worth an estimated—estimated because we have to keep the daily fluctuation in the stock market in mind—seven hundred thousand dollars."

My mouth fell open. "Did you say seven hundred thousand?" Heat rushed to my face.

"I did." He nodded.

With that amount of money, I could pay off the remainder of my father's debt on the farm. I could rehab the cherry orchard. I could even start thinking about the farm-to-table bakery I had been dreaming about. I let out a breath.

"The issue is," Maxwell went on, "You have to prove you are the rightful heir to the certificates. You have this letter and the stock certificates from your grandmother, but they could be contested. An attorney, or even a judge, will have to determine whether this letter could be considered a will. Did your grandmother have another will when she died?"

"I—I don't know. I was in college then. I can't say I paid much attention. My father and uncle would have dealt with all of that."

He nodded. "So who could contest the will?"

"My father, but I don't think he would. If I get money it will go to our farm."

"Anyone else?"

"The only other person would be my cousin Stacey. I suppose she has as much right to these as my father and I do. She's my uncle's daughter. My uncle died years ago."

"She could definitely be a stakeholder then."

I bit the inside of my lip. I didn't want to consider the

possibility of Stacey contesting my right to use the money for the farm. I didn't want to be in a legal battle with my family. Stacey and I weren't close, but I didn't want money to tear apart what little family I had. "What if I split the money with Stacey?" I asked, thinking that my dreams of opening the bakery right away were slipping away. However, I would still have enough to pay the debts and revitalize the orchard. I might even be able to start saving money again. It might be better to make those changes slowly than do them all at once.

"That's something you need to discuss with an attorney and your cousin. I suggest you meet with an attorney first and see what that person says about the validity of this letter as a will. From there, you will be better prepared for that conversation with your cousin."

I nodded.

He slid the envelope of stock certificates across the desktop to me. "It seems to me that this is good news for your farm."

"It's incredibly good news," I agreed.

"Then congratulations, Miss Bellamy. You have a remarkable find on your hands. Quite a remarkable find."

I held the certificates close to my chest, grabbed my coat and purse, and stumbled out of his office. I didn't think I'd been so wobbly when I used to wear heels. No, the news had made me unsteady on my feet.

Huckleberry waited patiently for me in the truck with the windows cracked. It was a crisp February morning, but warm by winter in Michigan standards. It was close to forty degrees. All around us I could hear running water as the layers of snow and ice began to melt away. It was a ruse of course—nothing more than the midwinter thaw. There was more snow in the forecast. Michigan had two months of snow left in its future if we were lucky. Three if we were unlucky.

I drove back home from the authenticator's office in Traverse City, my mind whirling. Even if I had to share the money with Stacey, the farm would be saved. I could make it self-sufficient, which is all I had ever wanted. My hands shook. I didn't even know how to tell my father all of this. I wondered if I should speak to the attorney before I did. Maybe it would be better to have all the facts before I told him.

When I reached the farm, I was surprised to see an Antrim Sheriff's Department SUV parked by my barn. Huckleberry set his two front paws on the dash as if he wanted to get a better look at the unexpected car.

Carefully, I slipped out of my father's pickup. Pencil skirts weren't made for trucks. Huckleberry hopped out after me just as Sheriff Milan Penbrook came around the side of the barn. He looked so handsome as he strode toward us. He was civilian clothes: jeans, a flannel shirt, and a bomber jacket.

"Hello, Shiloh. I hope it's all right that I stopped by like this. I knocked on the door and no one answered."

"It's fine," I said. "My dad's at play practice. My cousin is putting on *Death of a Salesman* this spring at the theater. Dad got a small part, but I can't remember his exact role."

"I might want to come see that," he said. "It's a good play."

He turned. "You have a beautiful piece of property."

"Thank you," I said. "Milan, I'm surprised to see you here. Is everything okay?"

"I just stopped by to see if you were all right. You had a traumatic experience."

Yes, nearly freezing to death in a frozen lake was a traumatic experience. "I'm all right. I'm just glad it's over and we can put it behind us."

"Me too."

"How's Sidney?"

"I shot him in the upper thigh. He had surgery and is in the prison clinic until trial. The judge didn't grant him bail."

I let out a breath. "I have to say I'm glad for that."

He cleared his throat.

I studied him. The usually confident sheriff was nervous. Why would he be nervous standing in my driveway? Maybe Diva the chicken had hassled him when he arrived and he was waiting for her to strike again. I couldn't put it past Diva to attack a police officer.

"I was wondering if you would like to go to dinner sometime."

I blinked. "Dinner?"

He cheeks flushed. "Yes, with me."

I bit my lower lip. Faces flashed across my mind: Logan's, Hazel's, and Quinn's.

"I'll pick you up tomorrow at seven?" he asked, sounding hopeful.

An answer caught in my throat.

SHILOH'S
Quick Farm Tips

I've learned a great many things from Hedy Strong about birds and how to protect them. One way to help birds is by feeding them in the winter. Suet is a great option because of its high fat content and because it gives birds energy. Something, I learned this winter is making my own suet, and I would love to share my recipe with you. Anyone can make this recipe. You don't have to live on a farm. If you're in the city, suburbs, or the country, your local songbirds will thank you. Enjoy!

INGREDIENTS

- 1 ½ cups vegetable shortening
- 1 cup peanut butter or a nut butter you have on hand
- 2 tablespoons coconut oil
- 3 ½ cups wild birdseed
- ½ cup cornmeal
- Handful of almonds or other nuts (optional)

DIRECTIONS

Melt the shortening, peanut butter, and coconut oil together in the microwave and set aside.

In another bowl, mix the birdseed, cornmeal, and almonds, and stir.

Add the melted mixture to the dry ingredients and stir until all are incorporated.

Use a plastic storage container and press the suet mixture into the bottom. Be sure to compact it as much as possible.

Freeze or set outside in the cold to allow to harden.

Once the suet is hard, hang it in a metal mesh basket in a tree for the birds.

It was a crisp mid-October afternoon. The weather was perfect for sweaters, light scarves, and riding boots. The air smelled of apple cider, hay, and pumpkin spice. It was my favorite time of year. Autumn in Michigan was something I had missed the fifteen years I lived in California. Despite the beautiful day, a knot was pulled as tight in my stomach as the ropes that tethered the boats to the dock on Lake Michigan.

Cars, minivans, and pickup trucks lined the half mile-long driveway as they waited to park in the open pasture next to my barn. When I came up with the idea of Fall Daze, I never for a moment thought I would have this level of response. It was overwhelming, and worse, I was underprepared.

I wasn't the reason all these people were here either. I had done my part by putting flyers up around town about the event, made an event post on social media, and bought a tiny ad in the local paper. However, my best guess was seventy percent of the hundred-some vehicles in my pasture were there because of my best friend, Kristy Brown. When Kristy endorsed something in Cherry Glen, people listened and lent their support.

Kristy managed the Cherry Glen Farmers Market. It was one of the most popular farmers markets in the region outside of Traverse City. She scored a spot on the local television station to plug the market, which she did, but she also spoke about Fall Daze at Bellamy Farm, calling it the best fall festival of the season. By the looks of it, people listened, and now I had to live up to her claim. That was a tall order. Fall in Michigan was serious business. It seemed that every town, city, and farm had a festival, and every weekend until the first snow was packed with autumnal activities. If everything went well, I had a real chance to save my family farm. If it went poorly, I might drive the farm further into the hole. No pressure.

When I was a child, Bellamy Farm was composed of four hundred acres. When my grandfather died, he divided the farm in half between his two sons. Years after my uncle died, Stacey, my cousin, sold the half of the farm she'd inherited from her father so that she could pursue her real passion in local theater.

She sold the land to a developer for a pretty penny, but then the development company landed in some trouble. As a result, that portion of the old Bellamy Farm was left to waste. As far as I knew, the development company still owned the property but had made no changes to the land. I wondered if it was just biding its time until the housing market boomed again and the second half of Bellamy Farm could be transformed into a subdivision. A subdivision on our family's land would make my grandfather do somersaults in his grave, and it made me a bit queasy just thinking about it. Ideally, I would have the money someday to buy the land back and put Bellamy Farm together again. However, since I didn't even have enough money to replace the shutters on the farmhouse, it wasn't looking good.

My father, Sullivan "Sully" Bellamy, stood next to me, gripping the arms of his walker. In his early eighties, he was perpetually cold and had a sour disposition that occasionally the right person could crack and make him smile. I was rarely that person. At the moment, he wasn't pleased with me at all. There were very few things my father enjoyed less than being around large groups of people. Hundreds of people invading his sleepy farm was his worst nightmare.

My father wore a black stocking cap that was pulled down over his bushy, gray eyebrows. The cap gave him a bandit-like appearance. He glowered at me. "How on earth are you going to feed all these people?"

It was a good question. My fawn-colored pug, Huckleberry, stood at my father's feet and cocked his head as if he considered this too. Then he glanced around with his wide-eyed pug stare. It looked like his round, brown eyes might just pop out of his head. I leaned over and scooped up the pug and hugged him close. I knew when my dog needed comfort. Maybe I needed some too.

Dad shook his head. "You've turned the farm into a circus."

"Dad, this is great PR." My voice was a tad shaky.

"Not if these people go home hungry. I'd say that's terrible PR. In fact, that's the worst PR that you can get. I don't know what it's like in California, but when someone shows up at an event in Michigan, they had better not leave with an empty belly or there will be hell to pay. I can tell you that!"

I glanced at the food table that was becoming sparse. When the festival began two hours ago, it had been piled high with plastic containers and bakery boxes of my organic baked goods. I used the festival as an opportunity to test my organic recipes. I had always loved to bake, especially with my Grandma Bellamy while growing up, but when I had been in LA, I had little opportunity. Too many people in the Golden State avoided carbs, myself included. Since returning to Michigan, my passion for baking had returned and I had wild dreams of someday having a bakery and café on our property that would serve real, organic farm-to-table fare that was produced right here on Bellamy Farm. The dream was a long way off, but the festival was a start, and I had truly believed it was a good start until it began.

I thought I had baked enough for the two days of the festival. There were over three hundred items ranging from cookies to muffins to cakes, but it would never be enough.

My assistant, Chesney Stevens, made a face at me. She was a tall and strong woman in her late twenties with brown hair that just brushed the top of her shoulders. She always wore a cloth headband to hold the hair back from her face. Chesney was a graduate student whom I had hired a few weeks back when I realized I couldn't do everything I needed to at the farm myself. She only worked as much as I could pay her, which admittedly wasn't a lot, but having her help for the ten to fifteen hours a week I could afford made a huge difference.

She was the perfect candidate for the job. She was getting her MBA with a concentration in agricultural business at my old alma mater in Traverse City but lived right here in Cherry Glen. She rented a small house in town with her younger sister. The little money I could pay would help her get by and supplement the stipends she received from the university for her graduate program. It all sounded too good to be true, so being me, I expected that it was.

Imagine my happy surprise when she turned out to be just who she said she was. There was no way I could have pulled off Fall Daze without Chesney's help. The last few weeks we worked tirelessly to make the worn-down farm presentable for this big event, and now it might be ruined because people would go home hungry.

I swallowed. "I have enough apples to make more apple cider," I told my father. "And I've called in reinforcements. They should be here soon. There's more to Fall Daze than food. There's the corn maze, yard games, and the hayride—plenty for everyone to do while they wait to eat. Don't worry, Dad. I've got this handled."

"Looks like you do," he muttered and shuffled away.

I sighed and went back to Chesney at the food table.

Chesney handed a customer her change. "Enjoy your cherry strudel!" she said with a bright smile.

The customer walked away, and while the next person in line considered what was left on the table, Chesney whispered to me. "We're running low."

"I know. I called a friend. She should be here soon with more food."

"You have a friend who is an organic baker?" Her blue eyes went wide.

"Not exactly…"

"Shi!" a friendly voice called to me from the pasture. Kristy Brown walked toward me, weaving in and around the people standing in front of the barn waiting in line for food.

Kristy pushed a double stroller. She was a new mom of twin girls, and she looked quite pleased with herself. "Look at this turnout! You did a great job getting people to come!" Her dark eyes sparkled. She wore a brightly colored handwoven scarf around her neck. The scarf was yellow, orange, pink, red, and lime green. The colors should have clashed with the rest of her outfit, but the intricate geometric pattern of the scarf just worked. I knew the scarf well. Kristy had had it for over twenty years, a gift from one of her aunts in Mexico.

My eyes went wide. "This is because of your spot on TV. I had very little to do with it."

"Don't be modest." When I didn't say anything, she studied my face. "What's wrong?"

I set Huckleberry on the ground. He walked over to the stroller, put his forepaws on the side of it, and peeked in at the sleeping twins. Huckleberry looked back at me with a whimper.

Kristy laughed. "Looks like he wants a little sister."

I frowned. "He has plenty of little sisters and brothers in the barn cats. There are the chickens too."

She rolled her eyes. "Your chickens do not qualify as siblings for Huckleberry. They are more like a street gang."

"That seems a little harsh."

"Shi, one of the chickens chased a woman through the corn maze until a volunteer caught the chick and locked it up," Kristy said.

I winced. "I thought they were all in the coop."

Hearing this news about the chickens, I was more grateful than ever for the high school volunteers who were helping Chesney and me out with the event. All of them were members of the high school's Future Farmers of America chapter. To be honest, they were probably a lot better at chasing chickens than I was. There were thirteen high school student volunteers in total. They guarded the corn maze—from wild chickens apparently—drove the hayride, supervised the pumpkin picking in the pumpkin patch, and helped park the long line of cars. I would be in a lot worse shape without them, including having to deal with a lawsuit over a chicken attack.

"I bet it was Diva," I said. Diva was a chicken who more than lived up to her name. "She's my most disobedient hen."

"I want you to take a moment and think about what you said just now, and then think back to six months ago when you were sitting in a fancy LA office."

I grimaced. The image was quite a leap.

"So what's wrong?" she asked.

I sighed. I had hoped she'd forgotten about that question.

She shook her finger at me. "Don't lie to me. I know something is wrong. You made that same face in biology class when you let Mr. Donalson's rats out of their cage and they ran out of his classroom. They never did find Gertrude."

I still felt bad about that. Poor Gertrude. Mr. Donalson was never the same after the incident. "I just wanted to pet one. I didn't know it would try to bite me. I jumped back for half a second, and they made a break for it. How was I supposed to know they were going to do that?"

"They're rats. They bite. Have you never heard of the Black Death?"

"That was a mistake. Fall Daze might be a mistake too. I didn't bake enough for this many people."

She grinned. "Not to worry. Jessa is on her way with more food. She's bringing pies! Deep-fried Twinkies too."

"I feel terrible pulling Jessa away from her diner. The afternoons there are always busy. Not to mention there's the issue of her food not being organic."

"Organic is in the eye of the beholder." She grinned. Her daughters cooed and kicked their legs as if they were in agreement with their mother.

"No, it really isn't," I said and then added quickly, "Not that I'm not thankful for what she's doing. She's really saving me. Whatever she brings, I know it will be delicious."

"Listen, you can just tell everyone Jessa baked and fried the organic out of her food. You don't have much choice. There must be two hundred and fifty people here. How many did you plan on?"

I sighed. "Maybe one hundred? I thought I was being outrageous to make that much food for that many people."

My father shuffled back over on his walker. I expected him to have gone into the farmhouse and putter with his collection of historical Michigan artifacts. It was typically how he escaped anything he found unpleasant.

"Hi, Mr. Bellamy," Kristy said with a bright grin.

He nodded at my friend. "It's nice to see you, Kristy. Congratulations on the girls. They are very cute."

Kristy blinked. "Why thank you, Mr. Bellamy."

I knew she was surprised. My father wasn't one to use the word "cute" for anything or anyone.

Dad turned to me. "You said more food is coming. Where is it? Chesney is about to be mauled for that last piece of pumpkin pie."

"What a terrible way to go," Kristy said.

I shot her a look and said, "Jessa will be here soon. She's the reinforcements."

"You're having Jessa's Place cater?" Dad said. "No one in this crowd is going to go for your hippie granola when they have a fried Twinkie staring them in the face."

"Dad, did you even look at what I made for today? There's no granola at all."

"I didn't have to look to know it was a bunch of hippie stuff you brought back from California with you. Organic." He snorted and shuffled away again.

Part of me really hoped he would hide in the collection room for the rest of the festival.

"I'm sure your dad is proud of you," Kristy said as she watched him go.

I gave her a look and then bit my lip. "Maybe I expected too much out of him and myself to host an event this soon after moving back to the farm. We weren't nearly as ready as I wanted to be. The fact that we ran out of food is all the proof we need of that."

"This soon? Shiloh, you've been back since July. You have to do something if the farm has any chance of success. Also, everyone who is eating your baked goods has raved about them. I think you should apply for a booth at the farmers market to sell them. I can get you an in." She winked at me.

"Really?" I asked. "I never expected to have a slot in the market this year. You said that all the spots are full."

Her face clouded over. "We have a vacancy."

I wanted to ask her what she meant by that when a shrill voice called, "Kristy Brown, I want a word with you!"

Kristy cringed.

From the pasture, Minnie Devani pushed her way through the line waiting to sign up for the corn maze. "Kristy Brown, you had better speak to me!"

Kristy sighed and turned around. Huckleberry galloped in the direction of the barn. I knew he was going to sit this one out with the barn cats. I can't say I blamed him.

Minnie was a squat woman in her sixties. She had gray hair that fell just above her ears and wore a plaid green coat over her olive-green pantsuit. The coat was a surprising fashion choice. Most of the time Minnie was precisely color coordinated.

Minnie wagged her finger at Kristy. "You had better take your lies back or I'll sue you!"

Kristy's cheeks flushed, and she stepped in front of the stroller. "I don't think you're the one who should be calling someone else a liar. Watch yourself, Minnie. If you want to revisit the conversation we had earlier today, I'd be happy to do that, but I don't think that's something you want to do in front of an audience."

"You can't tell me what to do." Minnie jabbed a polished pink fingernail into Kristy's chest.

Kristy clenched her jaw. I grabbed the handles of the stroller and pulled the girls away from the fray. By the look on Kristy's face, there was about to be some fireworks. I had seen the same look on my friend's face so many times. It never ended well for the person on the receiving end of that glare.

"Don't touch me," Kristy said through clenched teeth.

I pulled the stroller back even farther. You could never be too careful. It's not that I thought the two women would come to blows, but I wanted the twins out of the way just in case.

"I will do whatever I please after the way I have been treated," Minnie said. "You have ruined me, and you did it out of spite. You're a spiteful woman."

"After the way you've been treated? I have been nothing but kind and lenient with you. Do you want to tell all these people here that you are six months late on your booth rent for the farmers market? Do you want me to tell them that to help you pay off the debt, I let you work at the market while I was on maternity leave?" Kristy took a step closer to Minnie, so that she was just inches from her face. "Do you want me to tell them that when I got back from maternity leave, I discovered that you stole over six thousand dollars from the market and *still* didn't pay your rent?" She took another step closer to Minnie now. "Is that what you want me to tell them?"

Minnie opened and closed her mouth. Everyone in line for food, the hayride, and the corn maze stared at us. The festival grew deathly quiet.

I hurried forward and patted Kristy's arm. "Kristy," I hissed.

My friend looked at me, and there was fury in her eyes. I jumped back. In all my life, I had never seen Kristy this angry.

Minnie covered her face with her hands. The rings on her fingers sparkled in the late afternoon sunlight coming up over the barn.

"I think the two of you need to talk about this another time," I said in a low voice.

Kristy's face cleared, and her fury was immediately replaced with abject horror as she realized the scene she'd made. "I'm sorry, Shi. This is your event. I shouldn't have let her rile me up so much."

"It's fine." I turned to Minnie. "Minnie, I think you and Kristy should talk about this later, in private."

She glared at me. "You shouldn't be here at all, Shiloh Bellamy. No one wants to know what you think."

I put my hands on my hips. "That may be so, but this is my farm and I'm asking you to leave."

"I was leaving anyway. The only reason I came here was to talk to Kristy. I knew she would be at your little festival."

She made a dismissive gesture with her hand. "It's a poor excuse for one, if you ask me. My dear friend Doreen Killian told me all about you, and I can very well see why she doesn't want her granddaughter around such a bad influence."

My face grew hot.

Before I could fire back, she pointed at Kristy again. "I will make you sorry, Kristy Brown. Remember this day. I will make sure you never forget what you did to me!" She spun around and stomped back in the direction of the pasture that served as our makeshift parking lot.

Utter silence fell over Fall Daze.

I waved at the crowd. "Welcome to Fall Daze, everyone! We have more baked goods on the way and fried Twinkies! Who doesn't love a fried Twinkie?"

I don't think anyone was thinking of fried Twinkies at the moment. They were thinking that if anyone could make good on a promise to make another person's life miserable, it was Minnie Devani.

Acknowledgments

Thanks to all my readers who continue to follow me from series to series. I love writing the Farm to Table series and am so glad you have enjoyed them too. I'm an Ohio girl, but it has been so fun for me to write about beautiful Michigan, a state that I visit often and I hold dear.

Thanks always to my agent, Nicole Resciniti, for her continued guidance of my career and her unwavering friendship. Thanks too to everyone at Sourcebooks for all they do to produce these novels and promote them. Very special thanks to my editor, Anna Michels.

Thanks to reader Kimra Bell, for her sharp eye, and to my friend Sarah Preston, who has shared her vast knowledge of birding and owls. I also give love and gratitude to my husband, David Seymour, who bought the farm that inspired this series.

Final thanks to God in heaven for allowing me to have this amazing career.

About the Author

Amanda Flower is a *USA Today* bestselling and Agatha Award–winning author of more than forty-five mystery novels. Her novels have received starred reviews from *Library Journal*, *Publishers Weekly*, and *Romantic Times*, and she has been featured in *USA Today*, *First for Women*, and *Woman's World*. In addition to being a writer, she was a librarian for fifteen years. Today, Flower and her husband own a farm and recording studio, and they live in Northeast Ohio with their adorable cats.